More praise for *Jumping Ship*

"Exciting, revealing . . . Insightful . . . Like a colorful kaleido-scope, *Jumping Ship* changes shape and form at a moment's notice . . . Covers an impressive amount of ground."

—*The Pittsburgh Press*

"Kelvin Christopher James' stories form a vivid and often searing ex-ploration of Caribbean experience on the islands, in New York and in between. He writes about voodoo, dope, sex, friendship, children, and a host of other themes with unflagging energy and insight. He is a gifted writer with a salty imagination and a genuine understanding of the worlds he inhabits."

—Patrick McGrath
Author of *Spider*

"Beautiful, violent, and compelling stories—the violence is never gra-tuitous, the beauty is often unexpected and raw."

—Whitney Otto
Author of *How to Make an American Quilt*

"The 14 stories in this hard-hitting collection bridge the cultural and geographical distance between the tropical life on Trinidad and sur-vival on the mean streets of Harlem. . . . James has an ear for dia-logue . . . His stories have a tough physicality and an emotional matter-of-factness, meshing his characters almost cellularly with their environment."

—*Booklist*

Other books by Kelvin Christopher James

Secrets

JUMPING
SHIP
and
other
stories

JUMPING SHIP

and other stories

KELVIN CHRISTOPHER JAMES

Ballantine Books • New York

This edition published by arrangement with Villard Books, a division of Random House, Inc. Villard Books is a registered trademark of Random House, Inc.

The following stories were previously published:
"Guppies" in *Bomb* in 1989, "Circle of Shade"
in *Bomb* in 1990, "Tripping" in *Between C & D* in 1989,
"Transaction" in *Fairleigh Dickinson Literary Review* in 1990,
and "Succulence" in *Bomb* in 1991.

Library of Congress Catalog Card Number: 93-90476

ISBN 0-345-38283-8

Cover design by Kristine V. Mills
Cover illustration by Donna Perrone

Manufactured in the United States of America

First Ballantine Books Edition: January 1994

10 9 8 7 6 5 4 3 2 1

To mothers everywhere,
particularly my own and
those of my children

ACKNOWLEDGMENTS

Mainly to the posse who made this happen; good, good folks like Dougie-Doug, O-Joy-O, PaddyMc, Jackie DaBoss, SlicErik, Pablo-Ch, GeeB, Blusche, Dimsi, and Georg deSharpe. Also not to forget those extra-special, unnamed intimates who faithfully and variously provided encouragement and support throughout the roiling times achieving this manuscript.

High-priority mention to Joal Hetherington for her invaluable contribution in bringing together the initial manuscript.

CONTENTS

PART ONE

LITTLENESS

Quietly as a thieving mouse, Nipi eased off his bunk bed and went to the window. Remembering its risk, he pushed it very slowly open to mute its usual squeak. Then, with anxious eyes and craning neck, he leaned out to study the king-orange tree in the yard. A long, fearful instant teased him with other sights he wasn't looking for, like blinding blue sky and leaves greener because of the dew. Then he saw it.

A sighing feeling overcame him and softened the prickling tension that had slept like a burr in his head the long night past. Now it disappeared like a dream as he took ease from the soothing relief his eyes offered: The golden-ripe king orange was still there.

He had followed its life from a tiny green thing no bigger than a marble to its present gleaming ripeness, and for Nipi, the orange had grown from a private anticipation to an earned reward for patient nurture. He had fed it worry and care; look how just yesterday he had chanced it an extra day of ripening. Now yesterday's risk was a happy one. For in its yellow sheen, he could see the orange blushing that slightly pinkish tint that guaranteed special sweetness.

Abruptly, Nipi's mouth gushed full, and he guiltily swallowed the "eager water" (which Ma said sprang from a well of gluttony). But this wasn't raw greed. The way the sweet thoughts of the orange affected his mouth glands was more like magic, or something. Same as how it sent private glances, possessive glances, at him every time the green leaf-curtain trembled.

Two kiskadees floated into the perfect picture, and he tensed up. The gaudy yellow-and-black invaders alit on an upper branch and began performing their early-morning mating rituals, the male hopping from branch to branch following the serenading female. Every time she sang "kiss-kiss-kissss ka-dee," he echoed it and tried to jump her, and then she'd hop away through the air onto another branch. But it wasn't all this carrying-on to the music that had set Nipi's heart beating faster. The lovestruck birds were frisking nearer and nearer to his orange, and kiskadees, at any time, were known to more than favour ripe king orange. Yet, with all this hazarding, he couldn't go outside to chase them away.

Because Ma, who had ears like a bat, was up and dressing in her adjoining bedroom. If she knew that he, too, was up, most likely she'd make him accompany her to early matins. Normally, Nipi didn't mind that chore: It meant he was spared his normal yard-cleaning routines, and the church was a quiet place where he always resumed his sleep. But this morning was different. That reddish-gold orange was the only blessing he desired, and those screeching kiskadees were playing the devils for him.

Nipi looked around for help. Maybe there were some bluebirds in the other trees, or even a cocoa rachelle, natural enemy of the kiskadee. He did see some bits of feathered sky blue flitting about in the crown of the coconut tree, but they were paying no attention to the kiskadees. Before he could even damn his luck, a busy flutter of wings sounded his eyes back to his main concerns. Still nearer to the orange, they were persisting at their duet. Now they'd added somersaulting to the exercises. Nipi feared they were warming up to a sweet breakfast, while all he could do was watch from his trap at the open window. If only Ma'd hurry up and leave for church, he could go outside and make those blasted birds dance to a different music.

Unable to just look on, Nipi stretched his torso out through the window and began waving his arms about with extra vigour to make up for the absent noise he couldn't make. But the birds didn't notice him at all. He could've been any old whirling morning breeze. It would've been so different if only he had something to throw at them—and suddenly Nipi remembered his slingshot.

A scamper on tiptoe to his dresser and he'd got it, only to realize he had no stone to sling. He looked rapidly around the room. But his search made no miracles happen, and no stone upturned. Then his eyes fell on the marble on his brother's dresser. It was Diram's lucky doogle, his extra eye, as he bragged. Last night, just before they went to sleep, they'd been pitching marbles on the floor. Diram had won everything with his straight aiming. It really seemed the doogle could see targets on its own. Right now, though, an immediate glance showed Deadeye Diram still scrunched up in the bed like a baby, nursing some extra sleep from it. So keeping a severe gaze on his brother's resting face, Nipi seized the seeing-eye doogle. There was a special target he wanted it to take a look at.

The birds had now hidden their threat to his orange, but they had not stopped. They were perched in a basket of leafy fronds, out of sight for a clear shot. But armed with the doogle, Nipi had a new patience. He sat with the slingshot ready and kept his eyes on their general area, gauging their location by their singing. His left fingers held the marble loosely through the tongue of the slingshot. His right hand steadied the forked stick. He held the rubbers half-stretched in watch and followed the different rhythms of the couple's song. As he waited for the music to move, one thought gave him calm reassurance: Kiskadees were birds. Just as they had to sing, they had to fly.

Then patience delivered the female. She flitted into the clear and rested on a little branch to preen her yellow breast at him. Like a trigger, Nipi responded. He squinted his right eye and stretched the rubbers fully in aim. Then he gently sent off the seeing-eye doogle. It shot a squawk out of the yellow target, and down she came, tracing golden down behind her. Nipi grinned his satisfaction; the doogle had proven itself. As the kiskadee fell dead, the male flew a screeching spiral around her. When she rested and moved no more, he flew up to a lower branch, rocking back and forth there as if nervous at not flying away. But he didn't go. He just used the rocking as a rhythm to cry "ka-dee ka-dee ka-dee."

Nipi aimed the empty slingshot at him. His squinted right eye lined up the bird, and he thought, Yup, he could've had him, too. Then, without firing, he released the tension of the rubbers and glanced back up at the orange. It was safe.

Inside, Ma's shoe-steps told him that she was almost ready. So he relaxed again into contemplation. . . . Even the birds knew that his orange was especially sweet; should he peg it or should he peel? The male bird's crying intruded on his musing: "Ka-dee ka-dee ka-dee." Nipi studied him again from the valley of his aimed slingshot. He wished that he had another marble.

The slam of the front door announced that Ma was on her way to pray. Nipi remained still for a little bit until he heard the sound of her shoes in the empty morning street. Then, as if out of a cage, he jumped through the window into the yard. The gritty, cool dirt yard shocked a welcome to his bare feet, reflexively triggering an urgent call to void. So he trotted off to the latrine far up the backyard. As he passed the bathroom, he snatched up his toothbrush, intending to brush his teeth as he squatted and pushed. He had no time to waste.

Sitting and brushing in the fetid gloom, Nipi heard footsteps approaching the outhouse. He recognized them as Diram's and enjoyed a brief gloating at getting to the latrine first. It soothed the memory of those many other times, the times when he had been second. When he had been the one forced to tighten up and fidget on the outside.

"Nipi!" Diram demanded in an accusing voice. "You took my doogle?"

Nipi winced in his privacy. He had almost forgotten already that he had shot the marble. Nevertheless, his response was immediate.

"Which doogle?" he asked in a voice that carried complex messages. Right off, it denied that he had taken the doogle. Also, with some skepticism, it asked for clearer identification of the missing doogle. And finally, it suggested that Diram was very out of place even to question him on the matter.

This time Diram's voice was filled with convinced threat: "You'd better give me back my doogle before I bust your li'l backside." Then he heard Diram walk away.

Nipi sucked his teeth frothily. He was done, but he decided to remain squatting just to make Diram suffer. How dare he accuse him? There was no way he could find Nipi responsible for whatever mysterious things happened to the stupid doogle. Diram had been asleep like a watchman in a dream factory when he used it up as shot. Still, Nipi felt a bit nervous. Diram was one to hit when he got vexed, and Ma always seemed to support him. She was always saying that he was the bigger brother, so he had to get respect. When Nipi finally left the outhouse, he decided he'd be very discreet how he moved around Mr. Diram the Elder.

Diram was nowhere in sight. Nipi washed his hands in the tub of rainwater collected from the eaves around the latrine and was about to wash his mouth out also, but the sight of the many mosquito larvae looking big-eyed at him out of the surface offended him. Done with cleaning, he searched around the ground and chose a few smooth stones. As soon as he had the orange tree in sight, he began to locate Diram. With this fruit picking that he had planned, he wanted his privacy.

The sound of Princess Elenor's barking from somewhere in the front of the house made him feel easy. That was where Diram was. He liked to play with the dalmatian when he got up in the morning. So most likely the respected big brother would be occupied for a while. Everything was now right for him to load the slingshot and approach the tree.

Nearer to the tree, he made automatic note that, dead and alive, the kiskadees were still there. But his attention dismissed them to peer up in the tree. Then he changed vantage and peered again, and shifted his look about. Then his anxiety, growing in strength, almost choked him: The special orange had been nipped. For the first time and the worst time, it was not there.

He knew that it was Diram even before he noticed the long, slender bamboo rod left leaning against the tree trunk. Nipi could imagine how he had done it. He had used his long arms and the longer rod to reach and snap it down. Nipi felt a quick bitterness at the fact that he himself was so short, he couldn't have reached the orange even with the rod. He'd have had to shoot it down with his slingshot.

Suddenly, the rod represented a contempt for Nipi and his size. He felt a passionate hatred against it. He rushed up to it and kicked it hard. But he kicked soccer fashion, with the inside of his foot, and the hurt was extreme. And the rod just shifted, and didn't even fall.

The pain started his tears coming, and he ran toward the front of the house, screaming, "Diram! Give me back my orange!"

Diram was already half-done peeling the fruit. Shaking from the restraint of not snatching away the orange, Nipi went straight up to him. He brandished his left arm out like a sword, and said, "Gimme it! Gimme my orange!" He heard his voice, piping, high-pitched from his anger, but rushed on, "I marking it for a week now. Every day. So it's mine. I was just now going to pick it. You know by rights it's mine. You have to give it to me."

Diram sneered at him. Mimicking Nipi's shrill voice, he repeated, " 'You have to give it to me,' " then ended in his own voice, "I picked it, and I'm going to eat it. So leave me alone, you little bug." And he turned his back on Nipi.

Nipi felt his body thrumming from the frustration, and an awkward jig danced out of him. Diram's back was an insulting wall of disdain, as broad and unmoving as the huge world that besieged Nipi. Suddenly, the ghosts of a multitude of old peeves coalesced in his mind to form a just cause. Nipi realized that he was constantly wronged. He was a little mouse in a world of fat cats. They kept him at their whims. They gave him no preferences. He got the least food, the meanest chores, the most rules, and no privileges. None at all. It was, "Don't do this" or "Don't do that," as though they didn't want him to do anything except the jailwork they wished on him like a genie. Wasn't he people, too? They were just taking advantage of him! The provocations massed in his mind and mobbed him to the brink. And made wild from their manic energy, Nipi attacked the wall.

He rushed at Diram's back, swinging both fists like hammers, striking downward on the broad shoulder blades. But even as he pounded, he recognized that his rage was confusing his effectiveness. Diram just stiffened himself at the surprise assault. And Nipi felt his own knuckles hurting. But he was still goaded amok for justice, so he changed to another tactic.

With the aim to hurt anyhow, anywhere, he tried to simultaneously kick and knee Diram. Then, in the midst of this crabby attack, he suddenly felt himself grabbed by the waist and shoved aside. The force of the violence sent him stumbling, trying to regain his balance. Just then Princess Elenor entered the excitement with a rushing and a barking. Her first play was to collide with him and make him stumble back over in Diram's direction. And while still in this imbalance, he felt, hard on his ear, the jolting sting of Diram's cuff.

Abruptly, Nipi didn't want to fight anymore. He fled off in a cower, taking direction from the force of the blow. As he ran away, the tuning fork sounding in his ear began to fade slightly, just enough to catch the end of Diram's parting taunt: ". . . li'l mosquito, before I crush you!" Just the spark to flare his rage again. So Nipi decided to be nasty.

The thought of revenge banished his need to sniffle and redirected him to a slower circuit around the house. As he went, he wiped his face of tears and snot, then cleaned the mess on his pants. He aimed for the house corner next to the site of the scuffle, and as he came to it, he was careful to be absolutely quiet. Then, leaning his face against the wall, he eased a peeping eye around the edge.

Diram was leaning against the front of the house, tossing the last bits of orange peel at the base of the hibiscus fence. That glimpse was enough for Nipi to make his plan. He withdrew his eye from around the corner, and his forehead from the concrete cool. Thinking of the orange's sweet acidity made a spring of his mouth. But he suppressed the urge to swallow, and let the saliva well.

Nipi was almost up to him before Diram noticed. A flash of

satisfaction thrilled him at the startled speed he evoked from the respected brother. More important, as Diram spun around, he presented to view the succulent fruit in his hand. Still in full action, and with only a glimpse of the golden pegs of sweetness, Nipi hawked and spat his mouthful at the orange. The heaviest gob of phlegm missed, but the slimier spray nicely covered most of the orange. A good deal of it also bathed Diram's hand.

Nipi caught a glimpse of the dawning of a terrible disgust in Diram's face; but like a flitting bat, he was well on his way. A screaming erupted behind him. It was a yell that carried satisfying tinges of rage, frustration, and shock, among other angers. Only the effort he was expending at sprinting kept the grin from Nipi's face. His exultance showed, though, in his buoyant strides. He had got the big lunker back.

Nipi crouched low in the ditch behind the latrine and searched the yard for signs of pursuit, but he couldn't see the bully. So he stooped back down in the gravel-bottomed drain to think. It was certain that Diram would not let him get away with his wet revenge. But a stubbornness in him resisted the threat of that certainty. His actions had been just. The orange had been his by rights. So Diram had been wrong, and whatever he got after taking it was just darkness following daylight. It was fair Brer Anansi justice. Yet Nipi's experience advised him to run and hide a little first. It would be better to get as far away from Diram as sensible before he stood up for his rights.

Suddenly, with a muted "Aha!" Nipi spied his brother. He had been washing off in the bathroom. He now emerged in a crouching stalk. He had not dried off, and the water made his shoulders glisten in the morning sun. Diram's face was twisted with a determined grimace. Abruptly, Nipi remembered his brother's hunting skills. Once he had seen Diram stalk a nesting quail. Walking soft as a shadow, he had surprised the bird and wrung its neck before it could even cry out. This memory now served as inspiration for Nipi to get moving. He began crawling along the ditch towards the house. But it wasn't concealment that he sought now. He had an intuition that he should try to balance things out, so he was searching for something to help him make up for the five years and eight inches that made Diram bigger.

As Nipi started to scramble out of the ditch, some loose stones rattled in from the edge. Diram must have noticed the noise; Nipi heard him enter the ditch up behind the latrine, same place Nipi had. That Diram, the Stalker, had not bothered to conceal his movements convinced Nipi that bad trouble was nigh; and him without an equalizer. In the quick confusion as he realized Diram was gaining too fast, Nipi couldn't think of where to run. So, blind of direction, he leapt out of the ditch and into open flight.

As he raced around the back of the house, past the open kitchen door, a stratagem occurred to him. He stopped short, turned swiftly into the kitchen, and dove into the first dark space he saw, the cupboard-sized space under the fireside, where the firewood was kept. As usual, because this was one of Diram's most neglected chores, it was almost empty. As Nipi settled among the scant pieces of wood, he heard the pursuit arrive outside in the yard. Diram came around the kitchen by a few quick footsteps, then a listening pause, then another step or two, and another seeking interval, and then a move again.

Every time the footsteps stopped, Nipi held his breath and listened hard to trace the chase. An odd thought itched itself into his concentration: the way the rabbits stuck their faces out the cage-wire front of their hutch when he went to feed them. And the picture of long, sparse whiskers around a wet, twitching nose gradually became so irritating, Nipi could hardly stop from sneezing.

He pinched his nose hard; then, looking about himself, he realized the trap about his hiding place. He had jumped into a box with one door and was crouched unprotected, looking through it into danger. He couldn't change places now, either. For the quiet outside meant Diram was playing bat out there, listening to the airwaves for direction. Exposed as he was, his best move was staying put. So, carefully, silently, Nipi crept farther back under the fireside and huddled there, quivering and quiet. And tried not to think of rabbits.

The tentative footsteps came to the kitchen door and stopped. Nipi found infinite menace in the pause. Fear, joined with the rough feel of firewood under his hands, revived the thought of an equalizer. His left hand made a palm-spread scan of a small radius, then his right tried on its side. Throughout his questing, though, his stare never wavered from his boxed view of bright kitchen space.

Meanwhile, his hands suffered and searched, examined by feel and texture a broom handle, old spoons, a battered old pot, rejecting all except one pushy splinter. A soft gargle of frustration escaped him, even as he realized it might betray him. But his alarm pulsed more immediately as the outburst coincided with the creak of the loose floorboard at the kitchen door. Then there was no other sound.

Nipi was certain the kitchen was empty no longer. Diram was in there. He was tiptoeing along the kitchen wall out of view. Right then, Nipi, as he stared out into the too-quiet brightness of the kitchen in growing fear, could divine around corners. His right hand rapidly reconsidered and selected a stick it had just passed over. And then, with a shock, he saw his instincts had been right. Diram's unsuspecting feet showed on the floor before him, first one, and then a careful other, just a foot or two away.

They pressed silently on their balls with each step, toes spreading to push away the floor only at the very last moment.

Just so, searching, the feet passed by and right on through the kitchen, Diram never noticing Nipi crouched in his dim box. It was only when they were safely away that Nipi's left hand finally found the small wood hatchet; and he felt equal at last.

The smooth handful of hatchet handle was like a magic wand. Nipi was transformed into an awesome fighting being. Thus, armed and equal, he slinked on all fours, out from the murky belly of the fireside cave.

Assassin set, Nipi stole through the door the feet had taken, then stopped short. He had lost his surprise advantage. Diram, the thief, had seen him already. He was waiting under the shade of the sapodilla tree. He made a quick start to come at Nipi, but stopped full as though the air had turned solid around him. Glee surged through Nipi as he saw Diram acknowledge the power of the hatchet. Retribution swelled like an afterwave. Then his joy became perfect as he saw Diram turn and run to hide behind the sapodilla tree trunk.

Nipi shifted to the right, then to the left, trying to get a line on him, but he couldn't get a clear throw. Diram was shifting with him and kept the trunk in the way. Briefly confused by this tactic, Nipi just stood still in the open yard. He measured the foe behind the tree trunk. Diram seemed to be split into protruding shoulders and a left-side peering face, wearing a bit of a grin. Nipi wished he could throw the blade right through tree trunk and bully and all. It suddenly occurred to him that the hatchet was getting heavy. He rested it on his shoulder, blade up, threatening his right ear and blue sky above.

The enemy's face kept bobbing from side to side of the trunk. Its grin, grown big and cheeky, insulted Nipi back into rage. He shouted at Diram, "Come out! Come on out, you big coward."

He supported this with a winding rush towards the sapodilla tree. He stopped halfway there, as Diram had shifted with him as he approached, successfully keeping the tree trunk as his shield. His big face wasn't laughing anymore, though.

This respect overwhelmed Nipi with a feeling of power that left him wild and relieved and a little dizzy. He rushed the tree again and again in crescent patterns, not so much in attack as in an effort to maintain control of the situation, and partly for the thrill of seeing the concern in Diram's face. But after a while, seeing that Diram's parrying was keeping him at bay, his good feelings began to turn foolish.

It seemed he was making all the noise and sweat in this exercise; he pulling and tugging, Diram the oar's tip. He had a sneaky feeling that Diram was comfortably dancing around in the cool shade of the sapodilla tree making sport of him. Self-conscious all asudden, Nipi glanced quickly over at the neighbour's house to see if anyone was looking on. All in all, he was about ready to stop.

Then Diram taunted, "Going hunting, Li'l Beaver?" And Nipi felt the hellfire flare in him once more. He didn't think at all. He just rushed straight at the tree, swinging the hatchet. If he needed to, he'd chop right through it to get Diram out of his life.

But as Nipi committed his attack to one side of the tree, Diram left its security and ran from the other. Nipi was completely faked out. He was moving too fast to stop and set himself to throw a good shot. And Diram was heading for the full safety of the toolshed's open door.

Diram ran rapidly in a low, intent crouch. His move had been so well timed that by the time Nipi changed direction, he'd be through the shed's door, and safe. Frustrated and enraged by the neat maneuver, Nipi made a desperate try. In one unbalanced moment, he saw where the fleeing back would come clear of the intervening tree trunks. In the next, he fired off the hatchet with a smooth downward swing.

As the weapon left his fingers, Nipi knew the throw was perfect. Although he had to hop and twist so as not to fall as he watched its trajectory, he saw it all. He saw how the sharpened wedge rotated forward very slightly and proceeded on an arching pathway, assuming a fascinating grace in its swift flight, its true flight. For as Diram would fill the doorway's space, the flying blade would be there to enter his back as bidden. Or, if he was still stooping, his neck.

Still marvelling at the sureness of his aim, Nipi saw Diram run through the doorway. Then the door swung shut with a bang and accepted the winging hatchet with a dull *thunk!*

Suddenly, staring at the hatchet solidly stuck there in the cheating door, Nipi gave up altogether. He had lost. Everything was against him. There was no way he could've won anyhow. Even if Diram had been hit, the damage would've made Ma know they had been fighting. And any reported fighting meant a whipping from Ma, then a smirking from Diram, the newsmonger; and this morning's was too good a tale not to tattle. With another mental jolt, he realized that Ma must be on her way back from church by now, and all his chores were yet undone. Totally despondent at the hot trouble-pot he had fallen into, he hauled himself to the bole of the sapodilla tree and sat down. He glanced again at the hatchet stuck in the door. It looked good there, sort of mighty—the only neat scene in a bad picture. Then a hiccup erupted in his chest.

Nipi stood in waiting, swinging the wicket gate open, creak, and shut, bang; open and shut, creak and bang. The noisy activity provided background for his anxious staring up the street. Immediately Ma came into sight, he left his post and ran to the backyard, where Diram was busily feeding the chickens. He commenced lurking, like a loosely attached shadow, a few yards away from his brother.

Nipi tried on a penitent look and was approaching Diram when he stalled. He just couldn't do it, couldn't get up the gumption to beg the bully. Then, too soon, he heard the final sounds: the gate declaring *Creak, Bang;* the front door, *Slam.* At which Diram departed his gloat into the house. Nipi's next hiccup exploded in his throat, hurting as though it'd collided with the hope crashing to the bottom of his belly.

His immediate thought was to run away forever. He changed his mind when he could think of no place to go. Then his heart swelled with self-pity as a whimper and tears sought to share time with the hiccups. He crept around the house to his mother's room and pressed his ear against the wall. Indistinctly, he could hear Diram's voice. Its tattletale tones were clear, though. Briefly, Nipi hated him again, and felt sorry the swinging door had saved more serious trouble. The sounds of their leaving the room interrupted his spite. He darted back to the backyard, and was ready and waiting when Ma called for him. Instantly, he sprinted to his fate.

Nipi met her standing in the yard arms akimbo, impatient: not good. Her head was banded with a white cloth, her face sweating: neither here nor there, it was wash day, and hot. Most puzzling, but definitely good, she held no whip in hand. He stopped arm's length in front of her, and hiccupped.

She frowned at him and asked, "And what've you been doing since morning?" The "you" seemed selectively accusing.

Nipi swallowed to clear his cramped throat and tried to answer. Instead, he hiccupped again.

Ma frowned at him again. Then, irritation raising her voice, she commanded, "Answer me, boy."

Nipi had no satisfactory answer, but he wanted to say something before Ma thought he was being insolent by his silence. He tried for "Nothing, Ma," and helplessly hiccupped again. Frustrated, he felt the sting in his eyes turn wet and roll out hot onto his cheeks. Adding to his embarrassment, he knew that any try to talk would end in hiccups and make him look more simple. Broken by all this woe, staring at her stern frown, he began crying in truth.

Beyond the blurring of his vision, he saw Ma's face gentle. Then her voice, only remembered stern, said, "Stop the snivelling, and straighten up yourself, child."

With growing relief and fewer tears, Nipi corrected his stature. He pulled in an extra-hard sniffle. As he swallowed, Ma continued, "Now you better go attend to your chores, before I show you which side barley grows, okay?"

He'd never understood about barley's growing preferences, but that threat always suggested a hot backside for him. He nodded mutely as a more important thought was filling his mind: Ma hadn't heard about the fight. Diram hadn't told.

"Did you hear me, boy?" Ma demanded.

He went to answer, "Yes, Ma." Instead, he hiccupped again. Ma choked off a laugh and walked away. Nipi looked at the ground and shook his head. He wondered what they always found so funny about him.

On his way to get the yardbroom, Nipi passed Diram playing with Princess Elenor. He pouted his face sullen and walked straight past them. Diram's voice pursued him: "Go sweep the yard, Li'l Beaver." Nipi turned to answer, but had to grind his teeth. A hiccup was threatening. He tried to suppress it and failed again. He went on his way wondering which pointlessness God had invented first, hiccups, or being little.

He began sweeping, as usual, under the orange tree, working robotlike at rounding up the yellow leaves. Life's unfairness was on his mind. There seemed an enormous endlessness of days upon days until that unthinkable time when he'd be where Diram was. How would he bear the wait? The sweeping broom catapulted the kiskadee's carcass onto the pile of leaves and debris he had been forming. As the body rolled over, Nipi noticed something shiny about its wound. On looking closer, he found it to be the seeing-eye doogle.

Instantly, he forgave Life everything. It was sweet. It was fair. It dealt in Justice. Diram had bullied away his orange. Now his stars had given Nipi the magic doogle in return. Of course, it'd be trouble to ever use it publicly. But that was minor. Just hoarding it'd be fine.

SUCCULENCE

Another drop of sweat boiled off the curls of Gerrad's armpit and, tickling slightly, coursed down his side. The twitch broke his concentration from the exam paper before him, and searching for a breeze, he glanced through the big window to his left. Nothing there but the blinding glare of a hot young day. Barely past its ten o'clock stop, and I'm sweating steam already, Gerrad thought, as his eyes roved about the room.

He stopped abruptly, and returned tensely to his paper. But only a moment later, lids lowered as possible, he began covertly shifting attention up to the rostrum where the proctor sat. Where the heat had set her unconsciously fanning for a breeze with her wide skirt—slowly swinging her knees open and closed, and open, and closed.

Gerrad took one look, then rested his straining eye muscles. Then he went totally casual: First he made the casual reconnaissance, noting the others preoccupied with reading, writing, and pondering over correct answers. Then, most casually, he rearranged his posture, hunkering down, easing the angle for his now-so-casual eyes. Finally, all set behind the hand rested casually on his brow, Gerrad squinted sharply up the dark bellows of her skirt. And with familiar suddenness, the lighter shade of what he glimpsed undammed his pent-up blood into swift waves surging down his swelling crotch.

Somewhere behind, a commotion cut through, and she promptly stood up, roused by the scraping chair and overloud sighs—the gallerying of a first-finished test-taker. As she walked past up the aisle, Gerrad caught scent of her sweat, pungent in between the fragrant bouquet of bottled flowers she wore. Somehow the conflicting aromas unreasonably powered another fattening in his crotch.

Itchy all over, uncomfortably stiff in his lap, he rubbed his nose to forestall the sneeze that threatened. It passed, but left him afidget to a vague urge hiding in the back of his mind. Then, as the notion fully possessed him, he relaxed completely. Yes! he dared it. Right there in the aisle seat of the front row, he'd risk a quickie jay-o and get softening ease.

The immediate distraction was the proctor shushing the show-off-who-thought-he-was-first. As the fellow swaggered from the room, Gerrad ground his back teeth with chagrin. He himself could've walked out of the room at least ten minutes ago. The exam had been a snap—easy as peeping round his fingers. His recent dark glimpse brought back to mind, Gerrad began inventing situation around its scarce detail.

With a thrill, he could picture her legs flagging submission to the prickling heat. But going past the fascination above her knees, his imagination came up blank but for a fever of excitement. Was that valley cool? Moist? Was it sweating-hot? What would it do for him? And how would he test the mystery?

Meantime, slyly, Gerrad shifted in his chair, repositioning to conceal the bulge in his lap. He jammed his stomach to the desktop, so that by huddling over, his left hand supporting a heavy head, he assumed the slouching attitude of one industriously reading over his answers. His right hand, though, he fitted familiarly over the swollen pulsing in his lap.

Just at the ready, Experience began a worry about inevitable and embarrassing wet spots. That was like saying "Watch your step!" to a rushing mob, though. Already, just his close accomplishment was riding Gerrad, whipping him on. And pulling like the serpent powerful, the fleshed temptation probed and swayed longer down inside his leg. Under its pressure for attention, he glibbed to himself that he'd hide the spots with question sheets, notepaper—whatever shallow blind to block away his pipsqueak anxiety. Then, not fighting it anymore, he squeezed his handful through his pants, and thrilled to it . . . until an exquisite, bursting rapture had pained and passed and calmed him down.

A sigh escaped softly behind the draining relief, and he bent his head to rest on the desktop. He closed his eyes—wiped out by the empty power that had swept him over. As always, it had been so swift. Like a fleet hot wind, it had rushed over him, burning his passion away, leaving only a tiny consternation.

Ten minutes later, feeling flaccid as sails in a doldrum, he placed his answers on the proctor's desk and left the room. He had timed his move to coincide with her attentions to the anxieties of a late-finisher. And with his books held to his lap, he exited so smoothly, he felt certain no one had noticed the damp stains of evidence.

Gerrad squatted in the shade of a roadside tree studying the weeds and wondering what to do for company. His pants were dry now, and it'd be another half hour before lunch bell, when his two main buddies would get out of their classes. After lunch they'd return to their regular afternoon schedule. But since he had no more of these special scholarship exams today, he'd have four hours—until five o'clock—before being due home: a lot of free time to waste. Gerrad considered persuading them to make *l'école biche* and go river-bathing with him. After a moment's promise, though, the idea wilted when he considered the un-shaded two-mile trek to the river basin. They wouldn't like it either. In fact, beyond the tree's umbrella, the stinging sun dis-couraged every plan but staying in the shadows.

Thinking ease and cool, he got an idea that swiftly decided him not to wait for his friends. He'd go to the public library and browse. He recalled a book he had sneaked from the Adult stacks. In it were some really good parts about this country-woman and her crude gardener. Maybe the author had written another story like it. A frisson teased a journey downward from his quickened heart, and pulled him on his way.

Gerrad decided to meander two blocks out of his way and pass by the Girls' High. Although he knew it was not recess time, it was worth a try. A stray thrill might still be out there in tardy schoolgirls horsing about the playing fields. Those netballers wore skin-thin shorty-shorts that showed the most after perspira-tion.

This is how he was, these last few months past his fifteenth birthday. Where Gerrad's paths crossed femaleness, his attitude had assumed this gambler's hopeful nonchalance. On the spur of the moment, he'd alter any program for routes female in poten-tial. Alert as a stare, he prowled about clothing stores with their suggestive mannequins and piles of slinky underthings, and bookstores with racks of revealing women's magazines, and the jumping upper seats at stadiums, and women's wash-day clothes-lines. Wherever there was chance for a feminine charge, Gerrad tried being there.

This Girls' High was a favourite detour. On luckier days, he had caught sights of skin panty-high naked, in roughhousing juxtapositions that suggested dreams he could not imagine with-out such substance. When these good scenes aroused him, he'd press hot against the wall and jam there taut like a branding iron until his passion burst and doused itself to manageability. Then, afterwards, he'd rouse and droop off on his way, never fully bowed and ever ready to rise again and strike.

This time, though, when he came to the schoolyard, only it was bare.

Back on the road to the library, in the brilliant afternoon, Gerrad looked up and spied it. Against a background of black-green leaves, the mango gleamed like a sunset in shades of crimson and yellow. It was a ripe Julie—the premier grafted variety—and hung like a beacon above a formidable hibiscus fence about two meters high, with thick branching stems entwined to form a stalwart barrier.

Gerrad studied fruit and fence confidently, the beautiful Julie already so working his mouth pipes he could almost taste it. As for the fence, he didn't mind it much; getting beyond it was more or less taking a deservedly high step up to a grand prize. Gerrad believed mango Julie was—from aroma to swallow—the most delicious, totally satisfying fruit in existence. In furthering this theory of its excellence, he researched the Julie devotedly by gourmandizing every sample he could find.

He preferred to pick the Julies from the tree himself. Hefted, the best ones had a firm, sullen weight. And if the fruit was ready ripe, he'd caress it all over in the hold of his hand while it still hung pendulous and vulnerable, maybe drawing a final suckle from its mother tree. Then he'd pluck it, enjoying the reluctant snap. And then it was the bite, the squeezing teeth, the yield of succulent flesh, the warm, wet spurt and sweetest slurp. He sucked up a drool just from thoughts of it.

Barefoot now—having doffed and hidden his sneakers to better quarry the Julie tree—Gerrad tested a less dense spot among the tangle of hibiscus fence. Most of the individual trees were bushy with green leaves and hand-sized red or yellow flowers, and taller than he. Though it looked cushion-soft and pretty, the living stems-fence was so close-plaited, it took Gerrad's utmost strength to make it through this weakest gap. But finally, after paying well in determined striving and bloody scrapings and scratches, he forced apart some stiff inner branches and stole into the fence's garden side.

For a moment, he remained half buried in the cool leaves and reconnoitered his spoils. At least an acre of untended greenery lay before him. Wild grass and flowering weeds formed a pretty, continuous carpet until about halfway along, when this gave to an arbour of fruit trees promising cool shade from their lofty foliage ceiling.

As though sunstruck, Gerrad stood amazed at the sheer variety of fruit the garden presented. Like a fry in front a hook-shaped worm, he greedily scrutinized his prospects. About him were sun-faced guavas, blackly ripe sweet and sour cherries, several other varieties of mango, fat guanabanas, three—no! five—full-bunched yellow dwarf-coconut palms, clusters of pee-wah palms, and more, more, and much, much more. Bright, multiglobed grapes of purples, or salmon reds, or varied browns interrupted like extravagant pastry decorations on the generally dark green leafy background. And he was plumb in the middle of the party's cake!

He gaped about, making out what had to be a sapodilla tree with its sticky-juiced sweet fruit jutting directly from the stem like mat-brown breasts. He doubted only because never before had he seen sapodilla so big, so fat, so promising juicy. The garden's abundant variety was incredible, yet Gerrad sensed there was still more. Quite on its own, a smug, astonished, high-pitched giggle laughed out of him. But then, abruptly, at his own noise, before the rest of him could join the fun, his skin chilled and his hairs rose, and he became ultra-alert. It had occurred to him all this was too grand to be so available. There had to be some hazard here.

He slurped some spit around a mouth suddenly dry, and edged nearer to the cooler canopy of the fruity arbour, tensing even more. The whole place seemed too waiting: passive and quiet and biding like a trap. All the fruit—everything might be poised and ready like tasty bait. The only free movement in the arbour was the shafts of sunshine flickering hither-thither over the leaf-strewn ground like searching spotlights, or fleeing eyes.

Gerrad's cautioned thoughts returned to the Julie he had glimpsed. At least he'd try for that, then handle whatever developed afterwards. He ventured in its direction, and after peering up and about some, found it hanging on its branch at the outskirts of the treasure trove. A multitude of verdant leaves hid it so well that, but for the breeze and blind Luck, he'd have missed it.

Typically, the Julie tree was ridiculously easy to climb. Convenient branches made like a stepladder to a pantry. For a veteran conqueror of barriers like concealed spike-fences, vicious dogs, and watchmanning owners, this tree seemed begging for relief. So, not questioning Fortune further but still cautious, Gerrad was soon seating himself in the crook of the proper branch. Once quite comfortable there, he plucked, and continued his research of the unparalleled fruit.

While appraising a second Julie, he got to considering his promising fair tomorrows. He'd have to exploit his bounty very carefully. No one else must know of this garden of nectar. He must hoard it well, make it a lasting heaven. First job, though, would be to inventory the trove like a buccaneer wou . . . !!!

A silent scream seized his awareness. He was being watched!

Helplessly, he passed wind, then gasped through the stinking embarrassment. The flatulence had been a loud, sharp burst, a shot his watcher must've heard. Gerrad fought with a desperate urge to fly and jump and run out of there. He gritted his teeth and mustered self-control. He was not some simple thief. He must not scramble away like a scavenging stray dog. He had to face out this owner who tried playing him like a fly in a spider's trap. So with the sample's honey-juice forgotten and dripping all over his hands, Gerrad began searching out his watcher.

He felt a queer excitement as he doubled here as stalked and stalker. Hunting times before, during kills of iguanas and quail and even agouti, he had tried games of feeling both sides. Now he realized they'd been mere practice, training runs; nohow did they have the zing of this true experience.

Strictly, he kept the perfect silence of the garden. He was stiller than the trees, except for his tensing muscles. He kept fixed as sculpture, except for his slow eyes gleaning the sameness of the bush for minor shifts and subtle changes in its pattern. He searched the secrets of the dusky arbour, eyes sharp as glints of sunlight, nostrils aquiver at the air. He listened, too: hard enough to hear the leaves if they fell. Most scantily, he moved his search, and then only with deliberate purpose so as not to himself create the break of pattern that he sought.

And then, with a thrill, he discovered the eyes; although he was careful, and suppressed his wild satisfaction at the victory.

It was a woman, he guessed. She was standing among the stout, leaf-swathed suckers of a banana stool. Without knowing it, he had been looking in her direction all while eating the Julie.

He pretended to search as before he'd found her out; with every sweep, detailing her better from betwixt her setting. The hanging, dried leaves, with their shredded brownness, camouflaged her perfectly. Everything about her—her planted upright stance, her colour, and her clothes—blended exactly into the clump of plants. She didn't move, and seemed to be gazing directly at him. Then she did it again, and Gerrad realized what his hunting eye had caught to reveal her to him.

She had fluttered her eyelid. As Gerrad made another peeping sweep, she did it again, and he realized he was wasting his sneaking. The woman, indistinct behind the stand of banana shoots, was whore-bold winking at him. He strained to see her better as she remained surrounded by the palisade of fleshy sprouts. The only thing he saw clearly was the lewd suggestion in her distant eyes. A look so coarse and plain that already he was succumbing to its gutty message, and with sudden spasms close to hurting, he jetted spurt after fiery spurt of burning semen into his pants.

Bewildered, and weak in the throes of orgasm, Gerrad blindly grasped at a branch to support him. He held on, limply spent, his eyes a beam to the woman's face; caught there while she seemed to come into focus: the harsh domineering mask with gleaming, vulgar eyes, and cracked lips, and tangled hair, dirty with burrs.

Then the woman broke the thrall and turned away from him. Once, she looked back slowly, then went farther into the arbour out of view. Released from his *petite mort,* he stirred and listlessly climbed back down to earth.

With no intent to follow, he looked long at where she had gone. He felt sheepish and disgusted with himself. Who was she, and what'd happen now? Was she laughing at him? He had been so sudden, so inexpert, so quick, and so juvenile! Yet he couldn't have mistaken that look in her eyes. It had been a plain, leading-on look, its message clear and carnal. What he had done, she'd certainly shared and bidden.

He sighed, and hawked and spat in her direction, then turned to prowl—less pounce in his crouch now—back to his gap in the fence. All the way, spent semen slicked against his thigh, sticky-cool, and a sweaty lethargy resisted his need to be active again in the sunlit open.

Back in the street with his sneakers on, he looked at himself with the scratches and scrapes and semen stains and all, and one thing became certain. Library browsing was out of the question.

Twenty minutes later, Gerrad was jogging steadily homewards. From waist to knees, his jeans were sopping wet, as though sweat-drenched from a long run. This was the impression sought when he had poured tap water in around his waist until the semen stains were nicely absorbed in the blot. His jogging now was to work up a sweat to support that evidence. With the prevailing heat and two miles yet to home, such sweat was more than certain. He also endured the grind as self-punishment for his unmentionableness in the garden. All the same, every now and then an invigorating question sprinted through his distress to tease him: Would she be there another time?

It was two days before circumstances allowed Gerrad to visit the grove again. This time his destination was as certain as his route direct. He had also made some special preparations for the jaunt. Dressing for school that morning, intentions set, he had carefully chosen his pants: ones cut full and roomy, with two side pockets. The left pocket had the specialty of an enormous hole. The crumpled-up man-sized handkerchief in it now was one of the few things it could contain. One other item completed his equipment kit: a contraceptive rubber. Its label guaranteed it as "lubricated, ultra-sensitive, and featuring a reservoir tip."

Gerrad quickly entered the garden through the fat green fence. He stood there inside for a minute or so, enjoying the embrace of the soft hibiscus leaves. Although he glanced constantly at the clump of banana trees, he saw no one. His gaze never lingered there, however, but expectantly scouted the surrounding foliage. Gradually though, her absence soothing him, he relaxed and began wandering about. Close at hand, the honey-gold sheen of a ripe guava caught his eye. A little jump, and he was paid in full for his try. The guava's taste was well worthy of its colour, and it turned his interest to more flavorful research. Inevitably, however, his not-so-aimless meandering returned him to the banana-stool cluster.

From this close up, he was impressed by the robust vitality of the shoots and suckers: They reminded of sturdy, well-fed soldiers mustered at protective ease. Like a caress to his admiration, he heard a soft breeze sashaying through the shreds of their hanging dried leaves. It reached him, cool on his face, just as it bathed him with a frowzy, putrid stench. Instinctively, Gerrad snorted out the stink, held his breath, and swung around to head another way. And his heart almost burst itself as he did. Like a thumping drum, it drowned out the news of every other sense, announcing only the surprise his eyes had sprung. The woman was there.

She was sitting low down on an upraised root not more than fifteen feet away. She was looking at him that way, and seizing him fast with it. She had locked his stolen gaze right into hers, and he was more than powerless in his daze.

Again she was camouflaged, although discernible in her low-leveled recline. She wore something loose, earth brown, sacklike, that covered her completely—even to her hands. Her face, though, he could better make out, and realized he was mistaken in his earlier impression of prune-folds skin and cracked lips. It seemed now she was only as old as someone's mother.

The woman changed her pose unsubtly: Under her enveloping clothes, she boldly dropped her knees apart. And as if the suggestion was command to his plans, Gerrad's left hand homed to its two-holed pocket.

A fumble around the kerchief, through the specialty, and he could grasp the surging bulk and tug it in; feeling it so hard it hurt. He gloved the kerchief around its warmth and thrilled with the pulse of its might. A thought flickered that it could burst like a sizzling sausage, and that was fleeting distraction from the torrid fancy that the woman was deliberately open and widening for him under her earth-brown sack. He squeezed and wrung at this, milking the notion until it surrendered life. Until he was spewing his sperm like spit.

He became aware again in a happy lassitude, holding the soggy handkerchief around his lessened tumescence. Fingers spread apart like strangers in a bathroom, he pulled his hand from the pocket. Released, his penis slipped through the pocket's hole and fell thickly against his leg. He sighed long and closed his eyes.

In his pocket, he felt the mess soaking through. So he took out the loaded handkerchief and tossed it away near the banana stool. Then he stooped and cleaned off his hand on the grass. Close to the earth down there, he thought of the woman and, feeling very shy, half-straightened up to look at her. But she had gone.

It had been a long, hard one. Last night, after chores, homework, play, and a fight with his younger brother, Gerrad was exhausted when he went to sleep. Yet this morning found him strained and tired, not rested at all. He rolled over on his belly, and despite the intrusive sounds of his brother's toiling in the yard, he tried commanding some sleep from the new day. He closed his eyes firmly, and tried to think darkness and quiet. He thought instead that maybe he wasn't enjoying the sleep-late privilege he had already paid his brother for: Wanting an uninterrupted time for certain planned activities, he had bought this chore-free Saturday from his brother. The price was waiver of interest on an out-standing twenty-dollar loan. When he made the deal, a sweet anticipation was this luxury of late-morning snoozing. Now Gerrad felt cheated as his eyelids became belligerent at trying to avoid each other.

All the long-gone night he had been fielding battles. They had left him tender-skinned, sore-eyed, and confused. His dreams had been weird and crazy, unlike any before in how they seemed real without being actual. As if he had been split in two. Within and without, he could see himself be himself. And every sequence of the madness revolved around the garden-woman's face: a lingering etching in his mind, a mask framing the essence of his obsession. Every different dream scene had excited him further, was more erotic, more incredible, more disgustingly arousing as sequences and details switched, or repeated, ever-always dissolving without providing him consummation; abandoning him to lie wide-eyed tired with his chafing, absurd, swollen blood in hand, jerking it monotonously; futilely shifting the skin again and again; rubbing, polishing helplessly, anxious and frustrated for some kind of ease or climax. And all night long, he never won this simple peace.

Later on, when he left the house during the hottest part of the afternoon, he told them he was going to "cool out." He intended the phrase with private duplicity: in his brother's ear, to remind him of his stewardship. For himself, it meant his arbour of fleshy delights.

The day he walked was fine: bright with crisp sunshine lending every surface new polish. Gerrad strode along light as a bounce, feeling jolly and sharp with anticipation's energy. As if ready for a game, he wore a loose T-shirt, soccer shorts, and sneakers. When he arrived at it, he leapt onto the fence like a lion.

Once through, he headed directly to the bananas, slowing his pace to a stunned stop when he realized the woman wasn't there. He had so totally committed himself, he assumed her compliance. Now, her absence left him at a loss for what to do. He ranged around hopefully, special senses attuned only for her, searching, making sure. But she wasn't there.

His purpose in a vacuum, he was reluctant to leave this part of the garden. His eyes kept turning expectantly to the banana clump. Then he remembered his sodden handkerchief and went to where he had tossed it. A moment's searching around showed that it was gone, even as a piercing certainty declared that she had taken it; which set him speculating about her intent, and aroused the well-liked swelling. Within his thin, loose soccer shorts, it met no resistance at all.

And suddenly the vacuum filled as she arrived. He looked quickly at the banana cluster. She was standing a little farther beyond it, partially blocked by a hanging frond, and nothing else. She was out there in the open. He could see her distinctly. He shifted the sprig away and studied the faded brown sack for hints of her form beneath it. From the sag of the sack, all he could say was, she wasn't fat. Then his eyes were to her face, and all his attention was commanded.

But for a cast of demanding lechery, it was an empty place of ancient eye that hooked and pulled enchanted him. As he moved in closer, the woman, too, began shifting slowly, although not towards him but off to the side, as if keeping within opposite sides of a noose. Parrying in this manner, they danced well into the shady dome of the foliage. Then here, shrouded from the sun, she stopped and let him approach.

Her gaze, he saw, was riveted at his crotch, and reflexedly his groin responded. So much so, he had to stop walking as the massive erection forced itself out the side of his shorts. Rampant, it probed the air, unbalancing him as it quested with an ardour greater than he. Impaled by her imperious eye, he now recalled the dreadful dreams that had fired him up so without granting release. He knew a vague sense of danger, like a warning birdcall. But he shunned the presentiment. Her promise had him strong. It suppressed his natural fear.

Just her look devastated him with its suggestion of feral wantonness, of a willingness for crudest rutting. Gerrad could not resist. Desire had him strong in hand, stolid and slack of will. Yearning only to reach her, he arched his hips forward, straining like a bow, jutting out his crotch to her in offering.

Once more a tiny instinct of self-preservation recoiled. It hinted urgently that there was menace about the garden-woman. It bade him watch her mouth and how hungry it was set, to remember the decay stench that wafted through the pretty grove with her. He had never heard a bird there, he recalled, never seen a butterfly. Then that part of him fell quiet, as his attention for such concerns weakened and vanished. This macabre game was too far along for pausing now. The answer to the mystery was too close, and he craved it from a peak of passion he just could not climb down.

At that exact moment, as if she had divined his limits, the woman stuck her hand up between her straddled legs! With her shoulder slightly bent forward, she groped up under her loose clothes, and somehow the common, half-stooped pose suggested a surrender, as if she had given in to him. And at this unexpected, obscene perfection, Gerrad felt terribly little and lost, and trembling in anticipation, he squeezed his eyes tightly closed.

He remembered feeling this afraid of the sapping ecstasy when he had first started handling himself. He thought he had grown braver since. Now he knew a peculiar loss of dignity that the fear was still there; that it might go on too long and waste him up; that it had returned at such a time.

But now a clarion's peal was trilling every corner of his being and summoning every swift point of excitement he possessed. They roughed through him, rippling along his arms and trampling over shoulders, racing down his back, streaming up his calves and over his haunches. He sensed their brutish might as they massed about his groin. There, mob-eager, they rallied, garnering their power for a rampage.

Then Gerrad felt the forceful rush begin and exulted in an instant of lonely climax, before the rapture was shattered by a shock of draining pain. Something dry and sharp had punctured and impaled him. In a coffin of terror, retching tight-eyed from the agony, he strained and cleaved the hedge of his barring eyelids and saw the horrid *soucouyaun** was squatting before him, his own thick red gore spurting on her skull-hard face as it crowded his crotch with snarling, gnawing maws that were consuming him.

Then, as his soul shrank at the full horror of it, her hungry eyes glared up to his, and Gerrad knew a final keen despair. For all he found in her bleak pools of death was baleful mockery.

* succubus

OPEN CONFLICT

▐▌

". . . goin' t'chop a hunk out th' Humpback! Fiver goin' chop a hunk from 'is hump! . . ." The thought flitted out the dark of his sleeping mind: a fluttering, fluttering feather-soft bat brushing Boy-Strong into anxious wakefulness.

By the fullmoon brightness in the *'joupa,* all seemed in place about the open, single space. Outside, the air was shrilling with the first calls of early birds and croaking roosters claiming day'd be cleaning soon.

Above his head in the roof's thatch, something stirred stop-and-scurry, then again, another brief burst slithering through the dried palm leaves. Mr. Lizard hunting and eating well, Boy-Strong thought drowsily. Maybe dat's what rouse me. He relaxed.

Nevertheless, dreading the house slave's soft, fat, clammy body falling down on him because of some clever cricket's escape from a swift pounce, he scrunched up small and pulled the flour-sack sheet over his head. This set the hammock rocking a gentle, lulling wave. Boy-Strong rode it back to sleep.

". . . Fiver's bound t'junk a hunk from th' Hump's back. Ah

seen for certain!" Ma Tai's shiny face appeared in his mind, slits of eyes gleaming, bursting cheeks sweating malice, and grinning wide, white anticipation. . . .

This jarring prod unweighed the balance. Slumber fell away, and Boy-Strong felt his heart bring life into his day; heard blood's drum march it in, returning it from somewhere far, where it'd spent his sleeping. Heard it thumping about forefront, solid, there in his chest, harder and stronger, insisting, until Sleep dropped all its reins, and Boy-Strong was forced to take up that long, deep sigh of a breath that full-awoke him; at which he took another, just to hold living fast in place, until it felt belonged and risen.

Then Boy-Strong rolled out of the hammock onto the smooth dirt floor, and stretched aplenty of strength and youth. He recalled the foreboding of his awakening dream just as his bowels called, and, brooding, started towards the braided coconut-leaf curtain door, heading for the backyard track of dew-damp grass to the latrine.

A big fullmoon'd be floating low ready tonight, pivot point for the conflict in town. For a while, it had been his mind to break routine and go in today, Saturday, and linger into the night to personally witness the showdown, that depending on if he managed to sneak inside the rumshop at all. But yesterday as he was walking her home from school, Dina'd told him her father'd be working today, and that her mother was in bed not feeling well. She told him this with a sudden quieting of the normal mischief in her eyes, and the dicey idea of a town trip fell down dead. Heart attack right there; expired just like that!

He'd go in 'foreday morning Sunday as usual and sell his stuff all day; and just before sunset he'd firm up courage, go over by Ma Tai's pastry table, and as usual, the second-sight Shango woman would tell him the story her way.

Just as she had predicted last time: "Dat's when dey will be ready to dig into each other. Nothin' could make so not so. Y'd be hearing how it go when nex' the moon big, mi' chile, so you go practice some patience for de while," she'd said. And so said, just so it was seeming to be.

Today, though, was a put-aside special. Today was joy-with-Dina day.

A little later that morning, Boy-Strong went by Mr. Dennis to borrow Union Jack for the morrow's trip. He got over there seven o'clock early so to catch him before he left for his field-foreman job at the government's experimental farm.

Mr. Dennis was standing by the chicken pens, staring at the birds, sipping his coffee off and on. Boy-Strong greeted him, "Morning, Mr. Dennis."

"Morning, Nollis." Mr. Dennis never used his "home name," somehow formalizing his presence and reminding Boy-Strong of the ulterior motive for his frequent visits. It made him wonder if he was suspected, so he kept strictly sharp-wits around the older man.

He got right down to business. "Mr. Dennis," he began, "Ah come t'borrow Union Jack. Ah'm really sorry to have to bother you every time so. But Ah'm saving up to buy mi'self—"

Mr. Dennis cut in, "Oh yes, yes. I nearly forget is tomorrow tour ships coming in. Sure, by all means, take 'im. The walk'll do 'im good."

Mr. Dennis spoke so offhandedly, Boy-Strong felt relieved and piqued at the same time. He really was uncomfortable borrowing the jackass on such a regular basis, and would be peeved if Mr. Dennis took his genuine story as the simple blind of a borrower. He was saving up! Oh, how he was saving up! Only the horse-power he wanted was under the seat of a certain shiny moped he'd seen in the window of a dealership in town—an ambition he intuitively knew Mr. Dennis would disapprove of.

With his indignant conscience thinking for him, he said, "Thanks, Mr. D. But Ah'm really saving up, in truth, y'know."

"Sure, y're saving up, Nollis. Youth's always saving up before spending it all." He spoke this last part more swiftly and undertoned, as always when he made such double-meaning comments.

Although Boy-Strong had picked it up, he said, "Huh, sir?"

Mr. Dennis said, "Ah! Is nothin', Nollis. Is nothin' at all. But, listen me here. He have a sore where the harness pinching under his belly. On the right side, by here. Ah dress it and bandage it. But he might try to scratch it off. Y'know how jackass gain 'is name. So play eyeball f'r me."

"Yuh don't've to say it, Mr. D. You know dat. I wouldn't ever let Union suffer. Ah mean, we's close as family, me and he."

They laughed. Mr. Dennis sipped his coffee, and watched the moving carpet of yellow puffball baby chicks in their coop.

"So, how dey doin'?" Boy-Strong asked.

"Not too bad, y'know. Must lose two, three, dey so young. But don't you think I'm complaining. Not me."

Remembering a recent riverside conversation, Boy-Strong said, "Trellis tell me dat Jonas Bayne lose 'most all 'is batch. Chicken polio pass dem through, he say."

"Maybe, who knows?" said Mr. Dennis. "Jonas Bayne's a man dat wouldn't lean to storm winds. A man dat wouldn't give de chicken an' dem vaccine-water to drink. A man dat put 'is all in moon instead. So maybe is moon take care of 'is business. Maybe is moon dat pass dem through."

Boy-Strong hadn't intended to revive tired battles. Many older people didn't agree with Mr. Dennis's scientific ways. Half the time it was them not understanding; half the time it was Mr.

Dennis not grasping well the whole idea, and failing to explain its workings to them in a commonsense manner. Boy-Strong respected the man's belief in scientific ways, though, and enjoyed listening to him talk about Power through Knowledge and Conviction, and so on. But same Mr. Dennis never stopped criticizing any machine at all as noisy, and smoky; so Boy-Strong had his reservations.

"They's always some dat carn't give up dey longtime ways—" he began.

But Mr. Dennis cut in, "One time it used to be nice down dat valley. But it change. Down dere too damp now. Since dat brown mold take over, down dere damp like a rotten mop. An' dat mule of a Jonas Bayne don't even want to know 'bout de modern miracles we passin' out at de station. . . ."

Mr. Dennis had strayed into one of his favorite ruts. Boy-Strong knew the basic pattern of his grievance, and that Mr. D. could ramble along this groove for hours. So he relaxed his thoughts from Mr. D.'s gruff, convinced tones, and let his mind drift among its swells.

First orphaned at two by a hurricane, Boy-Strong felt Mr. D. came the closest thing to family ever since Grandma Mae and Pappy passed through the year he turned fourteen. Thinking about them months after the funeral, he realized they'd been attempting to model Mr. Dennis as father for him; always praising or criticizing his traits as compared to other men of the village.

He could remember darkening evenings when they'd be outside leaning on the 'joupa's tapia walls, or sitting in the yard slapping at gnats, and, after a wistful sigh, how Pappy'd throw weak eyes on him for long moments, then motion him close, and say, "Got a someting to tell you, son. A serious ting every man should hear. Son, live well and let live. Dat's how I say it."

"I know dat already, Pappy. You say it before. Don't

worry 'bout Boy-Strong. Ask anybody and wha' dey'd say is, 'Boy-Strong treat everybody fair.' Dat's wha' dey goin' t'say, Pappy."

Most times Pappy'd muse off before saying more. Once, though, he did give a working idea for being a better man when he said, "Y'know, son, what you gotta do is dis. It not so hard. Y'have to make up a man just as you like. A *doux-doux* of a man yuh could trust in de fair and de fray. Den, in yuh real life, whenever you get to crossroads, you just follow yuh man's footsteps. Y'see? So y'carn't ever get lost, 'cause is a masterman you following. Is yuh own dream man you goin' after!"

Boy-Strong had seriously considered the simple system, until, slapping at his neck, Pappy'd continued, "But make sure 'e tell you how to stamp out mosquitoes, okay?" Then and there, wet-eyed laughter had forever punched a joke through the plan.

Still, it was the only scheme ever spelled out before they passed through one Friday the moon rose new. Early that morning, Grandma had given him an envelope of papers to take to the government's land office in town: The trip was for his own good, she had told him. Against his protests, she had hobbled up and made coffee; he figuring she knew how his mouth ran rivers for her special clove-and-cardamom brew.

It was first dawn when he called, " 'Bye, Pappy," and heard a sleepy "Safe ways, son!" returned from inside.

Watching him away from the door, Grandma called him back. "Boy-Strong, son," she said sternly. "Do good the best y'could always. Y'hear me, boy?"

Cheerful, anticipating the town time, he had said, "Wha' else you expecting, Granny? Y'forgetting is Boy-Strong y'talking to."

Granny's face softened and grinned gums at him, and it didn't puzzle him that her eyes glistened so wet. Neither did he wonder about the last words she hailed at him: "Yuh right, son. Is me to forget, an' is you to remember. God bless you, child."

Boy-Strong remembered that trip all right. The seven-mile walk in was a blur of familiar forest tracks. In the several offices, he had waited eternities and finished all the land business; then, finally free of duty, he spent a great afternoon gawking about town. Mindful that they worried over him, he left early enough and, near five o'clock, returned home to howling dogs and a warm, ashy, but dead fireside. And a strange, stale, unplaceable scent that floated throughout the *'joupa*.

Worried and wondering where they'd both gone at that late hour, he lit the fire and the pitch-oil lamp. Off and on, to break the wait, he hurled sticks and threats at the constant-howling dogs.

As every shade of dusk fell into night, at every sound of movement, Boy-Strong craned and peered up the front track for sight of them. Ten thousand times he wondered where they'd visited, and when whoever it was would bring them back home in this dark.

It was about seven when in the midst of his worrying, the pale, close scent, the wailing dogs, and everything came together in a quiet, chilling thought. Trembling, already stricken, he tiptoed over and pulled aside the curtain that screened their sleeping quarters. They were laid out faces up, holding hands, dressed in their high-occasion Sunday bests. Grandma's eyes were open, glazed blank and dry; her face relaxed, a small overwhite smile gleaming from her too-even false teeth. Pappy's upper plate, never fitting right, grinned wildly out his lips like a thing escaping. Looking about the gloom in the room, Boy-Strong realized the source of the peculiar smell. It was their opened cedarwood clothes trunk.

For the balance of the night, Boy-Strong had watched his private wake over them; and early next morning he went to Mr. Dennis with his heartbreak and orphan's tears to tell of their passing. . . .

". . . Well, dat's how I see it. De new farming's a science. And dat's about how I say it," Mr. Dennis summed up, recalling Boy-Strong's attention to the immediate.

Trying for the respectful, newly-made-wiser tone, he responded smoothly, "You could say dat again, m'sire."

Mr. Dennis drained the rest of his coffee in a final manner. At which a thrill of anticipation birthed in Boy-Strong's belly, weakening him severely as it grew throughout too strenuously. He mastered betraying it, though, and, plain-faced, awaited the rest of Mr. D.'s parting ritual.

Mr. Dennis looked into the chicken coop and waved his arm at it. He said, "Well, son. Look at what I leave for what I go to."

Boy-Strong shrugged and snorted mock sympathy.

Mr. Dennis grinned and wagged his finger at Boy-Strong. "Y'must remember dis: A man mus' watch 'is heart to do 'is duty. Dat guard's always de realest man."

Boy-Strong furrowed his smooth face as if struggling with this wisdom. Then he wagged his point finger right back at Mr. Dennis, admonishing, mock man-to-man bold, "Well, m'sire, you watch y'heart, an' go do yuh duty."

They laughed fondly with each other before, with his usual brief salute, Mr. Dennis said, "Well, I'm off. You be good." And he went up the track to the house for his bike, and to work.

And as he departed, the tamped excitement raging within Boy-Strong lost all restraint, and rejoiced freely in anticipation of indulging its delight.

Extremely long minutes later, Boy-Strong's mucha-major reason for visiting sauntered down the track, carrying a basket of finely cracked cornfeed for the new chickens.

The vision turned his way, saw him, smiled, and transformed

into a promise of pleasure in subtle paradises. It said, "Mornin', Boy-Strong. How y'feelin'?"

"Oh God, Dina. How y'does take so long t'come down, when you well know dat I waiting." As he complained, Boy-Strong tried to put his arms around her. "Leh me show you how Ah feelin'," he begged.

Dina wasn't cooperating, maybe. She shifted about the wide-rimmed basket so that it shortened his reach. Then, when he sidestepped that, she wriggled and twisted herself about with much pressing and pushing and sliding against him, the contact of her warm, firm flesh charging him up before she slipped away.

From safe stance, she complained, "Look how y'make all de chickenfeed scatter-fall."

Boy-Strong was shivering hot inside from her touch. A larger part of the emotion was fattening down in his crotch. Embarrassed by the size of that passion, he readily knelt for concealment and began scooping up the chickfeed with cupped hands. "Ah'll pick it up for you," he said, working slowly at separating the corn from the dirt—as he had to, much in need of time to quiet down the heat bulging him out and burning him up.

A little later, Dina's chores done, they were dallying by the well, eating succulent king-orange pegs.

"Y'think he goin' to take advantage on that poor li'l man, Boyie?" Dina asked.

"You mean Onezy, de Fiver?"

"Yeah, who else but dat evil-minded brute."

"Well, I don' know, girl. But whatever have to happen, it happening tonight. Ah'll find out when I go in to town tomorrow."

"Well, I do hope nothin ent happen to th' poor li'l Humpback," Dina said. "It jus' wouldn't be righteous, Boyie. A big, strong brute like Fiver mistreating a little humpbacked midget so. You have to stop him. You just have to."

Boy-Strong had never mentioned their dimensions. Ma Tai had never provided any. But with this Fiver and Hump affair, some details just seemed to fall into mind. Boy-Strong himself had always imagined Fiver as a thin man with nice teeth, who'd begun to drink because he stopped smoking when he lost his right hand—just where it joined the wrist—to sharkbite. It was the match-lighting problem: He couldn't adjust his left to it, and was always too proud to beg assistance.

"I don't understand how you pick his side so," said Boy-Strong. "The Hump ent all goodness and grace, y'know. And in any case, I can't arrange or change what happen between dem. All I can do is parrot what I hear. As I buy it, I selling."

"It still not fair, though," Dina insisted with a pout, making Boy-Strong seriously anxious. Frustrating as she was about giving up an occasional hug or kiss, she could be ten times worse if she became fretful. And he hadn't cleaned and rewatered the animal troughs, put out their feed, and swept the whole backyard (most all of Dina's chores) in order to waste her liberated time arguing about the Humpback's fate.

"But if you want to encourage me a li'l bit, I don't know what I might manage," mollified Boy-Strong.

"Encourage you? Encourage you how? And with what? I don't've nothin' special," she said coyly, looking down into the well, and drowning Boy-Strong with her flirting prettiness.

"You shouldn't believe dat at all, darlin'. Lemme show you something . . ." Boy-Strong suggested. This was just the attitude he wished for, just the sort of position he wanted to prove out, there in the lush, shady grove of ripe-laden orange and banana and mango trees, with the sashaying breeze, and two precious hours of privacy ahead.

As always, though, time turned out no ally, and as usual, he soon gave up. She sealed off her softnesses in a fortress, her hands and arms becoming unbreachable walls wherever he'd try. And when, eventually, she brought up that she'd be missed if she didn't go inside, he was relieved to officially quit. His consolation was a sense that he might've conquered some meager ground. Several times during their fierce and silent contest, he had felt her pause herself on him; as if she was stealing a feel of him; as if she was tasting the tease in their struggling lovematch, and felt water in her mouth.

As they panted their way back to composure, Dina fixed her clothes and hair, while Boy-Strong turned away to rearrange the suddenly awkward weight at his crotch. He heard her say, "Boyie? Y'mean what you was saying?"

He spun around. "Yeah, is true-true, Dina. I really want you bad," he said quickly.

"Oh, not that, Boyie. I mean about saving the Humpback, and so."

Boy-Strong remembered his earlier promise. "Don't open dat bag o' stale fish again," he said quickly. "We talked 'bout it, an' I say wha' I had to say. I go do as much as I could. But only from nex' fortnight. And, remember, maybe I can't even go in de rumshop where dis ting happening. I underage, and dey mightn't let me in anyhow. So dat's why mih hands tied, an' why I've to depend on Ma Tai for de whole ting."

"But she's your friend, Boyie, and she know Obeah. So how come you can't work anything through her? How come y'don't ask her to protect 'im with a charm or something? I sure y'could give her some plan when you get in, in the morning. And then she'd have time to defend the hunchback. Couldn't you? Huh?"

Boy-Strong thought, Me?? Plan?? and didn't bring up how Ma Tai seemed to hate the hunchback. Or reassert that he had no influence in the matter. He wanted to get the conversation more personal. "Well, dat's a real good idea, and maybe Ah'll try it. But I still don't see why you getting so involved. Dat wasn't my intention in telling you de story. But whatever, matters pro'bly work out demselves already, anyhow. But, sweetheart, we should be thinkin' of us instead of dem crazy people in town."

"Don't come with all that 'sweethearting' me," Dina upsed. "If you could stop dat butcher from cutting up the poor boasie-back midget, den I might know for certain about all dat 'love you, love me' you does be preaching, and maybe den I might do anything you want." Her words after "maybe" were murmured as if she didn't really say them.

Boy-Strong blinked, her normal teasing frontline in mind. Except that, as if he had suddenly begun brightly shining, Dina's eyes kept flickering at him and darting away. And then, face flushed and strangling any lurking maybes, she whispered throatily, "I not making joke. . . ."

He stepped closer, held her shoulders, and found her quietly atremble, not pulling away. His heart-drum announcing Opportunity, Boy-Strong said into her cinnamon-scented hair, "You'll come over by mih *'joupa?*"

In the perfect fit of his arms, she stiffened slightly. "You crazy, Boyie? What if Daddy catch me?"

"He wouldn't."

Dina pulled out of his embrace and walked to the well. "You trying to get both of us killed? Y'know Daddy."

Boy-Strong went to her and covered her hand where it rested —waited—on the well's concrete rim. He said, "How y'daddy'll know? Mondays to Fridays he come from work six o'clock. Every day you come from school at two. Is ten minutes to my *'joupa* through de back trace. So how yuh daddy'll know?"

As he spoke, he tried to trap her flying eyes, now flitting about him, now straining in the direction of the house. Her hand, though, remained under his sweaty palm like a finders-keepers jewel.

"What about Mammy?" she asked.

"She not feelin' well dese days, remember? And she always sleepin' until fivish." He answered easily, certain, feeling strong to her hovering fears. Confident that she was wavering, ripe and ready to fall; knowing he was her net. He picked up her hand, damp and limp as if it had fainted. "Come on, Dina. Y'know how I love you. I so lonely without you. I jus' want to squeeze you up an' kiss you all over so bad. I only want you private an' personal to show all dis love I have for you, dat's all. Come by me Tuesday after school. Come and see my love."

She didn't answer, except her clammy hand clasped his tightly. After a bit, she tugged away and, casting a swift, shy look at him, skipped away towards the house. "Perhaps I'll try," she said, "but only if you stop th' brute."

She went, at ease again, grinning broad mischief at him, eyes bright in flight and fresh with promise.

Winded and turgid from seduction, Boy-Strong sighed heavily and leaned against the well's cool concrete rim; his anticipation shifting weights at playing fox with Mr. D., his anxiety tensing from Dina to Ma Tai and the conflict in town.

The sun one hour to go, Boy-Strong had tended and settled in the borrowed donkey before he went inside to take care of his own dinner. He threw some soda and flour together, set it to rise, and lit fire to his big iron pot, and in no time he had finished a nice-smelling roast-bake. As he prepared *bhagii* and sauce to grease it down, he also made peace with varied erotic, romantic, fantastic plans and dreams concerning Dina's possible visit.

Maybe it was the routine of kneading flour and making fire and food that steadied him and set him thinking on his straw— his craft that gave him self and pride, and good, good money every fortnight. Eventually, mind at peace after preparing the morrow's wares, he curled up in his hammock and rocked off to pleasant sleep.

With the first crowing of the cocks, as cool dawn blended into the moonlight, Boy-Strong left the *'joupa* feeling fresh and sharp. Along the forest's track, he breathed moist, earth-scented air as he peered into the darkened, silvered greenery, trying for glimpses of its life. All about him sounded the whistles and peeps and calls of night creatures, the underbrush rustling busily with its traffic—late sleepers turning in, early risers starting out, everybody circumspect about each other's space, but none he ever saw.

The jackass by his side, warm and rank, breathed a regular rhythm between its clomping hooves, and with the birdcalls and the hazy light and all, the walk grew peaceful, and made Boy-Strong meditative and unconscious of distance.

Ma Tai presently filled his mind, how it had come about between them. A year ago it was. He had just made fifteen, his granfolks passed, and Mrs. Dennis had suggested he go in town and sell the straw stuff he passed his time making. "One of those tourist stores'd take it off your hands. It's good quality. I've seen half as good in their glass cases," she'd said.

Mrs. Dennis was right. The stores were happy to buy his fine work, and in quick time he got to supplying two stores. That went on for about four months, until he noticed the stores were selling his stuff for five and six times the prices they paid him. So he stopped supplying them and began setting up his stall every other Sunday, when the tourist ships were in port.

It was the best move he could've made. For better prices, he plied his better handicraft directly to the tourists, and normally he sold out in hours. Did very well, thank you.

First few times on the wharf, he set up stall under the shade of a robust, fat-bunched coconut tree. His notion was that the generous shade helped his business by offering a moment's cool to the overpinking tourists. He noticed, though, that other vendors about him continued to set their trays and stalls square out in the blazing sun. It remained a vague puzzle for him, but, in his business mind, their due loss.

Then, one Sunday, this head-tied pastry-lady clued him: Sometimes, she said, a coconut, on its own, would drop from the overhead tree, and could kill the head it fell on. Five minutes later, Boy-Strong had moved his stall next to the heavyset, country-dressed older woman. Five minutes further, a coconut dropped with a crash where he used to stand. Stricken henceforth, Boy-Strong gaped at the woman with awe. Ma Tai—as she had given—just grinned smug as a witch at him.

Gradually, moon by fat moon, he found out more about her, much from other vendors' gossip. He also listened to Ma Tai herself, ever wary of her hinting manner, and scared extra polite by her constant references to Obeah ritual and managed spirits. Sometimes, going on about her jumbie business, a weird glint'd grow in her eyes: a flare of threat and power that made him gulp and shiver. Still, though, a sneaky feeling whispered that maybe she was just fooling with him, having her fun teasing with thrilling stories. On the other hand, there was always that deadly coconut, and how vendors who'd talk about her crossed themselves furtively when they did. So, about Ma Tai's strangenesses, Boy-Strong was always respectful, and considered her company a privilege.

Done with selling his stuff, he'd go over to her stall. In her bossy manner, she'd hail, "Hey, Tallboy. You finish already? I tell you y'should be raisin' yuh prices."

"I makin' enough, Ma Tai," he'd reply.

"Taste some samples from the tray," she might order him; and always impatiently, she'd ask, "Every time so I haveta invite you? Huh?"

Boy-Strong had learned to ignore the show of irritation. He divined it as masquerade for her liking him, and for her generosity. And, in any case, available from her trays was every compensation: sweet jams, honeyed sour fruits, tarts, *chillibibi,* boiled and roasted nuts, dried and juicy preserves, sugared cassava pone, molasses *tulums,* and coconut sugarcakes; all the sorts of things Boy-Strong could happily get sick eating. All from which she chose him samples.

It was while he dallied with her dainties that she got to telling him about the contention between the one-handed butcher and the hunchbacked shoemaker.

Except that the two lived next door to each other, Ma Tai never made it clear what set off the conflict. Once he interrupted to ask, and she went into a huff and stopped altogether. After that, Boy-Strong just kept his mouth occupied and his ears open, letting her fill him in as she wished.

One thing came clear: She didn't like the hunchback. Although, on the other hand, she faithfully related the more wicked scores he made on the butcher. Like the time Gibba greased the butcher's bike handle so that he broke his face falling because he couldn't hold on at all. Hoarse with outrage at the hunchback, she told full all of that funny episode.

By Boy-Strong's next visit, though, her glee had returned as she related the butcher's payback: how Fivers sneaked after the Hump and stole his pants out the rumshop's latrine, then hung them so high on the outside wall that the Hump, unable to reach up, had to rip them down grabbing at the legs while the drunkards ridiculed his nakedness.

This volleying of rancour and revenge was the set way between them, and lately, wicked returns went worse with the episode of Gibba the Hump's bloody leather soak.

Hump was a shoemaker could fit a dancing cricket. But was always busy working for rich people's pockets, without pride in himself even to put some beauty on his own two feet. Such was his miserly soul, Hump wore nothing but plain canvas alpagats. And it was mainly because he was so cockroach-cheap, Ma Tai wished him buried alive in his hoardings.

Hump used to soak his raw leather in a special potion that made it forever soft and easy to work and wear. Some said it was macawoeul oil, but common sense says it had to have more ingredients than just that. The soaking tub—a long wooden trough with a cover of nailed boards—he kept behind his shanty. He'd mix his mystery potion in the house, pour it into the trough, add the new leather, close the cover, then lock it. Usually, afterwards, and for Fiver's benefit, he'd shout, "Confusion to the busybodies!"

It took a while for Fiver's response, but with that constant needling, by and by he busied his body and replied to suit.

Thus, eventually, the morning arrived when the hunchback discovered two large white pig carcasses lying on the cover of his curing trough. They'd been cut at the throat vein, and were so drained of blood, their dirty, bristled skin was candle-wax clear. And all this bleeding had dripped through the boards and dyed Hump's soaking potion into an ugly, gory, stinking slush.

Hit and hurt at his core, the Hump bawled furious, red-eyed threats against Fiver's life. He screamed at the world, went into a fit of grovelling and rolling about in his bare front yard, and, in between snivels and gobby snorts of dirt and slime, dared Fiver to come out and play his endgame there and then.

Fiver let him rant and rave maybe half an hour before he opened his front door.

Reenraged at the sight of his tribulations, screaming like a branded bo'hog, the Hump rushed him. The neighbours, jurying the thrusts and parries of the conflict, corralled his charge and looked expectantly to Fiver for the next move. He, of course, pleaded ignorance and the innocence of flowers.

The hunchback didn't have but suspicion against him, he said. True, agreed the neighbours. Maybe it was his common sense knotted up that'd bunched into Gibba's hump, Fiver suggested. And the good neighbours grinned behind their hands and advised the Hump to go home and calm down. Which, roiling in his steam of tears, sweat, and humiliation, was exactly all he could do.

But he couldn't manage it long. Next thing heard by the neighbours was the Hump's challenge: Fiver was about to lose his last hand. The Hump was to be dread dealer. This rumour didn't stay long without response, as Fiver let it be known that all last night, Saturday night, he'd be ready to win or lose at the rumshop bar.

That's what it had come down to. From a fortnight ago, Ma Tai's conspiring voice returned to Boy-Strong's mind quite clearly: "Is de spirits' revelation. Onezy agoin' t'chop off Gibba's extra back. Be assured o' dat judgement. An' lehme tell you more, it'd serve th' tightback miser right, for the sky is the eye of common-man God."

That was as far as she'd say. She would betray no more of her second sight. Would only promise to tell him everything next time.

He had pressed her, "But, Ma Tai, y'have to tell me now. Ah mightn't come down, y'know. Ah mightn't 'ave any work done up to sell. Y'have to tell me de full story now. And if you really know it anyhow, why y'wouldn't tell me? Eh?"

Taking him the wrong way, she'd planted her hands akimbo, drawn her head back like a viper, glared her widened eyes, and hissed slow and heavy at him, "Well, hi-ya-yi here! So now you know what I have to do, an' what I don't have to do, huh! Well, Mister Know-it-all, you want me to plant you right here where you stand, never more no move? Never ever? Huh?"

Chilled to his soul with fear, Boy-Strong had apologized sincerely, "Is not so I mean, Ma Tai. I didn't mean no presum'tions, Ma Tai. Y'must know dat. I ent dat kinda fella, Ma Tai."

She glowered at him from the distance of her withdrawn neck for a long moment. But she had been satisfied. "Yes, is true. You was always a good boy. But sometimes you could be tryin' bold, too. So you better watch yuh ways well."

Then she had reached over her table stand, into the bowl with boiled *paymee,* and handed him one in forgiveness.

His dry, anxious mouth watering immediately, Boy-Strong began unwrapping the dark green boiled banana leaf. Still warm, the leaf's soft aroma didn't mask the delicious flavours of its contents: corn and coconut dough with spiced-meat fillings. Just before he shoved a full third of it into his drooling mouth, he remembered and looked at her face. "Thanks, Ma Tai. An' for the *paymee,* too," he said to the gleaming eyes he met in wait there.

She went back talking about it on her own. "De trouble between dem poised exact, pin-to-needle point. Pain must happen now. Have to. An' it goin' happen as I tell you. An' I ent goin' to miss out nothin'," she assured him.

He had responded carefully, "I only wondering why it wouldn't happen before, uh? Why not on some weekday evenin' when dey drinkin' in de rumshop? Huh?"

"Dem's moon people, chile. No spirit of dey own. Moon run all dey ways and dey means. Moon's dey momma and dey queen. When she belly full-out round an' shinin' brighty-brighty, dat's when dese men's waterbag of battles'll break, an' dere chile name Trouble will splatter from de confusion."

The grim picture quelled Boy-Strong's every query.

"Y'ent goin' to miss nothin' from me, chile. You's a good boy. I like tellin' you story," Ma Tai reassured. Then she clammed up tight and far-eyed.

Boy-Strong took the hint. "So, we go catch up full moon den, all right?" he'd said to her before swinging his gunnysacks up into Union Jack's panniers and beginning the half-moon trek home through the gloaming countryside.

Once in town today, Boy-Strong attended to his business directly. He set up stall in his usual spot and began selling. Everything went routinely; he being quick, smiling, and polite, as his tray emptied and his money pouch got fat.

Only thing wrong was Ma Tai being absent. All day, at every chance, Boy-Strong's eyes scanned to her usual spot. But, his apprehension growing, midday hot sun then afternoon clouds came and went, and still no Ma Tai showed.

Then, too soon he was finished, and still she hadn't appeared, and Boy-Strong became anxious. Not only about her welfare, and about the rumshop confrontation: Had the Hump had it? But most crucial of all, what was he going to tell his Dina? With her mind so set on saving the hunchback, she'd be pestering him about what happened. With bad news, her cooperation'd be a greasy pole to climb. With no story at all, she'd be that same slipperiness with a thick thorn fence around it.

As it neared sunset, Boy-Strong packed up and went along the roadside looking for answers. The third vendor he came upon gave him time to talk. She was a small, spry lady selling mangoes: rosy turpentines in pyramid heaps of four on a now-for-now box and tray stand. There were five heaps left. Boy-Strong selected one and paid for it, put three mangoes in his pockets, and bit into the rosiest; juices mingling with his, the too-much sweetness splurging from the sides of his mouth.

He met the vendor's eyes, bold and confident of a satisfied customer, and smiled at her. "Yuh right," he said, "dis is de real McCoy."

Relaxed another mango more, he got to asking her, "Y'know that lady who does sell treats up the way a bit?"

She followed his pointing hand. "Which 'un?" she asked. "Is more than one that selling treats."

"Ma Tai's her name."

"Y'mean the wildwoman they ketch in juju on the beach?" the vendor asked, excitement raising her voice.

Juju on the beach!!? The eerie scene he instantly imagined gave Boy-Strong a rise also, goose bumps racing a chill along his arms and back. He'd always had that weird instinct about Ma Tai, although generally she had been nice to him, telling him the story, and so on. Abruptly, he felt bound to defend her.

"Why y'must call she that?" he challenged.

"Y'mean that she's a juju-woman?"

"Yeah, as one f'r instance," he said.

"Because is so, mister youthman. Dat's what she is. You mus' be new 'round dese parts, 'cause everybody know dat 'oman does deal wit' spirits." She lowered her voice and, glancing about her, began talking so rapidly, Boy-Strong could scarcely follow.

He got her gist, though: Madam Taiama was one of her names; Madame Shashango, another. She was from Tophill County. Came down weekends with sweetmeats and things that she sold mainly to the tourists because people had it to say she put bush potions in her treats. Some to make life lucky, some to make love sweet. Some to give you charm, some to pass you talent, and some just to curse you with bad luck if she was in that mood. The mouth-watering tourists was bound to choose their destiny blind and go 'way. But not so those who know.

The mango vendor straightened up, looked around quickly, crossed herself, and finished in a normal voice, "Nobody don't take any chances wit' dat 'oman, mih dear. Not at all, at all. Dah'd be jus' plain foolhardy dangerousness."

Boy-Strong had never heard these rumors so plainly detailed. He listened, and remembering all the good treats he had stuffed from off Ma Tai's trays, he shuddered violently. He felt his belly souring, the taste of it back of his throat. He breathed carefully and palmed a sudden, clammy sweat from his brow.

The woman scrutinized him. "You feelin' bad, or someting?" she asked. Then, suddenly, she stepped back behind her tray, and squinted suspicious eyes. "Y'ent no sort o' hex from her, is you?" she demanded of him.

Boy-Strong snorted. "Come on, miss lady, y'ever see spirit eating mango?" He bit deliberately into the mango in his hand.

The woman burst out in nervous laughter. "Nor licking dey chops either," she said. "But I really 'fraid to tangle wit' dat juju-lady in any fashion at all. An' I ent shame t'say so."

"So wha' happen on de beach?" he asked.

The mango vendor once more cast her eyes over her shoulder at the crimson falling sun, rubbed her chin, and whispered rapidly, "Three days 'fore full moon, Tuesday gone, I tink it was. My eye didn't see, but folks saying how some night fishermen creep up on de witch on de windward beach naked as she born 'cept for she flab an' a wreath of blooded flowers on she head. She was in trance dancin' prayers at de moon."

She looked directly in Boy-Strong's face and nodded conviction at him. As she wanted, Boy-Strong asked, "An' what happen?"

"But what else? Dose men and dem jus' scramble deyselves back to dere fishing boat, and paddled deyselves away fish-quiet before she could come untranced an' notice dem an' fix dey no-business-dere behinds. Dat's what did happen. Wha' else y'expect?"

Alarm scrambling his mind, Boy-Strong grunted and contained his confusion. The mango lady's expectant eye beamed on him, inviting another question. But after a quiet moment, he said, "Well, thanks for dem sweet mangoes, ma'am. Hope you have some more nex' time. I goin' home now. Good night."

Mind adrift in a mist of consternation, his trusty feet found Boy-Strong to where he'd left Union Jack grazing. Then, consumed with misgivings about explanations to Dina, he wended the moonlit way home.

Next morning seven o'clock found Boy-Strong having returned, groomed, and penned up Union Jack. Mr. Dennis met him as he latched up the gate. "How tings went through?" he asked Boy-Strong.

"Easy as breeze in high leaves," Boy-Strong answered. "Made close a hundred, an' I still savin' mos' of de material I like. . . ."

He would've gone on talking his business, as he'd long learned how such bragging pleased Mr. Dennis; but this time Mr. Dennis burst in, "Look here, Nollis, we've to talk some man-to-man talk, y'know. Nadina talk, y'understand me?"

At her unexpected name, Boy-Strong understood only extreme confusion, although he immediately followed Mr. Dennis's meaning. Still, that didn't prevent his heart from leaping to a boom-booming start, as if trying to break away.

He gaped at Mr. Dennis, gulping to control his breath. "Talk, Mr. D.?" he blurted, as if it were a strange invention.

Mr. Dennis looked away from him, at the jackass in its enclosure. He said, "Don't feel nervous, boy. You is a good young man since I know you. I like you, an' I proud of how you handle yu'self when yuh folks passed. You close. Mih wife like you, an', most of all, mih daughter like you. Long time now she liking you. Long time now I know it. I'll be a stupid father if I didn't. I'll be a stupid father if I against it. You is a lucky man. You even have a special gift. You's blest for sure."

Boy-Strong felt he should say something in Mr. Dennis's pause. He opened his mouth. "Ugh, ahh . . ." he managed.

Mr. Dennis turned to fix chickenhawk eyes on him. "I know, too, that you like and respect Nadina. So everyting fine. An' I want it stay so. No messiness, y'understand? No mess-up-ness. I want marriage in a white dress. I want a grandchild in due time. Due time, I say. Y'get mih meaning, Nollis?"

Boy-Strong, flushed and dazed, was indeed rapidly absorbing meanings. He grunted, "Uh-huh, sir," and looked at the ground to steady his reeling mind.

Mr. Dennis gripped his shoulder, forcing Boy-Strong to meet eyes. "Nah, nah. Don't do dat. Nothin' to shame yuh face about. We's man together. I know you have blood. Young, cock-strong blood. But in this fowl run, you've to wait for what is yours. Even if it on the table already, is still grace before meals. When y'blood rising high, maybe you could go in town an' pluck some wild pullet, eh? But 'round here, you wash yuh hands. Here is manners before meals."

With that sally, Mr. Dennis slapped Boy-Strong's shoulder and grinned at him this wide.

Recent intentions in mind, Boy-Strong couldn't relate with the humour. He simpered an awkward try, and felt the fool for it.

Mr. Dennis went on, "In truth, don't feel bad, Nollis. Good-looking guy like you could catch plenty wild meat in town. Is jus' dat dis here pullet is only for home cooking."

"Only home cooking," Boy-Strong repeated, as if it were a lesson he'd just learned.

He mumbled good-bye and started back for his *'joupa*. Mr. Dennis called to him, "Hey, Nollis. Y'not forgettin' someting?"

"Huh? What?" said Boy-Strong, turning back.

Mr. Dennis was grinning wider, laughing even. He said, "You

lookin' shocked, man. But relax an' don't worry. An' don't be forgettin' she waitin' for you down by de well."

Only then did Boy-Strong remember that indeed his Dina was.

She was more in ambush: sprinting from the well as soon as he broke through the fruit trees and into her sight. Automatically, Boy-Strong thought that anyone back at the house could've, would've, seen her rush, then realized that his talk just now with Mr. Dennis had made all that no matter.

Dina grabbed his hand and pulled him towards the well impatiently. "So? Tell me quick. What happened? I gotta get ready for school," she demanded.

"Just talk," Boy-Strong replied, instinctively protecting his recent conversation with Mr. Dennis. "He jus' wanted to talk."

Then, seeing the puzzlement form in her eyes, he realized his misunderstanding. "Oh, y'mean de news from in town?" he said.

Dina looked at him doubtfully. "Don't try to back out, Boyie. You promised you'd help. So tell me an' done now. What happened?"

Boy-Strong paused for a minute as if taking a deep breath for a great dive.

Dina pulled at his hand, urging him on, drawing them face-to-face close. "Remember our bargain," she said, eyes bold and steady with his. "Well, I ready for my part."

So Boy-Strong held her hands tight, searched her surrendered eyes, and took the steep plunge. "Well, it turn out half an' half," he began. "De Hump surviving for now. But barely. He pay some little fella to put grease in Fiver's outside slippers jus' before he leave de house for de rumshop. So by time . . ."

As his Dina's eyes relaxed soft for him, Boy-Strong caught up the flighty threads of Ma Tai's conflict and, in his best fashion, carried on.

CIRCLE OF SHADE

With the first crowing of the old rooster that slept high in the thorny lime tree in his backyard, Striker! opened his eyes. Through the bare window space of his mud-and-wattle *ajoupa,* the fullmoon beamed its pale yellow gaze on him. He glared at it, sucking down his lips ugly, and abruptly rolled off the coconut-fibre mattress that slept him naked from the hard earth floor. As he stood up, he hawked and spat a mouthful through the window, high at the foredawn sky. A soft breeze came seeking past his face and left the single space of the room, still bearing all its comfort. "Don't need no moon eye fix on me," Striker! mumbled and, needing to piss, started through the door space for the snakepit.

Last new moon, as he set out on business deep in the night, the brightness at the doorway had stopped him for notice. Although the moon was blade skinny, starlight was so strong, shadows were forming their own colours. Taking it in, all of a sudden Striker! had noticed a glitter shifting just past the clearing of the yard; a sheen sliding along around the bole of the old red zaboca tree; a gleaming darkness that slipped through the underbrush with barely a rustle.

Striker!, smooth and silent over the yard's clean-swept dirt, had quicked over to see the snake gradually disappearing into a hole under the buttress roots of the old tree: a big macawoeul, fat around as Striker!'s lithe waist, and two, three times long as him. Judging from its sluggishness and the bulge of its belly, it had just fed, and was returning to its nest to digest the meal.

The two weeks since that morning, that's where Striker! pissed: right down the snakepit every morning, noon, and night. In the long run, when the snake came out hungry again, it would've grown to accept his scent and to take it as a natural part of its nest, allowing Striker! to tame it easily. In his business, a big old snake was always useful.

He targeted a strong stream and, thinking of business, pictured the land-grabbing woman he had woken up to deal with this morning: one of a settle of families who—despite his undermining efforts—had remained squatting in Striker!'s forests. This one a woman in her prime with two boy children, she had shiny, dark-chocolate skin, short-tempered eyes, a ready, rude mouth, and a long, bold stride. He conjured up her slim-thick legs, her pouting rump swaying defiant. He saw himself with her—on her —holding her wrists to the ground, pegging her, spreading those hostile thighs, licking the angry sweat off her breasts, absorbing all her struggle until there was just submission in her eyes. Then he'd tongue the salt of surrender from her belly, tasting her, teasing her, taunting her will.

Caught in his dream, flushed and panting, Striker! squeezed and tugged the thick shaft of his swelling cock. But when he imagined her hot chocolate face again, the disgusted grimace he pictured there abruptly curdled his passion. And his skin crinkled to the chill in the air, as instead he recalled the one real time he had gone by her board-and-concrete house to try courting.

It was a cool, sunshiny afternoon end of rainy season. Bursting cedar flowers were filling the breezes with winged seeds and woodscent. Broad-leaf tania had flourished like tall grass under the forest, and the hordes of wild pigs rooting tubers were easy to kill—they so dotish on the plenty. From the best hung in his *'joupa,* he had taken along a boucaneered haunch for the woman's kitchen. He had crossed the narrow gravelled cart road to their wicket gate, leaned over, and put the meat just inside their low bamboo fence. Then he called the house and waited.

He could hear them, feel them, scrutinizing him through their front jalousies. But only the dog came around: hostile, growling suspicion at his meat, sniffing at it with not even a try at a nibble, and glaring red eyes at him. Then Striker! sighted her younger son sidling along in the shadow of the house. Screwed-up-faced, he carried a piss-pot of whatever. Quick and scrawny, the ten-year-old had scuttled up and made his awkward toss, nearly splashing himself, most of the mess plopping on the meat, while Striker! easily jumped well out of range.

Half holding to hope, half holding back temper, Striker! had eyed his stunk-up meat and said to the boy, "Sonnyboy, tell yuh mother, I jus' want friendship. Is all. The boucan was a kitchen present." He couldn't stop his voice rising. "Is too much pride to foul good food so. All you shouldn't do ting so."

"I doh' carry message for no ol', ugly bushman!" the boy retorted, and scampered back to a side door.

Then she set the dog at him; it rushing threats and snarls but well keeping its place behind the bamboo fence. Striker! had given up. Not because of the stupid dog—he could always silence dogs—it was rejection had beaten him down, had dampened his anger like water dousing fired coal.

With half a year though, that same rejection had brewed him a bitter, smouldering resentment at her. While six times the night's pale eye went from golden goad to glittering blade, Striker!

watched her house and brooded on why she threw shit at him; on why she felt too high-blood proud and pretty for him. She would've made a fine female friend, but now he'd have to rid himself of her and her boy soldiers altogether. For as she chose to be, he had no need for such a formidable woman. And finally, he had hit on the manner of his revenge: his early job today.

Striker! went back in the *ajoupa* and pulled his hunting pants up over his nakedness and tied its leather belt tight. The coarse dirt-brown canvas fitted like a loose skin, supporting the weight of his balls, protecting his skinny legs right down to his ankles, shielding him. Wearing the hard cloth, he felt boarhog to the densest bush.

Next, from his special corner, and using his left hand, he concentrated on gathering materials he needed into a snakeskin draw-pouch. Same left-handed, Striker! put the pouch into a left-side pocket. Lastly, he hitched the knife sheath to his belt and slid his big blade into it. Then he left the *'joupa* for his home of forest.

In the foredawn darkness under the canopy, Striker! strode along swiftly and silent, his great callused feet familiar and confident of step. He was in his own place, where he was born free. Every crick and cranny, every pale green peeping bud, every rotten root and balding knoll, every grassy flat in the woods this side the mountain was his yard, his safeplace. He had come up here, nurtured to natural growing rhythms. Same was his father: born of girl stolen by a bushman grandfather run'way from the yoke fresh off the hellboat. They'd all grown up in these safe forests, all bred in remembered ways, all raised by free men honouring ancient gods of the ancestors and remaining ever untamed.

And now concrete house and engines were invading this sacred place; and among them was this high-assed, hot chocolate woman who felt she could spit on him.

Thinking bitterness, and with special needs in mind, Striker! headed for another squatter's claim a half mile past the sidetrack to the woman's place. This family—man, woman, four big boys, and a ripe young girl—had greedily boundaried off whole four acres. They worked the plot like oxen, making a garden of short crops like tomatoes, bodie beans, table greens, and such. Once a week, a noisy, smoking jitney groaned up the gravel road to pick up produce they sold in town. Every Saturday evening, the band of them returned grinning over the money they'd reaped out of Striker!'s birthright. Second on his list, he intended a harsh justice for them. For now, though, he only needed a sacrifice.

At night a guard dog prowled their yard, but time ago Striker! had made friends with it. Now he softly called the brute to him, and petted it some before giving it a bit of meat from his pocket. The dog gulped down the tidbit and came slobbering for more. Striker! cuffed it away roughly, stood up from his crouch, and started for the backyard trees where the fowls slept.

Easily, quietly, Striker! climbed up the tree towards the white cockerel. When it was in reach, with practiced moves he stifled the bird's head with one hand and twisted sharply, gathering its shuddering body close under his arm to smother the efforts of its flapping wings.

Quickly to the ground, Striker! at once ripped the young cock's head off, tossed it away, and drank deeply of the pulsing blood. It splashed warmly on his face and whiskers, his chest, where he absently rubbed it in, matting his hair into sticky clumps. When he had to pause, gulping to breathe, he felt the power from the libation rush through him and fill his head almost to a swoon. Striker! closed his eyes and thought prayers of homage to his ancient forest gods. With the grin of a hungry dog, he invoked ferocious Kutua Kalivudun, and frightful Culisha, and Tagwadome Fafume, the malicious forest wraith. From the cockerel's ragged neck, he relished the fresh, gushing blood for them, gorging their terrible appetites, and in exchange, he begged that the might of their fierce magic'd be on his side.

But already the blood was clotting sluggish on his palate. So he pulled the neckskin and feathers down and, using his teeth, tore open the bird's chest. The thick, fresh-warm aroma of the entrails filled his nose and his head, and made his mouth water. He swallowed ready, viscous spit and probed a careful finger around in the opened body until he located the gallbladder. He cut that out with the left little fingernail, and that done, gave in to gouging out the pink, bubbly lungs and stuffing his mouth with the sweet raw meat.

In response to the gorging, his bulging bowels suddenly rolled loosely, demanding immediate relief. He squatted down there under the fowls' roosting tree and shat, chuckling at the confusion he imagined the later-found turds would cause the land-grabbers. For, with their trust in their fence, and their watchdog, and their skittish, noisy fowl, they'd never stop thinking wild creatures. Wondering what monster of a hunting animal had made such a lump of shit. And that'd be only their lighter frightener. For what if they did think about the dread bushman?

Done, he wiped his asshole with the feathery pelt and, on the way back to his forest's tracks, tossed the cockerel's carcass to the slavering watchdog, smiling again at the trouble it'd pay for its choice early-morning snack.

Just as he had planned, Striker! got to the woman's place as day was cleaning. Opposite in the gloom of the forest, he squatted and waited for her house to come to life. After a while, as usual, the older boy emerged from the kitchen door, and went up the backyard to the latrine. In due time, the little wiry one followed suit. Patiently, Striker! waited until wisps of blue smoke told him the morning woodfire was lit, and the boys would begin their daily routine—the big one making breakfast, the other sweeping the yard. Then Striker! got up, ready to be contrary.

He jogged lightly across the gravelled road, approached their low bamboo fence with a burst of speed, and leapt cleanly over it —only to land challenged as their growling watchdog appeared from nowhere, and with a furious snarl launched itself at him. Quickly bracing himself, and swinging powerfully from his shoulder, Striker! punched the flying dog in the nose. With a brief howl, it fell heavily against the fence, and lay shuddering.

Striker! looked up from the brained dog to find the smaller boy, straw broom in hand, lip hanging slackly, staring in horror. Striker! bared his teeth and grunted at him. The boy shot off towards the back of the house screaming, "Mammy! Mammy! The bushman, the bushman! The dreadman coming. And he just kill Princess!"

Striker! grinned. "Damn right," he muttered, starting for the back of the house, "the dreadman is coming! And he coming set powerful to move out all a' you!" In his left pocket, his hand began dipping into the pouch to gather some special stuff he'd brought.

A window banged open side of the house, and the woman was screaming at him, "Mister man, what you doing in my yard?"

Striker! looked at her without answering. This close, she was even prettier; even though she was roused for war, and still rising. Her eyes were wide in her face—hard black marbles staring from white heat. Forming through her flush, sweat beaded rapidly and rolled over her cheeks and temples.

She screamed again, "Ah talking to you, mister man. What you doing in my yard? What right you have? Why you here stinking down my morning, frightening my children, and making my place ugly? Why the hell you deviling my yard?"

This was what particularly irritated Striker! about the whole set of them—this claim of the land they kept repeating. Where did she—they—get this right from? He said angrily, "Y'all think put up fence is all to do, and you inherit land, eh? Own it just so, eh?"

"I do what everybody else do, and for that matter, I do much less than most. So don't pick on me! You better leave me alone and go nasty someplace else."

"Is not me that have anywhere to go, madam," said Striker! slowly, "and is not only y'own hot mouth and y'own high pride that goin' t'have you goin'."

"Going? Who saying I going? Look here! Don't you threaten me, mister. Don't you mistake me. I ent no putty woman for you or anybody to shape up as they feel like. You don't frighten me at all. I's mih father one chile. Dead and gone, he jumbie still mih Tauvudun, and for man like you I have all strength. So you measure close the steps you take with me, mister. . . ."

The bigger boy interrupted, "Mum. Is true dat he kill Princess!"

The woman's marble stare blinked swiftly, and cleared to a dangerous cast. "What's that you saying, chile?" she asked.

The boy replied, "Princess dead. She neck break or something. She laying down by the gate, bleeding from the mouth, but she dead, or soon so."

The woman turned to Striker!, eyes glittering. She screamed at him terribly, "God blast your tricks! You evil fool. I warn you not to try to walk on me." She slammed the window shut and disappeared.

Satisfied, Striker! grunted: She seemed convinced he was serious. She'd soon realize her only way out now was his way. And to make the point, he started for the back where her yardfowl roosted in an old cocoa tree. This morning when they flew down hungry, they'd be gobbling up handfuls of poisoned corn he planned to toss from a pocket. The next matter'd be his knife to the yard animals. And, all or nothing, then it'd be the soldier boys.

Under the cocoa tree, Striker! looked up at feathered bellies and claws of chickens, guinea fowl, turkeys, ducks, pigeons; at all the snoozing yardfowl fluffed and huddled up against the early morning chill, yet unready to meet day, allowing Striker! time to summon support of his dread gods. The gods he needed to harden his mind to frenzy he could terrorize from, and to harden his hands into talons of stone to hurt and maim.

He stretched out belly down, humbling himself to his demons, grubbing his nose into the dirt and rotting leaves and fowlshit, fresh and stale. The soil's warm, stinky-sweet aroma rose up from the little gully his rooting chin and nose formed. He sucked the earthy breath noisily into his belly, holding the indraught long, bloating up himself, clearing way to his soul for the spirits he sought.

And he could feel them coming in. Low in his throat, he moaned into the ground—the vibrations travelling down his chest and guts to his groin, rousing and thickening his nature. And as his gods' grip took hold, Striker!'s eyes rolled up white and vacant. Then, serpent-supple, he slowly stood up straight and tall, entranced, unmerciful, a weapon cast.

From the corner of his vision, swift movement: The quick younger son, beginning a wail, was coming at him. From a calabash, the boy flung a cloud of powder that hit Striker! square in the face. That made him gasp for air, further smothering himself as the dry, stinging stuff crammed his lungs and forced his chokes and wheezing.

Overhead, alarmed by his hoarse, unstifling coughs, the startled fowl began clucking and squawking: a cackling and fluttering that faded gradually, and most strangely eased his breathing to a hollow-shell sound more and more muffled and distant, lazy, heavy-moving, as if his raging storm of discomfort were suddenly being squelched in a lake of molasses.

Striker! closed his bulging eyes to the confusing world changing about him—only to confront a multitude of weird shapes and commingling colours shifting through the black window of his mind. Without pattern, they stood or rolled and fused or weaved and thinned or danced and made him think of how the round green grassy once frolicked with the black ice smiles of sunny . . . shine . . . shine . . .

He shivered helplessly in the brilliance. The sky's bright grin was falling down, scattering about him in great cold chunks. From all around, the woman's voice came booming and scratching into him, words like needles piercing every hair root, screaming: "Hear now, bully man, I warn you fair to leave me be, and pass me by. But morning come or no, you choose to bind yourself to midnight. Well, dreadman, now I command you just so. Stay fast with your choice!"

A stifling darkness overcame his mind. Her sayings—massive, clammy—covered him like rain clouds, exploded heavy in his head like thunderbolts. Then, subject to their demanding sentence, his will dense, weighed down, Striker! at once commenced pacing round and round the shade under the cocoa tree.

Dully stepping. Steadfast stepping. Stepping a careful circle. Staying in the shade. Stepping where he dared not desert. Panicked yardfowl fluttered from their roost, colliding with Striker! in descent. Still he trod true at his circle. Wings and claws flapped and scratched his chest and shoulders. He only continued slapping his broad feet in their constant rut. One guinea hen's foot caught in his braids, clamouring with beating wings until it tore away a lock of hair and was free. Yet Striker! remained unriven from his wheeling way. Off and on, loads of steaming

fowlshit splattered down on him. No matter. Striker! kept steadily stepping. Stolid, stupid, step after step . . .

The world went around with a hollow rushing, like dry leaves
pushed along on a big *whooosshh* of wind. Yoked to the slapping-
feet rhythm of his trek, his mind caught wispy dreams about his
squatter-woman driver. He saw her standing arms akimbo in a
sunny field, dressed in men's trousers and banded for war with
white cloths about her head and belly. She straddled the ground,
fiercely guarding it as if it'd dropped from her womb, as if she'd
bloody the black dirt defending it, be ruthless for it. . . .

He saw her strolling in a garden with her shaman—a cot-
tonheaded man, short to her knees, who pranced about her like a
playful child, now this side, now that. The ancient carried a
square leather box under his arm, and every now and again he'd
peek into it and grin huge, toothless glee at the joke he saw
inside.

Striker!'s soul squirmed with yearning to know the contents
of the box: what powers, potions, secrets? And by enormous
striving, he finally got a glimpse: In the box was a cage that held
a tiny garden, and under a low tree with swollen leaves dripping
milk, a dark, hairy man was chained up like a slave. Big white
drops bathed his brow, but he could not drink; his lips were
pinned together with great curved spines.

Yet the desperate man, his head strained back and tears of pain
a stream into his ears, was slowly forcing his mouth open against
the cruel spines, gradually ripping apart his purpled, punctured
lips, so he could suck his own blood and slake his horrid thirst.
Then Striker! realized the poor, tortured slave was he. . . .

Long and deliberate as an old tree grows, vague time passed.
Weary, despairing of the endlessness, compelled to trudge the
shade of the roosting tree yet again, he went snivelling
around . . .

Beyond his stepping feet, the world was haze: a shimmering glare where things—animals? *vudun?* people?—moved about at odd angles and brightnesses. A nibble of fear, once cowering in his belly, had long grown into a consuming *corbeau* scavenging his mind peck after peck. . . .

Over and over, one main concern beat on him: She had him altogether now! He couldn't get away. This idea pelted down on him like rain. Only *it* was plain. He could not escape, although he was hardly there to them. . . .

The land-grabbing woman, her children, her fowls, her animals in the yard, all went about their business in the daze, treating him like a tree stump. They moved around him as though he were another lump of dirt in their yard. He felt empty of presence to them, the way his open *ajoupa* in its forest clearing was without him. . . .

Off and on, an enormous melancholy would rise up and choke him, and, without relief, Striker! would weep. . . .

Later still, blind in his swoon, unknowing whether he was whispering, or thinking, or heard, or not, Striker! cried out, "Oh, please, miss lady, let me go!" Through the mess of snot and tears, he begged, "Please, lady, lemme go."

More time later, Striker!'s world began slowly righting, and making sense in simple ways. Pain was close on him like sweat. All over—tired back and neck and straining shoulders—scrapes and scratches stung wickedly. But the distress made sense. . . .

He breathed the sweet, very cool air over his rasped throat, starting and flinching as it scraped down to his hot lungs. Still, it soothed. . . .

His eyes were sore, his jaws hurt. With every step, he now smelled the stale shit slicking in his pants. He tried to talk, only managing a hoarse groan. But it wasn't so bad. . . .

Eventually, looking about blearily, Striker! focused on the

spry boy scrutinizing him and, cringing fearfully, began a violent trembling.

"Mammy, the bushman waking up!" the boy boomed, each word erupting pain volcanoes in Striker!'s fragile mind. He could only cradle sweaty hands around his tormented head and trudge along drooling like a feebled bull.

The woman came out, dressed in men's trousers, her hair bound up, her head banded in white. She approached and commanded, "Stand steady, you!"

Striker! stood. His eyes fell to his foul, crusty toes.

"So! You still want to war with me, mister man?" she asked.

Every part of every word hammered echoing hurt into Striker!'s head. Afraid to speak answer and make more noise, he tried to shake his head in silent surrender, but at that, the world shimmered unsteady again. He felt himself close to being down and crawling before her, and grasped at the air for balance. And, dreading a fall to that final lowness, he just stood swaying, cowed, and quiet.

The woman said, "So, you is a cockroach now? You can't even mumble? And you want me let you walk and go, eh? And you want to go 'way and come back no more? And you want to leave me and mine in peace? Eh, bushman? Is that all what you want now? Eh? Nothing else?"

Striker!, drudged by the hot, jumping pains in his head and the punishing whip in her tone, couldn't answer. Instead, he began weeping again. After a bit, clearing his throat, he managed to whisper, "Just lemme go, miss lady. Please. No more."

"Listen to him, sons," the woman said, "look at him good. This is what man could be. No more! he says. Pleading now, he is. Remember him so! And you, mister man, don't you ever cross my pathways no more, y'hear!"

Then, from a bowl in her hand, she sprinkled some liquid on

his face. "Now, take all the bad yuh bring, and leave my yard in peace!" she commanded, and turned her back on him.

Then, and only then, Striker! felt free to go.

Anxiously, careful to close the wicket gate behind him, Striker! realized the crimson sun setting meant she had trapped and stolen his spirit for a full day. What a power she must have! he thought, shuddering as he slunk across the gravelled road and padded back into the forest. Just inside the sheltering fronds, Striker! turned and gazed befuddledly at her place one last time. Then, wearily, woozily, he homed towards his mud-and-wattle den, to huddle and to heal.

TRIPPING

Wasn't no difference they didn't know. Ignorance don't pass out shields. What they shoulda keep in mind was their place as tourists: strangers people putting up with. And anyhow, the guesthouse lady they was staying by had more than warned them.

But y'know that type of tourist . . . they who need the proofs for later on, when they showing off their two-week expertise about primal cultures . . . so they must have their photos at the right sites, and their shots hugging with the smiling natives, and so on. Well, in that far-out, high-tech bag, this couple was Mr. Click and Missis Flash.

So, when they and the Obeah ritual coincide, the only certain next guest was ugly Master Consequence.

You could imagine them on the way to the gathering spot. In the dark, sweating beads; gleaming creamish in the fullmoon light. Guided blind, but eager following over rough-and-ready trails, through underbrush waist-tall, the grass like razors, stinging salty every cut, and the bushes springing back, lashing them so, slapping them each step of track, making them pay for not knowing when to duck.

But they taking it strong—both of them, husband and wife; they so charged-up double-bound in conspiracy. This was rare and this was real: to witness Black Magic in truth. Actually doing the Voodoo. And nothing would stop them from sneaking some photos for later-on living-room proof. With the equipment they was toting, if they couldn't outsmart these superstitious natives, couldn't trick them good, well, may Shame consume their credit cards.

They certainly had equipment: each one with a hand-sized camera fixed-up ready, in the overbig pockets of their khaki bushpants. And superior confidence, yes, they had that, too.

They was almost in delight already. Could think a taste of triumph. "Dear" was eyeing "Darling," the beam broadcasting, "God, I can't wait. . . ."

Everything was going their way. Their strings from the guest-house had set them up prime. Front line in the circle. Firsthand on the action. That was them: spit-close to the stage. So close that when the flaming heat burst open the green firewood and make it spurt out sap-juice, is flaring-nose them who breathing in the raw heat of that aroma.

And if the centre-fire was hot, still it was nothing to the spirit of the crowd. That was heat and a half. Heat reflecting off gleaming skin, shaded from charcoal to burnished gold in the fire flames. But mood and color wasn't all to this scene. The tassa drum was there, too, filling up the dark space of night. Filling up heads, sounding out hearts. The tassa drum was cutting sharp and rolling deep and rousing. In between, the swornfolk chanted up their spirits. Clapped and jigged and pounded them up, yielding to the double-time beat jamming through them, tearing through them to wake their dancing jumbies; to loosen supple-waist spirits. And yes, readying them all for the Obeah-man.

All this time, black of the eye, the spy couple right there, middling the blast. It was hitting them that they was part of a big, big thrill. That they was inside the heart of this for real. With all the closeness, the freeness. All the rubbing, the touching. They could feel their blood sweetening, the red turning crimson, sending them high. And yes, making them, too, ready.

Then when everything was right, the Obeahman burst in!

A greased naked man, with a staff held in hand. A strutting mahogany man. A fine-figured man rushing round the flaring flames; glowing and grinning wicked, eyeing wild. Dancing free in the Night, whirling mighty in his sway.

And with that, the action jump up another height.

Right away the tassa start a power call that everybody pick up; the men low, the women pealing high; the Obeahman sending in his own chant to bind them. In no time, a spirit come free and take on a woman. It was a snake spirit, and the woman was heavy. But the jumbie was dancing her sliding smooth, and slippery light like sweat on skin. She was graceful as a cascabel in water.

When it let she go, and she swoon away, another woman ketch the trance. This one, ample as ripe fruit and limber like a whiplash. And Obeahman jumbie had her hips moving every way, without boundary in abandon.

"Jump, mih daughter!" he start singing out.

And she was a cricket! Smooth and easy, leaping up like sparks, flicking up high. Merry in the air, flaring out her skirts, up over a crowd open and happy like her face.

"Up, mih daughter!" they was singing, too.

Then, like brushfire spreading, one to one then another, swornfolk, man and woman, began to fly. . . .

. . . And it went further. So much, so fast, the tourists almost forget their plan. But then the sacrifices started and whetted up their needs for glossy memories.

Y'could hear the goats bleating in the back. But first it was the cocks: big, red-combed roosters. The swornfolk, man and woman half-naked alike, did it. One grabbed the cock's body, another the head; then they danced a jerky pull-apart. Then, while the head was tossed in the fire, the body handlers gulped from the spurting blood.

By the fourth cock, the couple was experiencing miles beyond their daringest fantasy trip. They was blood-splattered, and like everybody else, was probably tonguing off a drop or few of the bacchanal. Others around was much more than licking.

It was then a young fella, taken full by his jumbie, leapt into the bonfire coals to dance like a hell-crab; on his back, on his belly; though with not a burn, or a scorch, or a singe from the frenzy.

It was too much. The dazzle made the poor woman remember. "Oh God, I gotta get this. . . ." So out she slipped the teeny-weeny high-tech camera. A sly check around. No eye on her. Soooo, a little final adjusting . . . and noww! She sneaked the shot.

!!!CLICK!!! FLASH . . . WHIRRRR!!!

Suddenly that's all y'could hear. Everything else stop dead silent. The drumming, dancing, chanting, laughing hubble. All gone. Done. All to hear was this sneaky whirring of the automatic rewinding camera.

"Come out, Machine!"

Like a hammer, is Obeahman breaking the silence. Tourist man look at tourist woman. She eye-locked with him. Then, together, they turn focus on Obeahman. He looking straight past them. Nobody moving.

"Is now to show, Machine!" Is Obeahman again: not louder, but harder. He still looking beyond them like they tiny in his vision. But in the clear silence you could notice his gaze changing. The flames were sliding off different from his face, flaring now like they glowed toward punishment.

And still nobody moving.

Like the tassa was expecting him when he shout, "Drum me!" a rhythm came shocking out. A drivey one, quick as a whip. A wicked beat for a tourist woman who could barely tap toes in time. For the first with his eye on her, Obeahman scream out, "Dance for me, Machine!"

Then it was the poor tourist lady joggling out from her choice viewpoint, and prancing around the full circle, to stop right in front Obeahman. While all the time, by eyes and mouth and face, she was showing that she couldn't stop herself. That it was the drum making her. That it had got inside her, and had set her flinging about so; jerking around so foolish, out of rhythm, out of reason, gaping and gasping out of breath.

"Show me, Machine!"

At Obeahman command, she start stripping. Off shirt, then bra. Off belt. Ripping at her pantswaist. Busting off the buttons, tearing at the crotch enough to bare there. Then she started getting off the stuff in her mind. Shedding it good. Hard in the circle, round and round, stopping only for the deepest bumps, for the hardest grinds. Showing off how she could. How her waist would undercurl, and wiggle ride. How she could spread wide-wide, and shake. Give and take. Make blood flow and surge, and rush and rise.

Yes, she was doing all that. Her body was. But you could see dismay and shame brimming her eyes with the screams she couldn't utter.

Then, with all that action, the camera flipped out. It crashed on the ground and busted open. At this, the husband unfroze, and rushed to his woman; bared and bouncing, awkward and ugly in terror; helpless as her frizzy hair.

Obeahman had let her go, to collapse in a faint on her husband.

THE VAGABOND'S GENIE

He appeared in the wet night by a flash of lightning. He was on the coming-in trail and headed directly for my cabin. The angry light flickered him into view a second time: a tiny silhouette against the expanse of silvered, rainswept plain. The knee-high grass foreshortened him, so that I couldn't see his stepping feet, but an extra urgency marked his body's slope.

He was coming in fast and light. There was no load on his driving shoulders, and his empty hands were low and pumping swiftly. Another thing: He had used each flash to look back. Most odd—usually when they're running, their eyes are peeled forward, searching to prepare defense for what's ahead. Usually, they already know enough of what's behind.

The cabin is hidden about twenty yards inside the forest, which follows the line of the border. Since the other side is all grassy plain, at night it's easy for us to monitor large areas of the border by just sitting in the raised swivel chair at the hut's big window, and scanning the view between the tree trunks with night-vision binoculars. Fugitives a mile away are brought to touching distance. We can study them well long before they rush into the forest for haven at last, and come upon the camouflaged cabin.

Sometimes, to avoid the paperwork of a group-crossing, the guard will burst open the door and let them see his uniform in the sudden light. And then the races back are hilarious. They scramble over each other. They dive to the ground and squirm along in the grass like big worms. Or a single, sprightly one puts his fate in sprinting low-crouched, swerving and dodging, as though expecting bullets in pursuit. Fact is, they're giving a hearty moment without knowing it. This job of watching borders gets so lonely, most times they're welcome company, even in the holding cells.

But this one kept looking back, running from the Devil and uncaring about the deep, cold sea ahead. And such an ugly night he had chosen. I watched the rain exaggerate at falling and didn't envy him at all. As the darkness grudgingly surrendered his figure, it became distinct against the slanting greyness of the falling flood, racing across the coming-in trail.

We call it a trail, not that it's marked out or anything. It's just that somehow when they try to cross, it's along that same hundred-yard-broad swath of plain they come. It might be due to the geography of the river they have to get by first. Or it might be the grass's height and the seeming safety of the forest from their sneaking perspective. Maybe it's a factor of magnetic north. Whatever. It's why the authorities built this cabin here.

To realize the authorities' wisdom, though, requires conscientious uniforms with alert eyes. We who guard the border make sure that most who use that trail do it twice. Thus, we can also call it the return trail. We're proud of keeping a sharp border.

I put some water on the stove to heat, returned to the window, and scanned the glares of lightning for him. Caught him fighting the storm about half a mile away; doing well, considering the wretched scene. I thought to put on the cabin's light as a beacon through the slashing rain, but decided to wait some against the risk of scaring him off.

Tonight, I had my needs, and unknowing, he was running in to barter for them: warmth, shelter, and hot coffee for him, while I got company until morning. Then he'd be on his way back wherever, and I'd chug off to home in my faithful Bug.

Ten minutes later, I lit up the place, and once he'd got out of the pelting rain and into the forest, he came in like a moth as I swung the cabin's door open. Perhaps dazzled by the light, he never made out my uniform until he'd briskly climbed the six stairs and was sticking his hand out to shake mine in thanks and relief.

Then he stopped the reaching hand, the smiling mouth, and made an anxious glance backwards, out into the dripping night. He turned back, his eyes raced about the cabin, running into the desk with its record books and clipboards, and into the radio flashing its amber MONITOR ON signal, and into the three open, unlocked cells on the far side of the cabin. All the evidence that he was into a cage.

He took off his sodden hat and said, "I surrender, sir. You'll get no trouble from me." Then stuck his hands up in the air like a prisoner of war, dripping a stream on the floor, and looked steadily at me.

A special sincerity, too intense to be genuine, gleamed in his eyes. Or maybe it was something like amusement, or mischief, that sharpened the look and cast doubt about his earnest hazel-browns. There was that queerness about them. In an animal, I'd have called them cunning; in him, the first I could think was, they were liar's eyes.

I cleared the air about his status. "Listen up, pal, you can put your hands down. You're not under arrest or anything."

"Well, thank you, sir," he said as he complied. "As mih uncle used to say, 'Any bank in a raging river, any shelter in a storm.' But forget about that. This is the border, and you're the guard? Right?"

"Right," I said. "And let's leave it at that for now, huh. What you think about some coffee?"

"That's okay, too," he said, "but if I had a choice, I'd go for tea. It's a better caffeine."

I looked him over. I'd asked him to relax and all that, but all the same, he was being quite the man-at-home for an apprehended alien. I said, "Sure, I got tea bags."

He stood there dripping, and looking at the stove. Just as I was about to make the offer, he said, "Say, sir. Mind if I dry these off against the fire? I can wear a blanket from the cell."

"Sure," I said, and bettered it by offering him the government-issue coveralls. He emptied his pockets—a multibladed pocketknife, a bit of flint, a small ball of string—on the table, changed, and put his clothes on the radiator to steam-dry. By then, the hot caffeines were ready.

Halfway through his cup, he looked at the wall clock and said, "Excuse me, sir."

I grunted attention, and waited for his inevitable get-over story. He surprised me by asking in a chummy tone, "What time you going off duty? Huh?"

"What's on your mind?" I countered.

He put down his cup, walked into the middle cell, and spoke to me from behind the bars. "I really need about two hours' sleep, that's all. And I want to ask you a favour after that."

This either, I didn't expect. He crouched on the bunk so that the slanting shadows of the cell bars patterned his face. From one oblong I could see his monkey eyes shining at me. I glanced away, at the time. It was one forty-five. I was leaving at seven. I said, "Sure, you got it. I'll wake you at four, huh?"

He said, "Thanks," and rolled over to face the wall.

"Oh, oh, I'll get the lights," I said, switching off the bright overhead light, half in jest, half in defense against his certain manner. This guy was quite in charge of himself.

I worked the glasses along the raining plain once more. Sensibly, everyone else had stayed home: The wind-roiled expanse was bare, but for the falling water. I sat there, staring out the window at the night, listening. The wet sounds outside quieted the cabin strangely. I could hear everything: the man's steady breathing, a sibilant hiss from the radiator that was quite different from the softer sizzle of the drying clothes. As I tuned my ears outdoors, the rain's falling took focus. Farther away, susurrus like a swift-flowing river, was the constant rush of rain on the grass. Nearer, here within the forest, the sky fell more variedly, crashing about, sloshing in tiered patterns from the leafy umbrellas above. It dripped and dropped in gollops; jerkily, bucket-a-drop splattered on the cabin's roof, softening to subdued plops on the pad of forest's floor.

A sudden lightning ripped across the black sheet of wet sky. Although it was safe and warm here, the furious report chilled me. As if fresh-escaped from it, an angry wind then screamed through the forest, whipping the branches, lashing the leaves. The random violence cowed my ears back to the secure quiet within the cabin. Where the fellow was breathing peacefully, sleeping in synchrony with the tick of the clock. Their cozy harmony made the storm outside seem far away. And so inside of this I was, I closed my eyes to listen into my head.

It wasn't long before the offbeat splutter of my rebuilt Bug came chugging into my daydreaming, and made it perfect. I love that machine, and making it splutter just right is what I think I'm really good at. I'm intimate friend to each and every part of that car. It's like a baby I've made. It represents my tastes and scope and rangeability. For I have a plan that's more a happiest dream: that there'll be one day I'll have the bankroll and the time, and there'll be that sunny and windingest road through beautiful mountains with grand, gnarled redwoods, and aromatic spruce, or any kind of trees at all. And I don't have anywhere special to go. . . .

He happened into my mind brutally. One moment I was cruising at my leisure, floating through pine-scented hills. Next thing, the runner was in my mind, coming through wicked, slashing rain, looking backwards at terror. Except that, as the Bug's windscreen became the binoculars, and focused his desperate face, the eyes straining to push away what they left behind were no longer the liar's eyes now sleeping in the cell. No, I saw the frightened, fleeing eyes were mine, just as I realized it was my own terrified face the stinging raindrops helped at crying.

I awoke out of it with racing heart, surfacing with all the distress of that hopeless flight, plus a deeper, actual anxiety: What had aroused me? No sound or movement made a ready suggestion. I guessed then it must've been habit, and massaged my face, rubbing away the dream. The clock showed ten to four. Seemed time also had been fleeting.

With the bright light still off, I went across to the cell and was about to rap gently on the bars when he said, "Thanks, I'm all right."

His voice was well awake, biding its time, awaiting me.

That annoyed me some—him lying there in the dark cell, pounced, watching me doze, head back, mouth slung open. Me with my throat bare, him with that animal-wild in his eyes. All this independence of his was turning me off. I returned to my chair and sat. The guy was irritation in effect.

He said, "Sir?"

I grunted.

"Got a minute? There's something I gotta tell you."

Here comes the plea, I thought. To give him a hard time, I said, "No news you can give me I want to hear, pal."

"Maybe so. But it's interesting news anyhow. And it'll pass the time."

"No problem with my time, pal," I told him. "It passes light enough. And I get paid for it." I swivelled my chair towards the window, and scanned the scene outside while I fretted within. This guy's gall was something else again. His was exactly the wrong act to've adopted. He had nixed with me.

The bunk creaked as he got up to come out of the cell, and I recognized it as the noise that had awoken me. Too swiftly, I swivelled the chair to him, saw that he was dressed—his knife, and string, and flint in pocket—and, even as I glanced stupidly from the bared radiator to the table, I realized how seriously vulnerable I had been. Meantime, he just stood outside the cell, leaning casually against it.

I tried to keep alarm from my face by forcing on a severe frown. I said, "Listen, pal. I'm going to tell you straightaway, so you know the situation, okay? You gotta go back over. Nothing you can say, nothing you can do, can change that. You've got to return. That's the way the crumbs fall. And it's the law, pal. That's why we're here. We can enforce it, although we prefer to be reasonable."

He was nodding, and halfway smiling. "Yeah, I got it. I gotta go back. So it is written, and so, exactly, shall it be done." He raised his hands as if calming the tossing waves, and continued, "We're on the same side here, sir. We have the same ends. It's in going about them, I'm asking you the favour."

"Which favour? What asking?"

"I know, I know." He laughed easily. "Haven't got to it yet. The story I want to tell. Remember? I was saying there's something y'should know?"

I snorted out a chuckle. You had to admire the guy. There were no bashfuls among his balls. "Okay, shoot," I said, "I've got the time. What's the hot news?"

"In about two hours, you're going to have company."

"What company?"

"Female company. The female I'm escaping, that's who."

A bit skeptically, I asked, "You're running from a woman?"

"Mm–hmm."

Well, to say the truth, I was disappointed. I wasn't up to listening to his particular version of the common male fantasy. I'd heard many. Had my own. And, most of all, given early impressions, I'd expected more from him. But, well, I wanted company. I had the time. And maybe it wouldn't turn out stupid. So I said, "Fine. Let's hear it. But nothing changes. You're going back over."

"Promise?" he said, grinning as if he'd won a lottery.

He began, "Jack's the name people call me. 'Jack, as in jackanapes?' is the first thing she said when I introduced myself. It happened we crossed paths in the train station last summer: me shifting down South drifting to where the high-paying oil action was, she going home from some preferred situation here in your country. We two were the only passengers in the backwater station. So I chatted her up—anything to tickle her fancy. Pass the waiting. Y'know. Well, it was fun. 'Spite of her hoity-toity aura, she was nothing but friendly. We had a great talk. When I offered, she toked easy from the smoke I rolled.

"After a while, I got the urge and turned the conversation a little fresh. But she wouldn't go along, so I dropped it gentlelike, joking how for a fine woman like her plus some luck, I'd sell my soul to any lesser devil. She was gracious about it; grinned and said that one day, with a bolder angel, I might get my wish. Well, that piqued my respect for her. But to maintain the comfort level, I switched to telling her stories about my family—mainly about my Uncle Woody, my favourite person, dead or alive.

"I gotta explain about Uncle Woody. This was a man whose sole goal was never to work a day in his life. And, as far as I know, he never did. His philosophy was that any Tom, Dick, or Harry could work, but it took someone special to avoid that common, humdrum way. And he chose to be special. He was a hard drinker, a bad lover, and the buccaneer in the sedate harbour of his respectable family. He lived off them and his fallen women, wore his outlandish clothes, and died in his seventies a happy, notorious charmer, who had well earned his marvellous reputation. . . ."

The guy—Jack, as he said—had loved this uncle of his, I was sure. I could see his heart talking here. It was familiar with these feelings, and could say them anytime, and in many different ways. All he had to do was open his face, and the affection flooded out.

He sighed slightly, and got back on track. "Well, to make a long story short, when my train came and I was picking up my rucksack to go, she seemed wistful about her good-byes. I got a zing of, I don't know, zeal, desire, romance, whatever. So I suggested she let me send her a postcard. Keep in touch, and so on. An obvious, candy-coated ploy, but she bit like a sugar junkie, and gave up her address. With that encouragement and the train ready, I tried for a so-long kiss. She was awkward, but unresisting, and gave me some honey. Then, as my train chugged out of the station, she stood there, flushed and suddenly teary, waving at me. At the last moment, she called out, 'Jack. Jack, drop by anytime. You hear me. I want you to. I want you. . . .' Heard her clearly. Yep! Felt the offer zing in my belly. Must admit it: The sight of her there did sweetest things for me."

As Jack told his tale, I took the time to study him. I judged him older than my own twenty-seven. That I could say; by how much was harder. Might've been five, might've been fifteen—his face and figure didn't betray which. Other than his slick eyes, his narrow face suggested hard experience, a worldliness his even, boyish smile couldn't cover up.

The thought popped into my mind, and on impulse I interrupted him: "You have children?"

"Nah. Not as far as I know," he said, discouraging the idea away with large, barring hands. "If it goes my way, my race ends with me."

Noticing that he averted his eyes as he answered, I said, "Go on, pal. Let's hear the rest."

He continued, "Where was I? Ahhh, drifting South to my destiny . . . but, that episode's not for this story. Well, I did send a postcard or two to Leona. Didn't say much in them, except a mention of the romantic fancy of my last sight of her, and a promise to take her up on the drop-in offer. Which came through about four months later, when I rode a freighter up the coast and jumped ship in a port not far from her town. So, to test my stars, I set off to find her. I didn't expect much, maybe bed-and-board for a few days, if that. But I was hoping the hardest dreams.

"After asking directions a few times, I realized I was looking for 'the Hill House,' and found it at the southern end of this one-store country town. It was a grand old three-storied mansion that reminded of her hoity-toity aura. But end-of-the-road tired, I said, 'What the hell,' walked up, and rapped hard on a side door, where the steamed glass and window curtains hinted kitchen.

"I was right. That a motherly sort answered was pure luck. That type's usually generous-minded enough to offer ears and more, and soon I was eating without even having to mention my special invite. But, as Uncle Woody'd say, 'Listeners make you talk, and good food is no gag.' So, bellyfull happy, I told her all; and you should've seen the commotion that set off. . . ."

All of a sudden, I was skeptical. I knew what was coming, and I could miss it: a welcome worthy of a prince and lover, and so on. The usual, except for the individual seamy details. But this guy, Jack—it beat me why he'd feel he could run a soft story like this on me. Why would it change my mind about anything? Was he planning to ask his favour based on *this*?

Yet I remembered the stuff from his pockets: the string, the pocketknife, the flint. I thought of the rude light in his eyes. With this dumb story, these items didn't fit. So, benefitting him the doubt, I listened in again.

". . . happens gradual. That y'can smoke in your choice pipe. Yup. No matter how shallow or sharp the grade, everything comes on gradual. After she'd challenged the lawyers and they backed down, it was my wish equalled her command. Absolutely and all around. First week, I stayed in the guest room, and snuck up to her room after the housekeeping couple had gone to their cottage. But I'm sure they knew the score—that she was sweet on me. No way they couldn't. She didn't hide her feelings; daring indiscretion because she was so proud of me. She swore it was because of my influence—my presence and advice—that she was able to face down the lawyers. And later on, it was my masculine support. Y'know, with her brother choosing the priesthood and all, and she becoming woman's mistress of most she surveyed, and arbiter of Destiny for the folks of her village. She, the rich, kind woman. And I this good manager."

I regarded him scornfully. "And in every way possible. Right? And now you're running away from this, huh? Look, pal, that's enough. I got the picture. But I really thought you'd come up better than this."

He frowned down at me in my swivel chair. "So you're disappointed, huh? I don't've enough thrills? Right? You want a new, exciting angle from my experience for your thrill collection? Right? To you I'm just a thrills source." His voice turned bitter as he ended, "And you're the man controlling the border."

"And what's that got to do with anything?" I asked.

"Nothing, sir. It don't make a difference, anyhow. 'No road's a way without takers.' That's what Uncle—"

I ended it for him, "Woody used to say."

But he didn't take it as peace offering. Glumly, he returned to the cell and sat on the bunk.

On my side of the rueful silence, I was feeling guilty and stubborn. Despite his self-righteous mumbo jumbo, there was truth to his complaint. My using him, I mean. Yet, as much as I was willing to admit his point, I couldn't ignore my other instinct that everything he said and did was false: farce to sway me from the stated understanding—ploy to fool me.

Just then, from his cell, uncannily, he said, "I'll never be no one but mi'self, y'know. All I ever got is me." His tones mixed frustration, explanation, reconciliation.

I felt my judgement quiver, and resettle skewed that much in his favour. Conceding, I made the necessary move. "So, c'mon, pal," I said. "Tell me what happened. How come it turned out you're running from one man's heaven?"

There was a twist of triumph to his smile as he came out of the cell, though it could've been the bitter turn to his mouth as he considered what words to say. " 'S'not so easy to explain this. To make it convincing, I mean. One thing, it happened gradual. At the first, it was kinda ridiculous. Talk about indulgence—I mean, any whim, anything I wanted, was mine. I just had to speak it, and as soon as possible, there it was, and she's saying, 'Are you happy, Jack?' What else to say? It got so I was saying, 'Sure, I'm happy, Lee,' more than ordinary 'Thanks.'

"I'll give you an instance. She'd given me the keys for the place, right—a bunch, about five, six of them. They bulged heavy in my pockets, and I didn't like them hanging from my belt by a strap—that reminding too much of the choke of households. Second morning I had them, I went out walking and decided to leave the keys behind. When I got back about three hours later, she opened the door at my knock, all teary and flushed. She handed me a key—a single key. 'The house fits it,' she said, her voice catching with triumph as she grabbed and hugged on me to cry. Then she says, 'Are you happy, Jack?' I mean, of all the things to say. And this was just the downslide starting.''

"How's that?" I asked.

"Well, at the beginning, I sort of tested her. Y'know. How far she'd go. I mean, any natural body'd have. And I found no limits to her. She'd do anything. My comfort was the marks that made her head of the class. As a good student, she used mentor-me for every idea how to please. And as she became incapable of independent action, just so, the spice of surprise gradually went out of my life. Conversations became sanction conferences. She was Lee, who presented Options, as in, 'Can I?' or 'How many?' or 'Do you want?' or 'Is it okay?' I was Jack, of the Nod or the No.''

I grinned slowly, half-understanding. But Jack, his face quite somber, ignored that sympathy. "So, I started going in her woods of free, old trees, trying to be alone some. Y'know, just to think quiet, and watch the forest breathing the sun's rays, and smell the sweet sweat of living dirt, and so on. Y'know how I mean?"

This time I wanted to say, "Yes, I understand," because I really did. But he was going on so seriously now that I thought I was seeing his heart at last, and didn't want to smudge the peek.

There was that twist to his mouth again as he continued, "But she'd soon find me. Those many acres were her childhood playgrounds. She knew every nook and cranny and cave. Every hiding place. As if she had antennae, she'd locate me within minutes. I couldn't ever feel alone. Even my shadow was jealous. Then, when she found me, we couldn't talk—not sensibly anyhow, since her every opinion was a guaranteed reflection of my own. So we'd just stand apart, strained and silent. And I knew she was only being alert there, ready for any shift, or gesture, or statement I might make, so she could respond to it and *make me happy*."

Jack came near and crouched in front of me, looking up in my face. "So? Do I have to say more?" he asked. "Would you want to live with that? Could you?"

He took an anxious glance at the clock, then at the door. Maybe it was from my face, but he seemed pressured to work harder. So he played his big card. He said, "Listen, sir. You don't have to believe me to help me, anyhow. I'm not going to break your rule. I'll follow your instructions. I just want you to say something for me."

He slipped another glance at the door, and I saw the weak part of his heart. I had seen that furtive urgency before—mainly in trapped creatures, great and small. I could see then, it was his pursuer Jack truly feared.

"How's that?" I said.

"I just want you to say you let me through."

"Say . . . ?"

"Yes. Just say you let me through. Tell her that. Meantime, of course, I've gone back just as you wish. Just as the law demands."

" . . . !"

I thought I saw his scheme, though. With me lying for him and misleading the pursuit, he'd gain better time in his doubling back. It was a bold plan. I liked it right away. I made four eyes with him. I said, "Okay. You got a deal. As long as you're going back over, that is. I'll have you in the glasses all the way, y'know."

"Don't worry," he said, as we shook hands. "You bet I'm going back over. Just do your part for me."

I said, "Don't think about it."

Out the window, the world was silvering. I logged night going west at 5:30 A.M. while Jack used the toilet. Then it was my turn. When I returned, he was pacing the floor, rubbing his hands in each other worriedly.

"Take it easy," I told him. "You'll be all right. Have a cup?" I looked at him from the stove.

He was staring out into the blank fog of dawn.

He turned suddenly and approached me. "You've got to let me go now, sir. Please. The time is right." He drew me towards the window, talking fast. "It's like wool out there. I could get past her a foot away."

I saw his point, and another. I said, "Listen, pal. These here glasses're infrared. You can't fool them. I can pick you up out of pea soup, pal."

Didn't faze him. "I know, I know, sir. Don't worry about me. You'd pick her up too late, is what I'm worried about. I don't want her to meet me here." His voice went pleading again. "Please, sir. Let me go now. Please."

What could I do? I said, "Sure, feel free. Take off."

"Thanks," he said, and went. I felt as if I'd missed the trick.

My cup steaming on the sill, I followed him through the glasses. Sure enough, he was going steadily back over the return track. I took a sip, focused him again, then swung away to check the farther reaches of the trail. He had timed it just right. I got my first glimpse of Jack's genie.

I located Jack again, more vaguely away in the haze and fog, well to one side of her. Contrary to that, his genie—I couldn't recall the name—took on more and more distinct form. I followed her in some.

And, as I became certain of the evidence, I decided to betray Jack. I was set firm long before she reached the door. I held it open wide and very welcome. She came in, and looked around quickly. "He was here," she said, and turned around to go back out.

Except that I stood barring the door. "You can't go back out there, miss." I nearly gave it away right then, but caught myself, and said instead, "You look bushed, miss. Y'had to be walking all night, and in that horrible weather. You sure got to be tired, miss."

True, but she was still intent on returning blindly to the chase. She said, "You can't keep me here, sir. I'm sure I have all the documents." Her hands started for the inside of her long slicker.

"It's not that at all. Ten minutes off your feet, miss," I bargained. "A cup of coffee?"

She wavered at that.

"There's a mirror in the toilet" tipped the scales my way. Then Judas me added, "It'll be worth your while." I couldn't help leering encouragingly.

Why traitor to the race of man? Well, it wasn't because the genie was beautiful. She was. She was that, and rich, and strong, and determined, and foolish in love, and so forth. But most of all, she was pregnant. Plainly pregnant by that hotfooting vagabond. And that irresponsibility I'll never support.

I told her his plan over coffee, while she took tea. "It's a different kind of caffeine," she excused it to herself, then, hand on her belly, added, "It's just this once," to convince me. Then she listened without interruption until I was done.

"That's Jeremy all over," she said with a private smile. "Brags someday he'll fool the Devil. But thank you so very much."

"Jeremy!!?" I said.

"Yes, that's my man, Jeremy. Ownway, not to be trusted. Says anything, does anything, that jumps to his mind, that fits his purpose." She sighed. Not despondently, or broken—more like satisfied. Or maybe resolute.

I had to say it. "Maybe it's not a bad thing this guy goes

away." I looked out the window as if talking to the damp morning.

She got up and smoothed her clothes down about her. Too coolly, too politely, she said, "Well, thank you very much. I guess I'm on my way, now."

As she went to the door, I made one last, bold try. "Any man that'd make you go through this, in your condition, is a savage. You don't need a savage, ma'am."

That pulled her eyes back to me. They were wet, defensive wounds I'd bared, and hurt. She hunched over and hugged her pumpkin-belly. "We do!" she said. "You can't understand. You don't know him. But we do."

She went out the door, back to the trail. I didn't even bother to follow her with the glasses. There was no point.

I straightened up the cabin extra well—dried the floor, washed the cups—in the hour before my relief was due. It didn't help, though. They remained on my mind: he depressing, she a puzzle. I wondered if, in the long run, I'd really helped her. Would it be worthwhile to her when she caught up with him? I couldn't resist my wondering.

My musings stopped at the usual crash—which made it that sloppy loudmouth, Tomas Sands—of my relief's bike against the side of the cabin. He came in a minute later, boots dry, slicker folded over his shoulder, face excited and expectant.

"Tell me all. What's been happening? What's the story?" he asked.

"What you mean? How'd you find out?" I asked, confused. For I couldn't understand how he could've scooped my story.

"How? Well, it's parked up by the junction to the highway, had this note on it. Here we go." He searched his pocket and read from a note, " 'To whom it may concern,' it says. That's how I found out." Achievement had him giggling silly.

I took the note—on my own logbook paper—Tomas offered. "Who's it from?" he asked.

Unfolded, the note read simply: *Nice ride. Thanks for all you did.*

A queer thrill roamed my arms, my back, my belly, my being. I thought of her going back in vain, in hope. I thought of him doubling back to the clearing where I parked; his bright eyes peering through the windscreen as he guided away my Bug in neutral; him sitting in it, hot-wiring and jump-starting it, making quick distance, getting away.

I felt trembly, a bit faint. I'd so missed the trick, the very gall of him.

"You all right?" Tomas asked.

"Yeah. Just tired," I said, and went to the toilet to spit.

Tomas came after me. "So, what's about the roving Rolls-Vagen, and all? You're not fixing to tell me you loaned out your velvet-wombed machine?"

I didn't answer.

He persisted, a bit more thoughtfully, "It was pinched, huh? A runner got through, and nipped your Volks?"

I extended his reasoning sarcastically. "Then left a note, on official paper, to get it back to me, huh? Don't rave stupid, man."

Undiscouraged, Tomas raised his eyebrows at me. "Well?" he asked impatiently.

"Look, man," I said, "it's personal, okay? Woman problems. I'll tell you at the right time. But about last night—you should've seen the spitfire I had to send back. Pretty as a genie, she was."

That notion quieted Tomas. I was well familiar with his hot version of the fantasy. I left him to it, and went to get my Bug, my tour of duty done.

JUMPING SHIP

Bountin sat on the foredeck grinding teeth into his frustration. His eyes were fixed on the steamer's tie ropes as they sagged and tautened with the rhythm of the swells. They swayed a patient beat of tide rising, of sun going down. Of time moving as it would. Moving, and leaving Bountin stranded. The long summer day was moving on, and he wasn't. Binding him on this steamer's deck was his partner, him sitting over-shoulder behind on a bale of rope: Ruinsey, his friend, a man treating Opportunity like a slave.

Bountin, for one, never took on this last three weeks of stevedoring up the Gulf Stream to end it sitting on deck taking in orange-coloured sun rays. That was never the why he had ridden this seasickening steel bridge across the ocean. He, for one, had come here to get in the solid Land of Plenty.

Yet, for more than an hour now, he had been watching other ship workers filing down the gangplank, all just walking off and up the pier. Among them were some he suspected of having travel arrangements just like his. And none of his suspects had returned. So it seemed the gate into the place was working. And all Bountin wanted to know was why they, too, weren't trying it.

Bountin's generous resolve to bear up in silence slackened under this assault of reasonableness. He heaved a deep sigh, and his independent head twisted towards where Ruinsey was comfortable. Before he could complete his glance, though, Ruinsey hawked and spat a pellet between them; cleanly clearing the ship's rail six feet away, it seemed to banner rebuke in its comet's tail, making Bountin wrench his guilty attention back to the ropes. Although now the grind of his teeth could've crunched diamonds, and the response in his mind was, "Why y'don't spit up your stagnant backside?"

For the nth time, Bountin's eyes, restless as the sea gulls gliding above him, roved to midships where the gangplank joined ship to shore—his gangway into the American port city. . . . A swift tension ballooned within him. To stifle it, he forced a deep draught of the damp sea air, and at the back of his nose, the tension found a taste: a foreign tang suggesting machined air. The sort of taste action would have. . . .

Still, he refused to ask the question eating him, shy to because, in truth, the whole venture—the scheming, arranging, all and else—did belong to Ruinsey; Bountin himself being along for company, and to seek his own luck. With this thought, he shy-eyed at his partner with fresh indulgence, and tried harder to deal with the creeping time. For here he was, at the end of that master of a move: he country-wild and Caribbeano, jumping ship into America . . .

That they were so close! A thrill seized him, shivering across his back and chest, crawling like ants about his balls. He almost jumped to his feet, but caught himself. Instead, he tensed and stretched—his legs, his arms, his back—then yawned extra wide like the wakeful lion.

A hailing voice provided a distraction: "Yow, Coconut!

Ain'tcha goin' t'town? Afraid to lose yer monkey ass, huh?" The taunt ended with its owner's laughter, like a jackass braying after it had farted.

It came from a chubby brown-skinned fellow Ruinsey called "Flabber." He was an American, the ship's cook. He had decided that, of all the Caribbeanos in the crew, Ruinsey was to be jape's stock on the menu for the three-week freight run. So, at chow time in the galley, it was Ruinsey he pestered with "Coconut" and "Monkey" nicknames. Other Bloods wore hair in braids, or natural locks; yet it was Ruinsey's tresses that suggested "Golliwog" and "Snakehead" to Flabber. Every time they went to eat, Flabber became the pesky mosquito: bites and buzzings and all.

And what had Ruinsey done about all this? Nothing but play the statue. As if he didn't see, or hear, or feel. He just sat and listened. Still, on good sea days, when they were eating topsides, he would calm down Bountin's yearning to revenge him. "Man, I have a plan," he'd say. "Every fatted hog got his Saturday, and Flabber day is coming."

Now Flabber swaggered down the gangplank and, not satisfied with his joke, turned at the bottom and made an ugly face at them. Then he shouted something else. But the distance, and the gulls' cries, and the breeze, took it.

"Fuck you, Fat Lips!" Bountin screamed back, maybe in vain, as Flabber began striding away up the long pier into America.

When Bountin turned around, though, Ruinsey had stood up. His beat-up leather bag was swung ready over his shoulder. And in a flash the answer snapped into Bountin's head. That was why they had been waiting! Grinning with his insight, he gleamed a look in Flabber's direction. But the target was already gone, lost in the eight o'clock waning of the long and tired day.

Eyes full on him, Ruinsey cocked his head and asked, "You understanding now?"

Bountin nearly answered the lie that he had divined the plan years ago. Instead, being easy, he said, "Yeah, yeah, yeah."

And not wanting the lesson that might follow, he looked away —toward the narrow, sloping gangplank inviting them down. "So . . . we going now, right?" he said.

"Unless y'don't want catch-up to catch him!" Ruinsey answered.

For Bountin, the gangplank was no real necessity. His anticipation alone could've shot him across the space from rail to pier; he could've sprung up and glided over, like those after-hours gulls. But he was with Ruinsey, on his mission. So Bountin merely slapped at whatever might've stuck to his pants' seat. Then he bounced off.

All the walk up the long pier, Bountin stoppered his excitement and refrained from asking Ruinsey his intent for Flabber. He was still trying to determine it by himself when a chain-link fence surprised up out of the evening. He looked it over: where the lock was, the clearance at the bottom, the barbed overhang at the top. A sudden banging interrupted from his left. They turned and saw the window half of the sentry-hut door opening. A head with a guard's cap poked out and sounded a bleat in nasal pitch, like a goat enquiring after grass. There was a pause.

Bountin looked sharply at Ruinsey, fishing for a clue, or a signal. Ruinsey was staring at the man from eyes edged with blankness. Then his eyes turned to the gate, as if it could offer help, or translation. Bountin fixed on the gate also, now measuring its height, the size of the links, about how many steps it'd take to climb over.

The guard broke the silence. With the same accent, but slower, he said all in one, "Say!-y'all-speak-English-or-what? Habla-say-Español? Eh! ¿Qué-bota?"

Ruinsey cleared his throat, said, "Cargo vessel, *Flying Jenny*. Shore leave . . ."

His voice, sounding a little higher than usual, stopped short, interrupted by a purposeful buzzing, which continued long enough, as the guard pulled his head back in like a turtle. The window slid shut—*Thumptt!!!*

Nothing else happened. Checking Ruinsey for understanding, Bountin found Ruinsey checking him.

Vluuppt!!! The window slid open again. The guard's head popped back out. Glaring, grimacing, it jerked at the fence, "Get-da-gawddamn-gate!" it snarled.

The fed-up head disappeared. And the buzzing began again. It sounded more riled-up.

This time they both started fast for the gate, which, as it was pushed upon, clicked open and let them, easy so, into the paradise, America.

Their first scene was a long, wide, empty highway disappearing streetlight by streetlight into the darkness.

Bountin took it all in, looking about for some signs of life: for people, a car, anything. He expected more. Just what, he didn't know. He had this zest to shout at somebody. Or throw a stick. Or say "Hiya!" Yankee-style.

Ruinsey caught his arm roughly. "First thing is, we have to make Flabber remember. Right?"

Bountin came down to earth. He nodded, looked along both ends of the disappearing street, and asked, "Y'know which way he went?"

Ruinsey pointed to the left, a bit up beyond the streetlights. "That glow over there is the shining city. That's where he gone. And no car passing here this hour. So he gone walking."

It was such common sense, Bountin knew he could've figured it out also. He just hadn't known how high to look, or how to read what he saw. And all that was the stuff Ruinsey taught him. Every day, past and now.

On impulse he grabbed Ruinsey's arm and stopped him soft

eye to hard. Then he had so much thanks to say, he told him only, "Ruinsey, mi' man, this place ent so hard."

Ruinsey looked at him queerly and broke out his full smile that disappeared his eyes into wrinkles.

"I knew you'd like it, man. From the *f* in first, I knew it."

All their back-slapping dislodged the bag from Ruinsey's shoulder. And, as if that had knifed his mood, his grin turned down grim. "But I don't want to feel good yet, man," he said, then looked up the road to the city lights where Flabber was heading.

Bountin said eagerly, "Ay! man, I'm ready like Freddy." He recalled all the times Flabber had played the nettle for his man, and raked and stirred these angers into the working rage that'd drive him now to sting back. For yes! prickle cutting-down time was come.

Ruinsey adjusted his bag so it hung on his back. Then, muttering, "Now for his ass . . ." he set off at a brisk lope, Bountin easy at his side.

At first sight of him, they crossed from the far side of the overwide double street. Directly behind him then, they closed in with silence more than speed. Until, with a pouncing spurt, they were upon Flabber. Bountin kicked him behind the knees into a crouch, while Ruinsey caught him in a choke hold and wrestled him down to the edge of the sidewalk, crushing his face into the scrawny grass. So the first idea Flabber had of something happening was when he tried to scream. But his voice caught on too high and failed, and by then he lost his wind to a gargle. For with a pull, a rip, and a tug over, Ruinsey'd covered Flabber's head with his own denim jacket, leaving him well trussed up. Just for something more to do, Bountin kneed Flabber in the ribs, making him squeal and choke out, "Oh God! Oh God! Don't kill me. . . ."

Meantime, Ruinsey drew his gilpin: it with an edge like a new toothache. He, eyeing Bountin with silent strategy as he pulled it out. Bountin caught his design in an instant, and they changed holding positions slightly, allowing easier breathing for Flabber.

Thus he was begging for mercy more plainly when Ruinsey made his strike. As the blade sliced across his seat, a spitty wheezing joined with Flabber's cry, blending into an indrawn whimper, softer than the whisper of his splitting seating layers: the jeans blue one, the white shorts one, then the skin itself—a lighter brown than expected, and innermost, a pale, pink flesh springing tiny drops of blood that quickly flooded down the new-cut crevasse.

Henceforth, Flabber'd know stretching pains each time he stooped to shit. Good vengeance, since it was relieving his other hole that had brought this on. Bountin grinned at the logic of it as Ruinsey spat finally on his cringing victim. Then they walked off to the city, leaving him huddled and blabbering there.

They took a few false turns around long, wasteland blocks before they got near the source of the glowing. Then they could see headlamps flashing by cross streets not far in front of them. Here they paused to set themselves: to resettle the clothes on the body, to gather an easy pose for walking, to ready their eyes in their faces. Then, when they felt right, they walked up to the next intersection and turned into the flow of the actual, living American street.

"This must be a main avenue. . . ." Ruinsey kept repeating softly, more to himself.

Bountin had no contention with that, or anything else. He

was taking in the lights. The so many lights everywhere he gazed with bedazzled eyes. Not only sizes, but every shape! and colour. Blinking and flashing. Action lights. Sliding along picture advertisements. Popping on, emptying off. Pairing up in beams on shining cars, going and coming, red and brilliant. Shimmering the streets into golden streams, and rippled silver, and weird glitters, and hanging-tree shadows from the looming goose-necked lamp poles; lamp poles tall and aloof as royal palms.

Several times Bountin stared himself into collisions: with people, poles, poodly dogs, and potholes. After enduring some verbal abuse and vague pain, he marshalled his attention to immediate focus on the people flowing beside and about him like river sands eddying. They passed in multitudes of vital, plain, and regular sorts. Many carried a flair. Regardless of how it came out, they tried for a difference, in clothes, or makeup, or walking stride. No one seemed to care when the gimmick didn't work. No jibes, no embarrassment, even if frogface wearing silks was escorting pussycat in satin. Everybody was full of themselves, going along intent, overlooking any disturbance that'd vary their own destinations. Bountin marvelled. This was all right!

A girl coming past him was wearing cutoffs that never stopped. Just loudly enough he hailed her, "Hey, Sugar Juice!"

She caught the pass, together with his bold eye. Bold right back, she smiled full and close at him, then mouthed him a kiss as they passed each other forever, indulging him a lasting moment of honey. Hers was the City's welcoming kiss. It said he was among his kind of people. He was in his native place. . . .

Ruinsey's voice nudged into his attention, insistent about transport they needed to find, some "subway" train to get them to his contact in the city, to some woman expecting them.

Bountin waved an arm at his bothering, indicating the scene about them. "Which city? This isn't the city?" he asked.

Ruinsey let the question rise into the night. He only muttered, "Well . . ." and turned to searching through his bag, from which he took a notebook page and read it with many puzzled looks, as if the words were making strange signs at him.

"This could be any part of it. Look, man! I never been here, y'know. . . ." Ruinsey stopped, hmmm'd like a lawyer, then went on, "Listen! These directions say we *have* to get a subway . . . whatever it is."

Bountin couldn't figure why Ruinsey sounded so concerned. Finding the train couldn't be that difficult. It was a public vehicle. They just had to ask somebody, and he, for one, wasn't shy. And even if they missed the train, he was sure they could walk to Ruinsey's contact. It was one city, after all. They had all night, and he wasn't tired.

"You want me to find out from that papers man over there?" Bountin asked.

Ruinsey shrugged okay, and handed over the paper. Then he added, "But don't make show of yourself too much, eh? We've got to be inconspicuous. You understand?" His forehead was all frowned up in anxious ditches as he spoke, his eyes red with trouble lines.

All his show of dread was only firing up Bountin's temper. Why all this advice and concern? How come suddenly he was a cross to Ruinsey's shoulder?

"Since when you so worried about me?" he demanded, unable to keep the sarcasm and heat out of his voice. "You don't think your partner could handle, eh? Tell me!"

But he didn't wait for Ruinsey's answer. Didn't want one. The question was his point. He just stalked off to the newspaper stand.

With his partner's misgivings policing his mind, Bountin was strict on his politeness. He waited until the man was free, then said, "Good night, mister."

When nothing happened, he repeated it louder, twice.

Finally, the man looked at him and said, "Yeah, what?"

"Can you direct me to the train? Please."

"Which 'un?"

"The subway one . . ."

"Yeah, yeah. Which 'un?"

Bountin looked him over and saw the man was serious. So he tried, "Any one going in the city."

"Better y'take the bus," the man said. "Stops one block over."

Bountin leaned his elbows on the counter, and struck a pondering pose. He shook his head. "No, I want to catch the train."

"Same token," the man answered.

Bountin couldn't follow this meaning. So he remained the thoughtful one; began turning about the note he held and looking at it as if *it* had failed to satisfy.

The man took the hint. "Here, let's see that!" he said, and reached over his counter and plucked the note away. He waved it to arm's length and squint-focused to read. Then he returned it to Bountin.

"You'd be better off with th' bus," he said. "Your train's way 'cross town."

Bountin kept his pose; added a this-is-great-news smile. "Yes? Which direction?"

He spoke with much marvelling in his tones. The man pointed. Bountin nodded as if heady with a privilege. Then, as if afterthinking, he asked, "So, how far is 'cross town?"

The man looked at him curiously, grimaced a clown mouth, fingering down the ends while he considered. "Thirty, maybe forty blocks," he said.

Bountin smiled at him, straightened up, and put the directions in his pocket. Before he walked away, he said, "Thank you for your kindness, mister."

The man called after him, "Y'should take th' bus . . . same token."

Bountin, feeling champion, dashed into the street, noticed the red DON'T WALK while lithely skipping through some braking traffic towards the other side of the road. His satisfaction would've been really complete if Ruinsey had witnessed his handling the man. That certainly would've finished all the anxious nonsense in his mind: that the Bountin had lost his touch.

The man had pointed back along the way they had come. So they crossed a broad, busy one-way street, and went. Right away Bountin became spellbound by the lights again, all so close around from lamp pole to ground levels, while straight up above was opaque blackness. It was all upside down: as if the sky had upended its contents all around them, transforming the people, the stores, even the plain concrete he walked. The scattering star-fall had drenched the street with sparkle and changed the place into a bustle of glaze and glitter.

A glance at his partner striding alongside made Bountin realize that Ruinsey hadn't been sparking at all. Much more than his fashion, he had gone silent. Bountin began worrying for explanation. About Flabber? Not likely. They had done a good revenge—not even the victim was witness. In any case, Ruinsey never took on that sort of problem. His motto was "Make life simple, take it as it comes."

It occurred to him that Ruinsey might be tired. Or hungry. That just might be it. He himself, on thinking, was middling peckish.

"You slowing down, or what? How you so quiet?" he asked.

Ruinsey acknowledged him only a distracted, no-comment look.

They were coming up to a one-door store whose neatly laden stalls encroached halfway across the sidewalk. Pyramids of citrus, apples, bananas, mangoes, and other fruits competed colourfully for attention. Inspired, Bountin approached quickly, as he said to Ruinsey, "Man, what you need is some vitamins."

And with that, he crouched over the banana stall, and swiftly slipped a yellow-ripe hand into his shirt's bosom. Then, with a big grin, he sped off, surging through the sidewalk's throng, casting backwards looks.

It was a couple moments before he realized there was no pursuit. No one had come out of the store to throw even a look at him. So he slowed down to the pace of the crowd, which had just so calmly accepted all his shoving and rushing through. Finally, he stepped off the curb between two parked cars and waited for Ruinsey to catch up. The incurious crowd went by as if he weren't there. So he broke out a banana to munch while his partner arrived. And when he did, fell into step beside him, and offered him some food.

As if taking example from Ruinsey, the street was becoming quieter. The several past blocks carried less and less traffic: people, business, and otherwise. Bountin commented on this.

"It must be getting late," was all Ruinsey said.

Being patient with the man's mood, Bountin let that comment remain where it dropped. He himself hadn't been thinking of time, but of how the quiet streets seemed relieved, and freer in the more space they now had. And about how the air even had a lighter smell. And how the soft slap of the tossed banana peelings carried truer. And how he felt betting certain it was easier now to jump higher, or explode a lungful in a shout. But Bountin didn't bother bringing up all this. Not to a Ruinsey seeing the night only as a clockface.

It was a dimly lit, vertical sign placed abruptly next to some stairs leading underground. Involved with the rhythm of walking blocks and crossing streets, they nearly missed it. Seeing the stairs, right away Bountin realized that "subway" meant underground railway system, and with more excitement, that the trains ran through tunnels in the earth. That idea made him laugh out loud. He clapped Ruinsey's shoulder. "Y'see that, Ruinsey? And I was looking for a railway station, y'know, the water tanks, a platform, a signalman. Y'following me?"

Ruinsey nodded understanding, but didn't talk. Although, from the way his front foot was groping for the first tread, Ruinsey, too, had to be getting impressed right past his popping eyeballs.

Halfway down, at the zig in the zigzag staircase, Ruinsey took a packet of slugs from his bag. They were ten tokens, he said. Bought from his contact man on the cargoship, they were part of the stowaway job package. He handed five to Bountin.

"I hope these tokens working for this train, y'know," Ruinsey said, worried.

Bountin considered this. "Well, that ent the worst," he said. "If they don't work, we could just jump over. That turnstile ent a good three feet."

Ruinsey looked him over a long one. Then he said, "Bountin, you must stop thinking that way now. Okay? You not home. This is America. We can't be drawing attention so, or they will catch we. You have to calm down, man."

Ruinsey was being so solemn, Bountin made a check-up grin at him. "But how you so serious, Ruinsey? You sermonizing in paradise, man. I was only making joke. I know we not jumping."

Ruinsey didn't acknowledge him. Instead, back stiffened, token in hand, he led off for the turnstile. They put their tokens in the slots, and they worked just fine.

The underworld train ride was the final gate through which the City stormed to possess Bountin. Its assault began immediately, as with hurricane roaring, a one-eyed dragon-monster filled the tunnel, rushing up to them. Then, with a great shrieking, it turned out to be their grumbling train, restrained and shuddering, but, unnaturally, blowing steam nowhere. No sooner had it stopped than side panels scraped open and people tumbled out like finished batches. Doing as others who had waited, Ruinsey and he pushed into the carriage against the outflow. Then, inside, propped on hard, plastic seats, they watched the doors guillotine shut, and with a jolt, they were fast off, shrieking like a cross dragon again. But now inside it.

Under mountains? Under rivers? From what Bountin could make out of their passage, it could've been anywhere. Outside the row windows, the carriage's lights reflected off whizzing walls and sudden poles, where the checkered patterns of light strung into speeding bullets that disappeared for dark moments before returning to dazzle. All this was close to hypnotizing him when another charging rumble *vroomph*ed by, going the other way, and shattered his trance with a fist of sound force.

Bountin palmed away a slack feeling from his face. The dripping sweat was one thing; the bigger bother was a glazed view he tried squinting away. Yet it still seemed they were inside a bolt of lava, hurtling through the earth, aiming for eruption at some volcano, somewhere and soon. And very powerful they were; very dangerous, too. He had this sense that, although his feet were standing still, they were really flying, skimming over ground. One supporting proof was the wheel-whirring in his soles, which was also vibrating through his seat, and setting an annoying edge to his teeth. He stood up abruptly to change the pressures, and the annoying thrilling stopped; but on standing, he was unbalanced and almost fell. He only saved himself by an instinctive snatch overhead, where his hand found a securing hook. It was so exactly in the right place that Bountin realized it must have been put there for just that convenience. To him, it was such a practical forethought that he hung his head down close to Ruinsey's to speak his admiration for the designers.

"Isn't this something else again? . . ." he began, and couldn't hear himself above the train's roar. So he cleared his throat for the challenge, and shouted, "Ruinsey, isn't this something?"

As if Bountin's shout had caught him in a mean dream, Ruinsey jerked up, aggressive with alarm, asking, "What!!! What!!!"

This startled, fighting readiness put Bountin off his cheery mood. He was about to scream, "Forget it!" But right then his throat broke into a coughing fit from strain. And he could only hang there from the handhold, and rack his belly bones narrow with spasm after weakening spasm.

Meanwhile, Ruinsey kept repeating, "Calm down, man, you have to take it easy. . . ." as if it were mischief Bountin was making. As the seizure passed, Bountin felt the train slowing down. So he sat down to compose himself.

The door panels crashed open. Some people got up and hustled out. One or two rushed in as if under catch-up pressures. Then, through the door right in front him, three guys dressed up female sauntered into the carriage ever so coolly, as if they never noticed how the gates just missed smashing their shitting ends into skinny streaks. With lots of chichi and wiggling, they teetered their high heels to the plastic bench and sat primly, as if cautious of their hard ends testing against the plastic hardness.

Bountin was never so astonished. They were so weird, and so comfortable at it, he couldn't believe their boldness. He wondered at them, amazed. Did they never pass mirrors? Had they no family, or caring friends, to advise them of their appearance? Of their makeup caking between sprouting moustache hairs, of those muscled hairy calves, of those high-coloured, pointed-heel size fifteens. How could these guys stand up anywhere in public? Had they hidden in the toilet to wait for this train? Suddenly amused, Bountin decided these guys truly deserved a "Big-Balls Boldness" trophy. For with their display of gumption, they had to be carrying at least four sets of the daringest miracles ever.

The perspiration-moustache one stared back at Bountin. "What's your problem?" he asked in girlish tones.

Bountin could hold it in no more. He burst out laughing, weakening himself so, he leaned on Ruinsey for support.

"How quaint," commented the eye-shadowed one with scarlet lips, then closed heads with the others for a giggle chorus.

Ruinsey eased Bountin off as if he didn't know him. "Take it easy, man," he muttered.

Right away a part of Bountin's mind raged, *Take what easy?* But he was still laughing in part also. Only now there was nothing funny to his mirth. He just continued with the noisy grimacing from spite.

The plucked-eyebrows one was now staring him down. Then he proceeded to japing with flirting blinks, and moues, and tossing head. Bountin sprang up and stood over him. "You like me, Horse-mouth?" he challenged. "You want mih cock? Y'want it crowing in your face, eh?"

He hefted his crotch in Plucked Eyebrows' face, who pulled back and ladied, "What is your problem, sir?"

"I don't have none, you no-cunt monster," Bountin said threateningly. "But look yuh eyes on me again, and I'd fix your problems for you."

Bountin's hand was hot and damp on the blade handle stuck in his waistband. He was ready for anything. But before he could move, Ruinsey had arm-locked his neck and was dragging him away to sit close with him, holding him there.

"Don't let them vex you, Bountey. Y'have to take it easy. Forget them. Just take it easy," he repeated urgently.

As he spoke, the he-shes got up and sashayed downrange to the far end of the carriage.

Ruinsey had led them off the train onto a major interconnecting platform. But for the many pillars, so large it was, it could've made a full-sized concrete soccer field. They were standing now against a passage wall. Ruinsey held the directions crumpled in his hand. "Man, I can't see how we go make it, y'know," he said.

"How y'mean?" Bountin asked. "She didn't write down what to do next?"

"Is not that. . . ."

"Well, is what?"

Ruinsey looked away, slow eyes roving all around the big space. Shaking his head, he regarded the giant girders lying close over them. Finally, he said, "If those things break, I wouldn't even know where I die. Not if is east, or west. Or day, or night. And if is a crowd here when it come down, I'd die just like a common ant mashed up in a melee. . . ."

"But, Ruinsey man, they have all those signs about," Bountin said reasonably. "Look around. Look at all those arrows, and numbers, and colours, and lines you could follow. They could—"

Ruinsey cut him off. "Bountin, you can't see? You don't realize they only crowding you, steering people like cows, like tame animals. Y'think you could stand that? Y'could live so?"

He stopped and nodded in a final manner. Then he said, "Yes, man, we have to take that other track."

At Ruinsey's conclusion, a quaking notion zinged into Bountin's mind. Stubbornly, he pushed it away. Instead, he pointed up to the subway signs. "But, Ruinsey, that is the out-town track y'looking at. We going in-town."

Ruinsey shot him an odd look. And Bountin saw his partner's face in a new mask: one sharp and anxious, shining with greasy sweat; one with straining eyes that stared at everything too long. Then he acknowledged what was past working out. His partner really didn't want to go on anymore. For Ruinsey had turned and headed for the back-out track.

Bountin stared after him. He felt as if betrayed by some foolishness. As if his necklace charm had cut his head off, his whole spirit wilted. Vacant-minded, he stood there for minutes, until, in the distance, he heard the first urgent rushing, which before had roared into a train. That giving him life again, he sprinted off after Ruinsey.

Bountin found him before the angry dragon crescendoed past. On an inner track, it was skating farther into town. There was plenty of time for Ruinsey's train.

Their eyes made four, and all was said. They reached for and embraced each other. They were close as blood to skin, Bountin thought, and now they must bleed apart. Then they stepped back and, shy with each other for the moment, gazed together up the dark train tracks.

"I'll 'company you back to the gate, okay?" Bountin said. "I mean, if that's all right with you?"

Ruinsey worked his vanishing-eyes smile. He said, "Well, you settle your mind already, right, Boldman? So how could I ever stop you? Sure, make it back halfway with me."

He handed Bountin the crumpled directions.

TIES

I met a man in the joint. He was from Trinidad and mentally fine-tuned to crazy. But he was also harmless, and we all took care of him. A gentleman philosopher, and honest as sunshine, Trinee had a saying for every situation. You listened to him, and you'd think he was a hundred years old. Yet he was as young as any of us.

Once I heard him say how, when Lion gets old, common Dog fucks him. I cracked up when he said this to make a point in a funny story. But there's serious sense in Trinee's nonsense. And I, for one, never want to grow old so feeble. Not unless things change around in this town.

I went to the joint because I wanted to live the American Dream. Not too much, or too fancy. Just the ordinary American Dream, featuring food, good appliances, some fine clothes, and a steady income. No fancy cars! They're not for me. I will always pay the taximan. I'd even take the trains rather than have sanitation trucks, dogs, and vandals make my ride ugly. Yes, all I wanted was an average portion of the apple pie, minus the car.

Thing is, nobody ever showed me how to get it, except my brother, Stone. And he was a hard man.

Mama had named him Winston Shaka Jones. But his real name was Stone. He was six years older than I, and by the time I first could talk, he had the name already. He was a watchful guy, never spoke much about anything. That doesn't mean he was a thinker, now. Neither does it say that he was stupid. Stone was a one to do what someone told him. It had to be the right some-one, of course. Mama used to tell Stone to make something of himself, because his father had made him a ravager. She always told him that: "Your father made you a ravager!" It was as though she fancied the sound of it. Stone never said anything back. You ever hear a rock talk?

Stone's father had raped Ma when she was sixteen. He was her father's good buddy, and could visit the house when Gramps was away. He raped her twice in one week. When she told her mother and Gramma told Gramps, he said somebody had to do her the favor sometime. But then Gramps was a no-good any-how.

Once when Ma was upset, she told Stone what she thought of his father—mean, bitter things. Stone begged her then for per-mission to find the brute and end him. He was a fist-hearted fifteen-year-old man, but that night his tears were running full as he asked. Ma looked at him as if long lost, and then she said, "Don't bother, son." She hardly ever called us "son." Then she went over and held his face to her bosom. She was crying, too.

Stone was my man. From since I was in kindergarten, he was who I wanted to be. He was the nearest thing to Superman that I knew. He always got a job done, whatever the job. When I was about twelve, Stone took me under his wing. I was very careful to be cool about it. But I was happy as a soap bubble in summer. He taught me to play ball, to fight dirty, to steal and rob and hustle and con people. Even though it was much harder than school stuff, I learned everything. Stone didn't like to teach the same thing twice. Soon I felt I could do some things better than he. But we had no hassles. For a while, it was all good life. Then Stone decided to make a soldier of himself. So he joined the army to see the world, and they showed him Vietnam.

Sometimes, in the joint, time gets long. It's best then to just sit and think. I call it "monking," because you can become so inspired, with revelations and understandings. After a monking spell, you may get angry in a strange way. Every time you remember a wrong done you, a chill embraces you, forcing your belly muscles a little tighter, permanently. Make a check of all the brothers in jail. Those who look strong and lean, I bet they're either revenge-bent hating, or hugging madness close. If there's a difference.

Whenever I thought about Stone, I would read a book, any book. I read a good bit. I suppose I have a sort of angry prison education.

I admired Stone more than anyone else in creation. Yet he lived and died close to me, and I never knew him. Maybe I love him because I didn't know him. Maybe Stone was a mean guy. I don't know. I don't know if Stone had a sense of humor. I don't know what he liked in women. I never knew if he had a favorite beer. So now I get mad thinking of Stone. Somehow, someone stole my brother's personality from me. But then, I might've been careless with it. So I am cool.

Seven years in the joint taught me one or two tricks. A good one is how to be patient in anger. I learned patience from being bored working in the prison library. In a few years, I had patiently read every book they stacked. That way I picked up a liberal education, too. Otherwise I could've been a reluctant bookkeeper. That's what the authorities in the joint had decided to teach me to be. I guess they were trying to show me the pathway to upward social mobility. I didn't apply myself, though. I figured that if it was so hot, why weren't they all doing it? They wanted riches. And on the other side, I didn't expect many businessfolks would be eager to hire a bookkeeper with my record.

Watching the power of justice was another trick I learned. Up on the top edge of Central Park, like layers and layers of stubbornness, there is a great mass of black stone, a hard cap to the natural heart of the city. I always picture it when I think of the Justice System in this town. Being involved in that system is like being stuck in the middle of that unfeeling mass of hardness. That's if you don't have power: to slip, to slide, or explode out. And to folks like me, power comes in different guises. It's not easy to hold, or even recognize.

I have seen guys pray to the jailhouse lawyer as though he were God. Just because he, a prisoner like them, could comprehend that unnatural legal thinking, those traditional laws that changing times have made foolish. So, to them, the jailhouse lawyer is a great man. Guys would beg him to listen to their cases. They'd approach him as though it were Judgment Day and they have a fifty-fifty chance of getting in, and he's the one with the deciding vote. They're so reverent! You find out that these "common criminals" are men who could tell a good joke. Or movie buffs who want a good education for their kids. And it's the prison lawyer who has power to change them so. For to many a brother in jail, he is the best and last hope.

This lord of promise was no help to me, though. I had an open-and-shut case: accessory to murder of an officer and a civilian, attempted robbery, assault of all the officers who tried to kill me after they had handcuffed me, and a few misdemeanors they ganged up as the writing space ran out. The trial didn't take long. The prosecutor mentioned my address, and the judge became red in the face. Then his lips closed up tight like a disturbed oyster. My legal-aid defense counsel was like a little boy on a big seashore: You hardly noticed he was there.

What saved me some was my minority. I qualified as juvenile, unschooled, unable to understand the best ways to progress in regular society. So I got life, meaning three-to-ten. Not too bad. It kept me out of wars and other trouble.

When Stone came back from the government's war, we had begun some serious hustling. The difference from before was Stone. He moved with incredible smooths. This was from his Vietnam training. People who saw him armed knew he was dangerous. They did exactly what he said. Which was very nice, since we were able to stop mugging poor folks, and lived off the high-priced little stores, and such-like. It was quicker money, less time on the streets, and easier on everyone. We never hurt a soul.

Stone spent a lot of money on Mama, giving her a good time in the fancy life. I sort of let him. They had their special thing I stayed out of. Once he bought her a fine mink coat. Mrs. Saunders, who had a true eye for style, said Mama wore it like she was born to mink. And Mama seemed to believe that. For you wouldn't have believed her graciousness when Stone and I took her to those fancy-named restaurants. I'm sure Ma went to every Caribbean country boasting a hotel and an airport. Yes, she did make merry of her little self. She knew that Stone was trying to make up for his birthright. Just as she had to know we were robbing and stealing. But we never spoke about such things. What was there to say?

I got the idea for the numbers-joint takeoff by accident. It came on a cool fall day. Angel and I had been playing ball in the park, him in dungaree coveralls, me in jeans. He was going to show me the mightiest dunk shot ever by a six-foot-one, unknown high school player. He started fifteen feet right of the hoop, driving in powerfully from an angle, then he leapt for height and—only managed a mighty miss.

The ball took off, ricocheting over the fence and into the street. Then a telephone repairman ran out from behind a repair truck and tossed the ball back to us. The freaky thing was that the guy, even down to his coveralls, was Angel's double. We agreed that it was some kinda weird, then ended the game and started for the bodega to get something to cool down over. As we passed the telephone-repair van, Angel decided he'd play the van's license-plate number. And surprised me by going into a little doorway almost blocked by the repair van—a new but thriving numbers joint.

Half hour later, Stone was satisfied with my answers. I had told him that, yes, there was a fresh-dug, open trench between the curb and the truck. That the men were working on it. And that, yes, the numbers man with the gun sat his protection well inside the joint's door, as he didn't want to be conspicuous to the repairmen. Only then did Stone agree to go shopping with me. We bought apparatus that telephone repairmen carried: coveralls, two yellow hard hats, oversized plastic goggles, pliers, and some colored wire. And we were ready.

Next day, there were no newspaper stories about the stickup of a numbers joint. To street people, that meant no one had died, so the police were staying out of it. But the street also had it that the numbers people had lost about $100,000 worth of quite spendable money. They had no idea who'd taken them off. The two robbers had entered saying they were from the telephone company. Every man, woman, and child who heard the news wished they'd been the heroes.

About three hours after that nonstickup, two quietly dressed young men stepped into a small hardware store on the East Side. If anything was remarkable about them, it was that they were so circumspect in deportment. They virtually trod the pavement softly. The younger, more outgoing one asked the storekeeper for some rubber bands. He was courteous and spoke nicely. The other young man stood by silently. He remained just inside the door and carried in one hand a large, filled shopping bag. There was something magnetic about his silence. He seemed charged, alert, set like a rattleless viper. This quiet one was looking at the store's only other occupant: a brown-skinned, middle-aged woman. In that neighborhood, perhaps somebody's maid. She was in the store's phone booth occupied at frowning as she concentrated on her conversation.

While he was bagging the rubber bands, the shopkeeper glanced over to the watchful young man. The gesture was more of curiosity than caution, as if he didn't like the boy's quiet but wasn't threatened by it. The transaction completed, the young men turned to leave.

Then the door opened, and a new customer entered. Instantly, the quiet one fastened his gaze on the new man. And right then came a moment when time paused on the brink, before the events of its smooth flow jumbled on together. Some things went so fast, they had to be recalled with effort to memory. And some things happened too slowly for ever forgetting.

The new man wrenched around to face the intense stare. Then he spread his legs and put his back to the door, defending it against the boys' exit. His reassuring voice announced, "All right, everybody, take it easy." The take-charge tone identified him. He was a well-trained plainclothes officer who knew trouble when he saw it.

The nice young man was quick in his response. "No trouble, Officer," he said, "no trouble at all. Ask the man." And the boy looked over to the shopkeeper.

The shopkeeper was smiling nervously. He didn't want trouble in his store. Meanwhile, the nice young man leaned privately on the hard one. He urged in a whisper, "Let's go, man. Chill out, chill out!" The defiant one responded reluctantly, like a rock shifted by a great effort. But he was moving. The nice one reached for the door handle. He was trying hard to be casual.

The new man now seemed embarrassed by his overreaction, and relinquished the door slowly. The nice boy moved aside for the other to leave ahead of him. But as this young man passed, the man reached over to poke suspiciously at the bag. He demanded, "What you got in there?" At that, the hard young man flowed into action.

Stone released the bag most gently. With no other motion, and before the bag had hit the floor, he was holding the poking hand. He twisted it somehow, and the officer's face was jerked down to collide with Stone's rapidly rising knee. At the same time, Stone's other hand reached for the man's hair. He grabbed it and twisted violently. And I heard the muffled, crunching sound with which life deserted the bewildered man. It was all done faster than I can say.

I was fascinated. I couldn't speak, and tears rushed to my eyes. I had never seen physical action so perfect. He had performed the brutal act of killing with a graceful finesse that was wonderful. He must've felt my emotion, for he glanced oddly at me, his face set proud. Then, as our eyes met, I saw him flinch and go dead. Same time, I heard the shot.

A big hole had splattered out the top of his chest. It went from a quick jagged white to a brown flowing red. I spun around to see the shopkeeper with the shotgun still in his hands. He was trembling badly, and spitting white froth from the side of his mouth. He looked older than he had just a moment before, and shook his head as though violently negating the scene, dislodging his glasses. He clutched the wavering shotgun with one hand,

and snatched to right his glasses, but only succeeded in completely knocking them off.

My bullets must've hit him somewhere in the trunk region. I saw no wounds or bloody spots appear on his haggard face. He tried to brace unsuccessfully against some invisible, avenging whiplash. Then he crumpled down across the counter, and with a sobbing, gargling sound started to die.

I felt Stone pulling at my pants cuff. My eyes were rivers, and snot was running in between my open lips. I looked for something to blow my nose and wipe my face with. Stone kept tugging at my pants cuff. Impatient with the irritation, I blew out my nose onto the bloody floor. Then I dried my face with my jacket sleeves, and I looked to attend my main man.

Stone's left shoulder and arm were almost blown away. The thick blood was surging out of him and onto the floorboards. It seemed so much. Stone wanted something. He was trying to tell me what, but all I heard was a gurgle. His face showed a lot of damage, but mainly it looked sweat-dirty. Then he looked at my hand, and I understood. It was the gun he wanted. So I put it on his shoulder and let some blood run over it. Then I pulled up his good hand to hold it there, making him look like some macabre marksman at rest after firing. Then he did the one thing that could break my heart. Stone cried.

The tears were seeping through his half-closed eyes and running down the sides of his face into his ears. I thought it must feel uncomfortable. But I was at a loss for what to do, unable to move, or comfort him. All my life, he had taught me to take care of business. But I didn't know how to comfort someone when he was dying. So I just sat there in his sticky blood, crying and feeling protective.

He was trying to talk again, and couldn't because the blood was in his throat. After a while, he began to cough and cough and cough. I said, "Take it easy, man," concerned that his shoulder couldn't take such a jarring. Then he said something. It sounded like, "I ain't no rapist." But it was a wheezing rasp of a whisper. What was clear in it, though, was the righteousness of the innocent. Then Stone died.

I never told Mama about that part. I didn't want her to know what he was thinking last. For no one loved her more than Stone. I didn't.

I never found out what happened to Stone's body. I was in the hospital recovering from the arresting officers for a month after he died. Mama lasted about two years more. When I got to jail, she used to come see me once every month. But we didn't have much to talk the hour out. She really wanted to know more about Stone. She was asking me something I couldn't tell her.

After she passed, they took me once to see her grave. Her neighbors in the building had buried her. They had also petitioned for my pass to visit the cemetery. At the gravesite, no sadness came to me. Instead, I found myself wondering what had become of the mink coat, and all that jewelry Stone had bought her.

Jail was good to me. I was educated there. When I went in, I was like that officer Stone destroyed: just an average dummy with minimal education and a lot of good instincts. I learned to think in the joint. I came to understand that time is friendly if you keep yourself ready. And I had one joy there: a pleasure I fought with every day. You see, I didn't want to become dependent on it. For I had no control over it, "it" being the letter I got every two weeks.

Men in jail become pathetic in their dependencies. Without ever realizing, they make themselves into puppets. They are manipulated by everybody—by other prisoners, guards, officials, by chaplains, by entertainers, by their children and their women, and most of all, by their hopes.

This can cause some strange changes. I've seen lovermen go weird. From Romeos who broke and balled the ladies outside, lovesickness turns them into lisping, stubble-chinned, prison-yard queens. For salvation from prison, men have been born again, lost themselves in hobbies, developed occult philosophies, become militant or mental defectives. Sometimes they seek death with rash cunning, smiling all the while. Sometimes they just go mad. But they hardly ever recognize they're dancing for an uninterested puppeteer named Hope. For in prison, salvation is not your own to find. They have no saviors there.

Sometimes when I knew my letter was due, I would begin to avoid mail call. I learned to enjoy the pain of avoiding mail call. I'd do it gradually, a day at a time, holding myself in check when I felt the anticipation rise. After a while, I learned to like the thrill itself, minus the gratification. There were times when I suspended pleasure until I could pick up two letters at a time. Once I did three.

The letters always got to me looking old in their cream-colored six-by-three envelopes. Regardless of postmarked origin, which changed frequently, the return address was always one word: Harlem. I liked that. I read it as a defiant camaraderie. They were addressed in liquid black ink, used by an old-fashioned nib pen dipped in an inkpot. Fine lines were impressed on the envelope so that the writing was neat and straight. Yet the handwriting was nervous and unpracticed, a crochet of words formed letter by letter and linked by flourishes. It was mostly this time and concern in production that made these letters my constant comfort and solace.

They always began, *My dear son Othello* . . . They always ended with, *A Prayer for Those Awaiting Deliverance.* I never said the prayer, but I respected it. The letters themselves didn't give anything much in the form of news. I usually flushed them down the toilet just after reading. I kept the stamps, though. These I dated and put under my mattress in a prison envelope—my treasury. What these letters unspokenly said was that the old cleaning lady was keeping up her end.

After Old Man Death had walked away with his full bag, the shop knew a moment of relief. That was just a feeling, though. The fact was, I was sad and very frightened. There were blood and dead people all around. One of them was the law. There was also a shopping bag containing $126,000 wrapped in a bath towel. It was a bad spot to be in. I knew I should get out of there, but was too listless to move. Moreover, there was blood all over me. And I really didn't want to leave my man. But neither did I want to face those officers who were radioing their rapid approach.

As if from a distance, I heard Mama's voice saying softly, "You'd better soon get away from all this trouble, son." For a moment, terrifying thoughts of angels and the supernatural overwhelmed me. I actually gasped for breath. But immediately I realized she wouldn't have said that, or in just those tones. So then I was only surprised. I looked around. The old lady who'd been in the phone booth was walking toward the front door, carefully avoiding the spots of blood and disorder. She was obviously leaving, intent on minding her own business. In a confusion, I also knew there was nothing I was going to do about it.

Suddenly, without thought, I said, "Wait! Please, wait." She paused, one hand on the doorknob, and the words spilled out of me. "Here, take this," I said, grabbing the bag and holding it out to her. "Please, ma'am . . . Use whatever you want. Please. Keep the rest safe for me. Anyhow you want. Here! These keys are to safe-deposit boxes. Take them. This is all my ID. Please, ma'am, hold it for me. I love my brother. I have to suffer with him. His name is Stone. Please!"

I was moving all the while: rushing things to her, handing the bag to her, explaining, pleading, and crying again. Sniffling like a baby. At last she said, "Okay, son, okay. I'll take care of your business for you, just as you ask. But now I need a change of air."

She had been peering at me head aslant, still half facing the door and looking uncertain. Then, when she said, "Okay," she smiled at me and winked. It was a spry wink, an okay-let's-do-it wink. And with that twinkle, she gained my absolute trust. Then she took the loot and walked out the door, still being careful to avoid the gore. The only things that I knew about her were her voice, that she'd worn a red scarf around her neck, and that her accent was Caribbean.

Leaving the joint is an emotional experience. Some men can hardly take it. They ask their people to come and meet them to help them go through the gates. You're glad to leave, of course. But if you've been in for a while, you're leaving old friends. Sometimes they're your only friends. And they're glad to see you go, but they also wish it was them leaving. So in the morning or the night before, when you tell them good-bye, you feel the coldness of their envy. Yet you ignore it. You're too glad to be getting away from that cage of anger and despair. And you know, too, that they're really glad for you. There's just no way they could show it.

But that's not the hardest part of regaining your freedom. The most difficult is stepping into that strange, spacious, glaring world again. You're like a country boy walking first time into a slick, big-city nightclub. Everyone is looking at you. And you know they all think you're a piece of shit. And you have to be cool, 'cause you're not sure about it yourself.

In addition to the usual "Harlem," there was a real address on the last two letters. It was near Marcus Garvey Park, and this was where I headed when I hit the city. That afternoon it was the only certain place in this world. Everywhere else was just a blurred understanding. I headed there express, no stops nowhere. Just having that place to go to made me forever owe the old lady. Lagniappe was that she let me come out on my own.

The house was a four-storied brownstone. It looked solid and secure—as Trinee would say, "as though it there since Hatchet was Hammer." I rang the super's bell as instructed in the letter.

After a minute, an older man opened the door, put his head out, and asked before I could speak, "You Othello Jones?" I didn't answer right away. After such a long time locked up, the sound of my name, public and free, was soul music. I savored its song, the cadences: la-la-la laaa.

"Yes, sir," I told him, "I'm Othello Jones."

The man smiled at me. "Well, sir boss, your room is on the top floor. It's nice, spacey, private. Can see the park up there. Lots of light. Mrs. Dean said I must see you have everything— even unto the fatted calf. . . ." He chuckled at his reference. I smiled away, too. Although not so much at what he said as for his manner. He went on, "She said you'd see her two weeks from tomorrow. She left some things with me for you. Looks like she's . . ." And he kept on talking, treating me like family and making me welcome.

GUPPIES

The intercom's blast, big and commanding, woke Natty. Y'd think there's a fuckin' fire somewhere, he thought irritatedly. The alarm had made him start up from his bed—the living-room sofa. "Damn," he muttered at the summons, "somebody'll haveta fix that fuckin' bell! Th' shit's enough to . . ." He shook his upset head as a horrible enough image failed him, and crossed the room to the speaker, jammed his thumb hard on the Talk toggle, and bawled into it, *"WHAT?"*

He released the toggle and listened, glaring at the intercom as if it were some drooling fool harassing him. Although he well suspected who it was downstairs bothering him so early in the morning. He would bet his balls it was Swooney: the early man of the crew he'd recently got down with. Swooney's folks (unlike Natty's father) had no idea that he scrambled. They were strict churchgoing people; he had to show them school report cards with aces. If not, from the way Swooney acted, they'd probably sell him as a slave or something.

Because of all this dangerous living, Swooney had to be out in the street every morning by six or seven o'clock, supplying the early dope fiends. His folks, meantime, thought he was in training with an athletic club.

And all this was cool with Natty; except that he had noticed that since he began scrambling with the crew, Swooney'd been fucking him up like a cheap whore's pussy—as if he planned on proving his reputation as a bully by messing with Natty's sleep, and waking him up long before . . . Natty couldn't finish the thought as Swooney's impatient voice came loudly through the raspy speaker: "Yow, Natty. Come on *down,* man! I *gotta* go!"

Like the rush of a familiar high, Natty's irritation swelled to anger. He jammed Talk again and screamed, "Okay! Okay! Just get off the fuckin' bell. Y'fuckin' asshole!"

The edge of the toggle caught painfully into his thumb's ball and forced him to release it too soon, so even as he was finishing his retort, he heard the hollow click of the intercom returning to neutral and nullifying his response. His anger wanted him to jam it again and repeat, but his sudden pain was wicked and sharp and surrendered him to sticking it in his mouth and sucking it away as he turned, sore and ugly, to get ready and go down.

As Natty went to the bathroom, his father's voice, hollowhoarse like a weak jalopy's horn, warned, "Tell them motherfucker friends o' yours, 'A man's gotta rest,' y'hear me!"

Natty sucked teeth derisively and grumbled, "Yeah, Pa. Right!" He slapped a dismissing wave at the closed bedroom door, thinking, What th' fuck're you fussing at? Just's always, talking for wolfing sake. Y'still'll be here resting up all fuckin' day, anyhow.

He turned the frown in his mind to speculating about hot water in the faucet. The cold flow confirmed his expectation: The super was probably drunk again. Natty muttered, "Business as fuckin' usual," spat his disgust into the bathtub, and left without bothering to wash up.

As he rounded the corner he connected on, the first person he saw was Black, the crew's lieutenant. In his robot-motion manner, he was leaning on the light pole, staring past Natty, up the far end of the street. He must have, but gave no sign he had noticed Natty's approach.

Natty greeted him, "What's up, Black?"

As if he had to plan it, Black turned slow and stiff toward him, and stuck his palm out. Natty exchanged a casual touch. Still without a word, Black then resumed his pose, leaning stiff against the light pole as if thawing arthritic joints.

But Natty knew the attitude was only Black's play. When on the street, he moved slowly and didn't talk much. He looked on at everything from behind his wraparound sunshades and dark clothes he wore night and day, keeping his mind behind that mystery fence like the killer monster in some cut-'em-up horror movie. Because on the street, he was the man in charge. But get him on a basketball court, don't think "sneakers" because, that quick, he'd dribble past and lay you up.

Even so, Black's street mean wasn't *just* play. He had become lieutenant after Freddie Dingle, the big-time dealer, had got busted, and Black took the possession rap for him. Being only fifteen at the time, he was in Riker's for only four, five months. While inside, Black never had to give up his sneakers, or his ass, or suck nobody's dick, either. That was because he didn't drop no dime on Dingle, or make no turn for the Man. And Freddie Dingle had weight. Nobody fucked with his business. So that was why Black could be so cool. He had proved. He had people. They had his back.

Natty stood there thinking and looking around for a few minutes. Then he asked Black for his dope: "So wha' y'got?"

With great effort, Black replied, "Quarters."

"Lemme hold a deuce," said Natty.

Black sauntered across the sidewalk, away from the building, and looked up at a second-floor apartment. "Yo, B's," he called up.

Immediately, a girl's head poked out a window, looked attentively at Black, then went back in to return a minute later. A packet fell down. Black picked it up as if it weighed a bus, and handed it to Natty. "Quarters, each twenty jays at a dime, awright?" he drawled.

"Yeah," Natty said, "y'got it." And stashed the dope in his inner clothes. A minute later, he broke out for his safeplace, Pepito's.

Pepito's was a candy store up the block from where they did their main scrambling. A Puerto Rican man they called Señor P. ran it. Natty's crew had an arrangement with Señor P. that he held their daily working stash for them. When they made a sale, they went and got the jays from the candy store. For this, each of them, Black, Swooney, and himself, gave Señor P. a twenty a day. It was a good deal all around since Señor P. was dependable. The few times the bulls busted his store, they never even found an aspirin.

Tall and athletic in dark gray warm-ups, Swooney was already there. As soon as Natty saw him, he went off again. Two schoolgirls from the nearby junior high were at the counter, buying from Señor P. But Natty's rage was a train taking him past his stop; he was helpless within it. Right on throw-down distance from Swooney, he stopped, arms wide and aggressive, and said, "Why th' fuck y'always leaning on m'bell like that? Huh?"

He got everyone's attention, and an excitement from their notice fanned his anger. He felt flushed from the tension that charged the store. He was about ready to do anything at all and release his power when Swooney backed out of his own ready stance and, glancing at Natty warily, walked out of the store.

Natty watched him with no relief. Instead, he felt strained and queer, and that he had gained nothing at all. One of the school-girls tittered, and he was about to go after Swooney when Señor P. got in front of him and began shouting the new excitement away. "Hey! Hey! Take it easy, my friend. Let him off this time. Don' bother no more, *amigo*. Let it go."

He spoke as though he exactly knew Natty could've and would've torn up Swooney's ass. Natty took to the manner and quit as if reluctantly.

Immediately the girls left, he did his business with Señor P. Throughout their little talking, Natty played the mean avenger calmed by Señor P.'s peacemaking. All the time, though, Natty suspected the quick-eyed, smooth-faced old man knew the real deal: He knew who had been saved.

At a spare five feet ten in sneakers, Natty knew he couldn't tangle with Swooney. Although the same age at sixteen, Swooney had cleared six feet and was growing. He was also built solid, like a longtime Cadillac. But still more than all that, Swooney, with his straight A's and handsomeness, was kill-crazy. And this is what Natty feared in truth, because he himself didn't have that in him.

Natty called to mind one late spring night when a gang of them had gone blockbusting over in the Flagg projects. About nine or ten of them went, two carloads, with everyone carrying weight. Redblood George was one of the older guys. He was sort of in charge. Del, Natty's cousin from uptown, went along because Natty asked him. They had come up on some Flagg project guys hanging out near a fireplug, about six of them. The cars had pulled over really slow, one behind the other. Soon as the Flagg project guys noticed the slow-down action, they fig-ured something was wrong. They might've thought it was the

Man, so they tensed up to watch. Then, as the lead car stopped, out of it jumped someone wearing a white ski mask pulled down over his eyes to his nose. And he was covering them with a glinting sawed-off shotgun held braced against his hips.

In his car, next to Natty, someone sighed, "Shiiit . . ." drawling it out long and slow, as now a few other of the guys stepped out of both cars, backing up Ski Mask by pointing their guns at the Flagg project dudes. Natty himself remained in the car loosely pointing his .38 at them. Like everybody else, though, he was really watching Ski Mask. In the half-dark and the excitement, he hadn't yet made out who it was. Then he had heard the crazy sniggering in between Swooney's voice taunting the Flagg project guys: "Sooo . . . who'll start the races? Huh?"

The whole night went quiet then, until Swooney was telling them, ". . . at the count . . . okay? Here we go. One . . . two . . ."

But by then the Flagg project guys were off—gone *WHOOSH!* like a crowd in a Flintstone cartoon. Then, as Swooney counted ". . . three!" he shot a blast behind them. *BOOM!* Natty was certain some of them got pellets in their rearviews. And that was really just funny, for if they hadn't jumped the gun, and had been ten yards closer, someone'd have definitely been blown away.

When the Flagg project guys set off fast away, Natty and some others, just for the waste and noise, shot off a few rounds at them. Then they shot out a few windows and some streetlights before driving away. They were all still charged up, though, so they went to a party and got dusted up some. Except Swooney. He had them first drop him off—shotgun in a sports bag—near his house. It had been close to midnight: "Y'all know my hours," he laughed as he stepped out of the car.

As they drove off, Natty looked back and found Swooney

waving at them. He looked the perfect TV picture of a bright, college-bound kid being dropped off. Then Natty thought of what was in the sports bag, and could only shake his head and grin. Swooney was brave, or crazy, or something. Whatever it was, though, he wasn't all right. And Natty never wanted to suffer from it.

Back out Pepito's, the street was becoming nine o'clock busy. Droves of schoolchildren were coming out the subway shafts and buses on their way to either the junior high or the elementary schools close by. More important to Natty, though, were the many dope fiends standing about in small groups waiting for their methadone-maintenance clinic to open doors. They reminded Natty of hungry vultures in black-and-white westerns, except that in this case, the vultures were the rotten food he and his crew scrambled on.

Swooney was talking to a regular customer—a temporarily outside prison-yard queen, an ugly thing. His hormone treatments had grown him small, sudden bumps of breasts and larger, blotchy lumps on one cheek and his neck. Today, despite the cool, he wore a short coat and a thin, shiny dress over skinny, man-hard knees. And he still managed to bare some of the chemical breasts. He was complaining in a high falsetto backed with heavy hand movement, "Listen, darling, I have to say it. This product ain't quality. I mean, I don't know, but it doesn't do it. I could tell you personally that, like, what I get from those nice fellows across the park is, er, like definitely nearer the mark."

"Well, go across the park," said Swooney.

"Who? Me? Go across the park alone?"

"Y'afraid of rape?" said Swooney.

His sarcastic tone seemed to convince the fiend to stop bullshitting as he slipped into a regular man's voice and asked, "Come on, tell me what ya got, huh?"

They put bodies together and were halfway private, although Natty could see the dopehead palming over money and Swooney checking the bills. Then Swooney said, "Yo! There's only nine here, home!"

The fiend went back female, conducting air with his fingers again. "Y'gotta gimme a break, darling. Y'know I'll take care of that little thing. I mean, it's just a dollar."

Swooney sucked his teeth and started to hand back the cash, just as the fiend added, ". . . I'll bring you by some business with it, later. . . ."

Swooney abruptly put the cash in his pocket. He told the fiend, "Wait here!" and went down the block to Pepito's.

The transvestite leaned against the building, preening debris from his shortcoat. Some schoolchildren passed by. One quick-faced kid commented deliberately loud, "Look at that he-she faggot with a beard and a bustline!"

The fiend cursed, "Fuck all y'all!" and faked a ladylike lunge at them as the group raced off, charged by fear and laughter. Then Swooney was back, warning as he handed over the dope, "I don't see you later with some business, and you get a fuckin' sneaker up your ass, y'hear me?"

The dope in his hand, nothing frightened him; the fiend was walking away shaking his ass like two bricks in a bag and talking feminine again. "You worry too much, darling."

Then he split for his morning methadone looking so weird and funny, Natty couldn't help remarking, "Fucker'd prob'ly *enjoy* that."

Swooney burst out his strange giggle and slapped palms with him. On his part, Natty was even more relieved than the grinning friend now that the unspoken understanding was that their earlier hassle was done with. The least of all was he could now concentrate fully on business.

Once the clinic opened, the fiends came for their dope, and Natty's quarter moved fast. Then, after about half an hour, Swooney handed him a dime bag. "That's all I got left, man. And I've got a ten o'clock class. A seminar thing. Do me a big favor and handle it for me, and hold the bank until later. I'd really appreciate it."

Natty was glad for the chance, and said, "Bet," and Swooney split for school. Watching him go, Natty had an urge to laugh at him. Not because *he* was funny, but because *it* was funny that Swooney did what he did—his very idea, being an ace scholar scrambling part-time. It was like thinking of shitting in heaven: Nobody did.

A little way down the street, Black was also doing his business. Being lieutenant, he could never leave the street while his crew scrambled. He did his own dealing by having one of his girls— Tira Jemson—fetch from Pepito's for him. Tira was one of the several freaks and younger guys who hung around the crew, happy to do whatever for them. Until a few months ago when Black put him down, Natty himself was one. Other than fetching, Tira also kept on the lookout for rollers (in patrol cars), and DTs (in unmarked ones). As a girl, she sometimes stashed weight for the crew (in her drawers or pussy) during emergencies like narco raids and so on. Before Natty was really down, his job was to walk with the music—an expensive stereo boombox with equalizer and double automatic-repeat cassettes, sponsored by Black.

Margo, the dickwit now doing this chore, joined Black and Tira, then motioned Natty to come talk with them. It was to find out what light dope he preferred for their coming lunch break. Black was about sending Tira to connect. Natty gave up ten dollars for some budda.

By one o'clock, lunchtime, Natty had sold all the dope he

held. After putting aside the $10 he did for Swooney, he had $494—$6 short of two quarters' worth, because of some breaks he'd given regulars. He gave the money over to Black, who returned him the $94 as his own. Then, business settled, they went to a Chinese restaurant for some takeout, after which they headed to the park to get high and gamble some.

They met Del and Tomas there playing ball, and got them high on the smoke Tira had brought back. Then someone suggested craps.

After a while of playing, Natty was holding the bank and rolling his point as if Lady Luck was living with him, when a politician-looking man walked into the park leading a group of well-dressed people. A few local senior ladies in heavy coats were sitting around airing their faces watching the world happen. It was these folks the politician approached and, no questions asked, began speechifying.

When Natty paid close attention, he found the man was criticizing the location of the methadone-maintenance clinic: ". . . is a bad policy, from a cruel politics. A cold politics. A politics of selfishness and bigotry. A system in which we are used up, consumed by abuse. A system that's callous, dishonest, and falls short in humane aims. These politicians who allow this dumping of methadone clinics in despairing communities such as this, they are profiteers from narcotics. They are criminal when they convert our already trying communities into magnets for criminal elements. They corrupt our Hope with the trash. They organize the crimes against us. . . ."

His little crowd of followers and the bunched-up ladies agreed, "Yes, yes. It's a shame." The senior ladies, however, since they lived around the area, knew the crew as scramblers, and were sending informed glances from the speaker toward the crew where they grouped near the hoop listening.

The politician continued spouting. After a bit more of it, Tomas raised his voice and suggested, "Maybe someone oughta burn th' motherfucker down. Huh?"

At this, the politician, either from misunderstanding the ladies' glances, or interest in the simple solution, led his well-behaved crowd over to the crew. A couple of the seniors followed.

In his same speechifying volume and tone, he greeted them, "Hullo, young fellows."

Tomas answered for the crew, "Yeah, man. How y'doin'? I think y'got it right."

The politician started right in. "We're with the community task force seeking to close these methadone clinics. We think they represent a corrupting influence on our young people. . . ." He had everyone's attention, and continued by asking, "So, do any of you have views on this important matter?"

Tomas, grinning hugely, repeated, "Yeah, man. I say give th' shit a light."

Del chimed in, "That's right. Them firemen shit around all day planning on their pension. They need some work, man."

Natty added, "That's right. They play Ping-Pong. I seen 'em."

Now, everyone in the crew, even Black, seemed ready to bullshit with the guy a little bit. But then a serious-looking man behind the politician asked, "What do *you* fellows do?"—And, glancing at his watch—"Shouldn't you all be in school?"

It was Tomas as spokesman again: "You blind, mi' man? Can't you be seeing it? Look, I am in school, and this is break time. Uh-huh, I'm studying to be a warmonger in big government."

At which Natty offered, "And I'm going to be a nuclear physicist, so I could nuke up the whole fuckin' world, especially the politicians."

The uneasy expressions on the faces of the main speaker and his proper little crowd settled into determined let's-get-outa-here looks, and they began to leave.

Meanwhile, Del had thought up his ambition, and now shouted it after their receding backs: "I'm goin' to be an explorer so I could search out you suckers' bank accounts."

By now the crew was laughing outright. Tomas had changed his mind and was screaming that he now intended to be a "task-force asshole" designer, as the man and crowd got into their cars and escaped. Even the senior ladies were laughing.

Then Black, becoming serious again, suggested it was time to get back to business. Natty didn't mind at all; it'd been a fun lunch, and had left his pocket winning.

It was about eight o'clock, and the whole crew was out there: There was Black, Swooney, Natty, Del, Tomas, Tira, Margo-with-the-music, Margo's sister Dee, and Fat Noleen. Business was sporadic at that time of evening, and Black, Swooney, and Natty were standing apart talking, while the others attended to the entertainment, and the occasional junkie copping.

Between his scrambling and gambling, Natty had cleared about seven hundred dollars, his own money. Swooney, too, was flush, and Black had just proposed they go see the latest horror movie downtown. He would take Tira so he'd have some pussy afterward. Dee, the younger sister, liked Swooney, so he was fixed up. Natty, however, with neither Black's cool command nor Swooney's good looks, had no one. So Swooney was on his case, teasing Natty to take Fat Noleen. "You'd definitely get some pussy, once you find it between them monster legs she got."

Trying to laugh it off, Natty replied, "Man, I don't fuck with frogs."

At this point, Margo-with-the-music joined them. She was high, and Tomas was boldly fondling her breasts and ass as if he were searching for cancer lumps. She was acting uninterested, as if she were one. Lowering the volume, she explained that she wanted to leave the music. She had something to do, she told Black. Tomas grinned and elaborated: "She's got a nut to crack."

Immediately, Swooney upsed with, "Let Natty hold the box. He don't've nothing else to hold."

Sensing the point, Tomas suggested, "Why don't he go'n fuck Fat Noleen? Del swears she sucks bone like a vacuum-cleaner snake."

He and Swooney began laughing and slapping palms. Natty, seeing it getting out of hand, began blustering, "All right, all right. Stop fucking with me. Okay?"

Between howls, Swooney said, "But who . . . ? Who's fucking with you? . . . Nobody's fucking with you . . . not even the frogs."

Everyone was dying with laughter.

A rage beginning, Natty shouted, "All right, Swooney. Y'd better stop right now, okay? Before I really fuck your shit up."

He was so hard and serious that suddenly, as if a tape had ended, all the laughter ceased.

Swooney's voice came softly and too friendly for its quiet. "How're you going to fuck my shit up, Natty-Nat?"

Still angry and vengeful, Natty challenged him, "How about if your fuckin' old people find out you're just a fuckin' dope dealer, huh?"

As if he'd just said the Secret of Life and Death, Natty felt everyone staring at him; even stoned-eye Margo-with-the-music was blinking for a better view.

Swooney, muttering "Shit-faced motherfucker . . ." through his grin, moved fast, his fist poised to throw down before Natty could react. But Black had flashed in between them and shielded him, saying slowly as ever, "Y'can't do that, Swooney." And Swooney stopped, as he had to. If not, he'd have been punching Black.

He tried getting around Black. But shaking his head no, Black shifted to deny him.

"Get out m'face, Black," Swooney warned him, "I ain't bull-shitting."

Black didn't budge. "Y'can't do that," he repeated. "All week you been fucking with mi' man. And you won't be hitting no-body while I'm around."

Swooney let out his crazy giggle then. He asked, "So that's how it's gonna be, huh?"

Firm as a sentencing judge, Black answered, "That's how it's *gotta* be!"

Throughout all this fast action, Natty was more confused than anything else. Although he felt safe, as if surrounded by a solid wall just about his height wearing black clothes, he knew he was also looking wimpish and protected from Swooney; and now the commotion had attracted the rest of the crew and brought Dee running excitedly to Swooney's side, grabbing him and pulling him away possessively, as if he were the last man on earth. Tomas and Margo joined her and dragged him away. Then, after advising Natty to go home and cool out, Black and Tira went off, leaving his cousin Del and Fat Noleen to console with Natty.

Uncomfortable with them and still slightly confused about what had happened, Natty started away alone. But they hurried to catch up and walk with him. Del asked, "So what's goin' down, Coz?"

Before Natty could respond, Fat Noleen asked, "Why y'want to be fighting that crazy fool for?" Then, with heavy distaste, added, "Y'know how he wantsa be trying to bully over every-body?"

Her point of view, with the sympathy in her voice, was just what Natty needed. He didn't feel so much in the coward's shadow of Black's big wall anymore. He answered them both with a determination he was uncertain of, "Well, I ain't taking no more shit from him."

They all stopped, and both of them looked at him. He shook his head decidedly at them. "I just ain't. That's all. See y'all tomorrow."

Then he went home.

Next morning Natty was dozing on his sofa bed, vaguely expectant in his half-sleep, when he rose up abruptly as he remembered the hassle with Swooney and realized that his bell wouldn't be ringing. Before his relief could settle down, he became anxious about how Swooney would react to their beef. He speculated on this as he prepared to leave and finally decided to carry along his .38 to work today. He took it from its house spot, and stuck it next to his skin in his pants' waist. The moment before leaving the apartment, he thought of talking to his father about it. But earlier on, he had heard a double set of snores through the bedroom door. So there was a woman in there. She would be a stranger, and this was a family matter.

Over at the spot, Black told him Swooney wasn't down with them anymore. Natty asked, "Who told you?"

Black looked at him: Blank.

Natty asked, "Dee?"

Black looked at him: Maybe.

Natty asked, "Y'hear anything 'bout what he goin' do?"

Black shook his head: No.

Natty nodded as if he agreed. He said, "You worried?"

Black looked at him blankly. Then he changed his mind and said, "Look, man. Swooney ain't stupid. This is Dingle's business, 'n' he don't fuck around. Swooney's hip."

Natty nodded as if he agreed with every word. "Yeah," he said. "Yeah."

Black said, "Maybe y'should double up for a few days, huh? Them early dope fiends should be going wild over in his spot. If y'want to handle them."

Natty felt the weight of the .38 in his waist, and his resolve not to take any shit, and he felt serious. He said, "Yeah, give it up. I can handle it." He collected the dope and headed for Pepito's.

Señor P. had heard about the trouble and had advice for Natty: "Hey, my friend. You must try to fix this thing up. What you say? Huh? You such nice fellas. Why spoil it with the fighting and trouble? You have a good li'l business. No? Don't foul your nest, *amigo*. Huh?"

Natty never looked at him or answered. Back to the counter, he kept his eyes on the door as Señor P. spoke to the back of his ear. He wondered why the old man was so concerned. Maybe it was his twenty every evening. Maybe Swooney had asked him to quiet and cool down the trouble. Think of the Devil. Señor P. was just saying his name: ". . . that Swooney fella. Now he's not really a bad fella. Maybe a little, you know how they say, *loco*, maybe. But he's mostly mischief. That's all. He's a good *amigo*. You must try with him."

A group of schoolchildren trooped in for their junk, interrupting Señor P. Natty saw it as a good chance to break out. But just in case the busy Señor P. was playing the Kissinger, he said, "Hey, I don't want no hassles either, *señor*. But y'know how it is. Right?"

Then he went to work.

A Viet-vet junkie was giving him a hard time about some dope bought earlier in the week. "Yo, listen up. Yo, listen here. The shit ain't shit. This is the worst dope I've ever, ever gotten next to. It ain't worth shit. And the bags're too small anyhow. It's a fuckin' rip-off, man."

Natty was hardly listening to him. He said, "Don't know about it, man. Can't help you."

The junkie went on, ". . . an' how th'fuck y'all c'n call this shit 'Devil high.' Devil shit, I say. An' what th' fuck you motherfuckers cutting the shit with, huh? Last bag put a hurting on me. Cramps and shit and everything. Man, I was sick as a motherfucker. . . ."

Natty knew the junkie as Onezy. He had lost his right arm at the elbow in the Nam, and was a dependable booster. He worked the nicer Fifth Avenue stores, and usually paid for his dope with fine clothes, or shoes. But he was a complainer— always dissatisfied, always grumbling, always threatening. Natty was trying, but he had things on his mind this morning, and no patience for the fiend's usual bullshit. He cut him short, "Look here, Onezy. I never sold you nothing, okay? I don't know nothing about your gripe, okay? So quit yer fuckin' crying in my face, okay?"

The junkie walked about fifteen feet away, and from that range proceeded with his whining attack. It being near nine o'clock, the street was busy with schoolchildren, folks going to work, to the Laundromat, fiends, regular people, and so on. Thus, Onezy's loud complaining was drawing attention. Two fiends made purchases from Natty, then, as they went away, paused to listen better to Onezy. After a bit, one returned to Natty. He didn't want the dope because he felt it might be bad. Onezy just told him it was cut with something dangerous.

At that, Natty went off.

He took the pistol from his waist and, holding it concealed in his pocket, rushed up to Onezy, and had collared him and shoved him against the wall before even thinking if he should. "What're you doing, sucker?" he bawled into Onezy's face. "What th' fuck y're trying to do, huh?"

From in his pocket he rammed the pistol's barrel hard into

Onezy's stomach, and felt as the fiend's thinness surrendered away from the jab. Immediately, Onezy's whine changed into a frightened pleading. "I ain't serious, man. I'm cool, baby. I'll go, I'll go. Please."

Something offensive about the junkie's smell, and his attitude, and his flinching frailness combined to disgust Natty. He wished to rid himself of the nasty pest. In his pocket, he squeezed the trigger hard, then deliberately again in surprise at the mere muffled clicks he heard instead of the blasts of gunfire.

But Onezy, too, must've felt or heard the misfire. He suddenly began screaming, "Don't shoot me, man. Don't kill me!"

And the curious who had so quickly gathered began scattering every which way like roaches busted by sudden light.

Next thing Natty knew was Black dragging him off the junkie and stumbling him away, asking him angrily, "What th' fuck is wrong with you, man? We can't have no trouble here. You know that!"

Natty still wanted to get off, but was a bit bewildered also. In a rush, he began explaining, "You wasn't here to see. But I was right. Onezy was right there in fronta me, bad-mouthing the product to th' other fiends, making them return it. I couldn't deal with that no more. And then the fuckin' gun won't fire. Y'know what I mean, and fuckin' Onezy there fuckin' around. That's too much shit. And I ain't taking shit no more. . . ."

Black said, "Okay, man, okay. But y'got to cool out. Cool out. It's all right. He ain't nothing but 'n angel-dust hero. You can't get fucked-up over him."

How Black spoke suggested a special looking-out between the two of them. Natty was willing, wanted to be contrite and pacified. He listened to his main man's advice, and took a walk while Black took care of Onezy.

He had just rounded the corner away from the fracas when he met Fat Noleen coming his way. She blocked his way and asked,

"What's on, Natty?" Then, looking at him more closely, held his coat's sleeve and asked excitedly, "Something's going down 'round the block? . . ."

Still stimulated by the hassle with Onezy, Natty fattened his answer: ". . . nearly popped a fuckin' dopehead. He was fuckin' with me. . . ."

Her eyes widened with thrills and fright. She held on to his other arm and cried, "Natty. How y'always gettin' in trouble, huh?" but crooning as if she were applauding a bad baby. Then she said more specially, more closely, "Where're you goin' now?"

"Just cooling down . . ." he said.

"Why y'don't come up to my house, huh? Y'know you should get off the street."

Natty hesitated. He took a sly glance around. As he met her eyes, she turned away slightly and said, "Nobody's home . . . and no one'll be seeing you."

Seeing by that, that she'd understood, he said, "Bet," and went up to her house.

She had her own bedroom. The main thing in it, bigger than even her dresser, was a wall unit of three shelves with many large fishbowls set along them. The fish in the bowls were tiny things with oversized fantails of blues, and greens, with spots of silver, or black, and any color at all. So impressed was he, Natty instantly forgot his uneasiness about being seen. He realized she'd arranged the bowls in rainbow order of fantail colors: the whatever variety of reds, then oranges, then yellows, and so on. The fish were totally happy and spry, darting in between water plants, parading their pretty spots, or rays, or stripes of color on their outrageous tails. Natty sneaked a glance at Fat Noleen as he checked them out. He found it hard to fit the two sights in the same room: lumbering Fat Noleen and these skimpy flashes of color. She caught him looking at her. He said, "Hey, this is really the joint, Noleen. These shits're stupid pretty."

Her eyes popped as she flushed. "Lemme get a jay," she said, and went to a cupboard.

Natty could see the big blush forming all over the soft brown skin of her fat neck and shoulders, giving it a raw look. He grinned to himself and asked the bulging sacks of her backside, "So what kinda fish is they?"

"Guppies," she answered. "That's what they call them in some books. But their real name is millionfish . . . they's from the Caribbean, Trinidad, I think."

Natty, half listening, studied her sitting at the table cleaning the chiba, talking fancy fish. It was the first time he'd heard her even talk that long in one burst. Suddenly, he felt compelled to show that he also knew something about fish. He couldn't think of anything but began talking anyhow. "Tropical fish is something else. . . ."

But she had continued, ". . . a pastor, an Island guy named Guppy, he saw them as a special type, and sent them to England to find out, and the white people in England named the fish guppies. But he had called them millionfish because was so much a' them. 'S what the local people used to call them, anyhow."

She stopped and concentrated on lighting the joint. She dragged deeply and passed it over. "They look real pretty," Natty said before he pulled on the sweet-smelling budda jay. He held it in long and sighed it out slowly. He passed the joint and said, "Different kinds in each bowl, huh?"

"Only the males pretty," she explained. "All the fancy-tailed ones're male. The females're plain. I only put them together to breed."

The budda had given him an enormous rush of clearheaded

cool. He became precisely aware of everything about him: the spot of bright sunshine on the crystal fishbowl; the soot-soft lines of the different levels of water in each bowl; the flicking darts and frilling pauses of the male millionfish; and Fat Noleen's smooth voice, deep and charged like the rich flush that had recolored her. He had to laugh. "Yow, Noleen," he said, "y'got some good shit here."

Natty had the joint again; he toked and passed it back. She hadn't answered, but just sat looking fat and soft at him. He figured that the chiba must be getting to her and recalled what Tomas'd said about Del's comment about her vacuum-cleaner snake head. Abruptly turned on, he became interested in finding out.

Noleen began talking fish again. "The females make babies every month. Makes it easy to experiment with them, if y'feel like it."

"So they's easy to breed, huh?" Natty followed up, trying to get her attention. Her eyes only fluttered at him and fled back to the fishbowls, and Natty realized she was shy about looking at him in the way that said he could have her.

She replied, "Uh-huh, and bold, too. Y'see how they always come up to the bowl face begging. And they'd eat anything . . . even their own babies. The store guy sez that in Trinidad, in the countryside, they eat wigglers and keep the mosquitoes under control. . . ."

Her voice got softer and softer as she talked away. Natty kept his eyes hard on her face, but she wouldn't look at him. Just sat there soft and flush and fat, as if he could piss on her and she wouldn't move, staring at the gulping fish as if they were sending code signals to her. He went up to her smooth, fat face and pulled out his dick. He shook and rubbed it about on her soft cheeks. Then he held her head steady and shoved it at her mouth. Her take-me lips were still shaping on how "guppies can live with little oxygen," when his dick slid in and she was forced to turn to slippery sucking.

It was a morning about two weeks after that when Natty's bell rang sudden again. When he answered it, however, no one was there. He figured someone had made a mistake downstairs. About an hour later, sevenish, he rounded the corner to Black's block and saw a small crowd milling, mostly junkies and younger street people. They were gathered around someone laid out on the street. As Natty got closer, someone at the crowd's edge recognized him, and shouted, "Natty! Natty! They jus' done fucked up y' man!"

And hearing that, Natty broke to the middle.

Black was lying on his back with his face twisted oneside and spit drooling from his mouth, past his ear and into his naps. From that side of his face, other than the spit, he could've been sleeping. But as Natty stepped around and peered closely around the ear resting on the street, he could see the sunk-in part where Black's head had been crushed, and the blood was leaking out slowly onto the asphalt. From that view, Black looked dead.

A fiend had seen it all. Nothing to say to the police, but he had seen this guy creep out from the corner of the building where he'd been hiding. He had ambushed Black with a baseball bat when Black came out to lean on his lamp pole. When they asked him who the guy was, the junkie said he didn't recognize him. But from how he said "recognize," Natty knew he could easily clear up the fiend's mind with a jaybag.

It took two bags, and as he had expected, it was Swooney. He had worn the same white ski mask, and had giggled while he batted Black a second and a third time, after he fell. That's mainly why the junkie spoke up at all—". . . th' mutha didn' 'aveta be so dog-mean on mih man, see?" he said. " 'E'd crunched 'im firs' strike. Ah 'erd it clear crost th' fuckin' street. Y'un'rstan'?"

When he got this news, Natty didn't fuck around. He knew exactly what he had to do. He hailed a gypsy to Freddie Dingle's place. All the ride he thanked his luck that he had such a rich chance to see the Man himself; depending on how he showed right now, he might get a big play.

Natty left Freddie Dingle's place feeling very good about himself. One of Dingle's crew had called the news to Freddie. Then the guy had called Natty to the phone. He said into it, "Hullo . . ."

"Lemme hear it."

"Is about Black, Mr. Dingle. A guy, usta be with th' crew, Swooney his name. Well, he batted Black this morning. Black looks real bad. . . ."

"Swooney?"

"Yessir, Swooney. A fiend seen it all, an' he tol' me."

"Hmmn."

"He had a beef wif Black, sir, and me, too."

"I know . . . you did good coming right away, Natty. We'll take care of it. You did good."

"Thanks, sir."

"I'll be in touch, but you should get off the street now, Natty."

Natty hung up in a triumphant daze. He'd hit a final-second three-point-play winner: Freddie Dingle said he'd done good; Freddie Dingle knew him by name, had said it twice; and Freddie Dingle'd be keeping in touch! As he left the lounge, Freddie's man handed him a bill. Natty blinked at two zeros, heard the man say, "Go to the movies, champ." He stepped out the door into bright sunshine. A service car was waiting, engine running, at the curb. The driver stepped out and asked, "You Natty?" in a way that said his ride wherever was compliments of Freddie Dingle.

It nearing eleven, Natty eased into Fat Noleen's building and rang her apartment's bell. As usual, it was no problem. She buzzed him in. They had worked out this rendezvous since the millionfish day. Now he had her every day around lunchtime. On the street, they acted distant as usual.

When he was inside and they had talked about the millionfish and that he was cooling out for the day, he asked her for a joint.

She said, "Maybe y'shouldn't be smokin', Natty. Can't do nothing today, y'know."

Natty didn't get her meaning. He looked at her.

"Friend's here," she said. She was apologizing.

He didn't let on his relief. She being so big around and heavy, fucking her was clumsy and awkward. He much preferred her to just suck him off. That he couldn't complain about.

She was standing near the cupboard with the chiba when there was the sound of heavy boots landing on the floor somewhere else in the apartment. Noleen said, "Ma's bedroom . . ." and Natty knew instantly what had happened. Someone had entered the house through the fire-escape ladder. Then, before he could even get up off her bed, Swooney and two other guys had filled up Noleen's bedroom.

Natty didn't know the two guys. The shorter, dark-skinned one looked older—maybe twenty. The other was skinny, kid-faced. All three of them looked blank-happy dusted. Swooney was giggling and talking crazy-friendly: "My man, Natty-Nat. My main man! Now my man's getting the pussy big time. Fattyfroggy Noleen piggy-pussy. An' it all belongs to Natty-Nat. My main man . . ."

The long, light-skinned one interrupted, "Come on, Swooney. We goin' to fuck 'im up, or what?"

Natty measured the skinny shit and decided to try to kick his balls in. Then he noticed the stocky guy and Noleen staring dead at each other; she with her mouth trembling open and closed like one of her silly fish in the bowls. The stocky guy said abruptly, "Let's fuck her!"

Right away the skinny dusthead said, "Bet!"

Then Swooney agreed, "Yeah, let's run a train up the fat cunt."

A rush of closeness from being with her reminded Natty of how Noleen had just been embarrassed about her period. Feeling protective, he put it to Swooney, "Hey, man, she's bleeding."

The stocky guy cut over him, "Shit, I don't care."

Natty caught her eye. He shrugged. He had tried. Noleen just stood there springing tears from her big, soft, empty face as they went at her.

They made Natty sit in a chair while each rode her three, four times until they got fed up. Then they shoved makeup bottles and other stuff up her. The room became stinky with a stale, rotten smell from her blood. Once, when Natty tried to sneak away, they pushed him to the floor, and wiped her dirty pad all over his arms and clothes. Swooney and the stocky guy punched him around some, while the skinny one pissed in some of the fishbowls, and hawked and spat in the rest. Then he joined in and tried to kick the shit out of Natty while Natty rolled himself in a ball, minding to protect his nuts. They didn't seem at all tired out from their raping, and only stopped when Noleen began screaming and swearing that her moms was due back any moment. Then Swooney and his boys called it, and left through Fat Noleen's front door.

After they'd gone, Natty was so hurting he just lay down on the bed while Noleen, crying and sniffling, did all the cleaning up, even of his own body and clothes. Every time she found a new daub of blood on the floor or the wall, she started sobbing anew. "Oh God, if Ma sees this mess, I'm dead, she'd be crazy mad," she'd bawl.

Partly to distract her, Natty said, "Them fish're fucked up, girl. Look, them at the top. Like they're gasping."

"I don't care, Natty. I can breed guppies," she almost screamed at him. Then it was back to her clean-up moaning, "Ma sees this shit 'n' I'm dead. . . ."

It was a month before the doctors were allowing anyone but family to visit Black. As soon as Natty heard this, he went to the hospital; wanting to avoid the rest of the crew, he went morning hours. Black was in a private room decorated prettily in blue. But he himself looked fucked up among all the flowers and nice sheets, and so on. His whole head was like a cloth egg with bandages. His eyes were swollen tight-lidded, and running pus. In a hoarse grandfather whisper, he said, "Yow . . . Natty."

The sight of him brought back afresh to Natty that Swooney had done this, and that Black had got into it protecting him. It made him feel so bad, the tears were burning up his eyes. He abruptly stepped up to the head of the bed where the bottles and tubes hung, and where Black couldn't turn his crippled head to see. There, he quickly dried himself. To cover the time, he asked, "So how y'feeling, man? When y'comin' out?"

"When I could move . . . mi' hands again." Black forced the words one at a time, more paralyzed than in his slow, slow way; with his two-toned whispers, only sounding sadder longer.

They talked around, Natty bringing him up-to-date about this and that: Swooney being nowhere to be seen; Señor P. sending flowers; Tira bugging out because Black was hurt; how he, Natty, was carrying his careful .38 ever since; that the dope fiends were going off all day by the clinic, now that they didn't have dope; in response, DTs were covering their former scrambling corner and standing out like pork in a drugstore.

The cop story made Black laugh, but it hurt him somewhere to tears. After the pain passed, he went tired and motioned Natty nearer to croak a number into his ear. "Freddie Dingle sez y'should call him," Black whispered. "They found Swooney."

At about eight o'clock, the intercom sounded three short blasts. Natty, already dressed, was up and off his sofa bed by the time the third blast had ended. He went in the kitchen and reached in the oven to take out a .38 Special. He'd got it yesterday from Freddie Dingle as the job was lined out. Now Natty was careful to remember, and loaded the gun with the special bullets Freddie Dingle'd given him. That done, he shoved in the safety and stuck the gun deep in his waist. Then he went downstairs.

As planned, the car waited a little up the block with the engine running. Natty went to it and got in the backseat. The driver didn't look around, only raised the music loud and bassy as soon as Natty slammed the door. The driver wore extra-big warm-ups with the hood pulled low over his forehead. All Natty could see of his face was a side of jaw. Driver tossed a parcel over to the backseat. "Put it on, man," he said, "just like mine."

It was another warm-ups top, monster-sized, with a hood. Natty put it on just like Driver, with the hood pulled low down. Then Driver rolled the tinted windows completely up, and they sped away.

It was a high school in a nice area, in another borough. With the engine running, they waited near twenty minutes before they finally saw Swooney walking across the playground. Immediately, Driver geared up and cruised slowly toward the blind corner. Natty shifted nearer to his door, took the .38 out of his clothes, and put it on the seat next to him. Driver spoke in a calm, reminding voice: "Wait till he's alongside the fence so's he can't run in nowhere. Move in quiet, he might be carryin'."

Natty sensed Driver checking him out through the rearview mirror. So he didn't swallow the spit leaking into his mouth. He said, "I got it, man. I'm awright."

For that's how he felt in truth. The action coming down was set in his mind like a learned play, simple as a pick-and-roll, easy. Driver stopped the purring car a fifteen-foot jump shot blindside from where Swooney would come out of the playground. Then he switched off the engine, and the jamming music went silent. And the play was set, waiting for Natty to make his move.

Swooney walked onto the sidewalk and seemed to look directly at the silent, tinted-glass car. Then he continued up the street carrying some school books in one hand and a small shopping bag in the other. Natty, right hand on the gun in his pocket, opened the car door without a sound. He was quickly out of the car and alongside the school building's wall. Then he sneakered up to Swooney at a fast walk. As Dingle'd made him practice over and over, in his pocket he gently released the safety. When he was close enough, he took the gun out of his pocket, and putting it near behind Swooney's head, he called softly, "No school today . . ." And as Swooney turned around, Natty blew his face away.

The kick from the gun jerked back his hand, hurting his wrist sharply. But Natty sucked in the pain, followed Swooney's flailing body down and, hand-to-wrist police style, put another jolting shot into the head.

The car horn blasted close beside him. Driver was shouting, "Homey. Call it, now! We outa here!"

Natty ran back and was swift in through his still-opened door. Before he could shut it, they were revving up the street, tires screeching, powerful, and around the corner flying, just as Natty felt as he met Driver's eyes in the mirror. Driver's shifted away as he said, "Y'fucked 'im *up*."

"Said I would," said Natty.

Two weeks later, up at his place, Freddie put Natty down with his main crew. He handed Natty a handful of fifties and some quarters of dope, and told him the setup. Bottom line was, Black might never make it back, so Natty was now lieutenant. He'd get so much dope and had to bring back so much basic bank. He mustn't mess with the supply: What he got, he sold. Prices on his block was whatever his business could make it. He made seven and a half a day, plus whatever. Natty thanked Mr. Dingle and assured that he wouldn't disappoint.

Afterward, sitting in his cab home, he thought of Del, Tomas, Margo-with-the-music, and the others, and tried to select his crew. When he came to considering Fat Noleen, what he remembered was the train Swooney had organized on her. It made him feel soft for her, and he decided the one thing he'd do for certain. Tomorrow he'd give her some money to get a brand-new crop of guppies.

ONE NEVER KNOWS

It had been one of those intoxicating days Winter grudgingly offers as reprieve after six grim weeks of blizzards, frost, and unrelenting cold. The sun had come out into pure blue skies and crystal-clear air. Now late afternoon, it still shone spiritedly through branches laden with last night's snowstorm. Nearer the earth, brilliant rays and shifting beams reflected from the snow-drifts, sparkling winks seducing me along the path.

Off and on, I passed other sunshine worshipers, strolling, playing, animating Christmas-card scenes. Shame all of it'd be too soon a memory: the gloam of evening close, the passing moments' pleasant reminder how Winter begrudges but so much.

Up a slight but continuous incline led me to the knoll near the center of the park, and I was decidedly huffing it by the time I had trudged there. I should go on more, the heart needing just such deliberate stress to grow strong again. But doctor's orders or no, my bellows apparatus needed pause. So, the first bench at hand, I sat and gave my sturdy cane a rest, while I puffed my hip-hopping heart back to a fox-trot beat.

It was a tranquil spot presenting a pleasant panorama of the park. The gaze could linger on the blank flower plots near the front gates, on my exercise incline with its snow-blanketed pathways winding up through heavy-branched firs and pines. The far end of the view found a thick, continuous green of well-forested hills, any of which'd be fine vantage to watch the moon rise, or the city's evening light up: a best window for any sort of busybody.

Nearer by, the parka-clad folks frolicking in the snowy flats were colorful teddy bears to me without my glasses. With puffs of breath, they semaphored fun to each other; word-clouds of closeness that remained afloat in their departed space.

All about, the air was alive with children—their keening screams, their snowballs, the delight of their laughter. They were romping and tumbling and frisking and falling in a manner that assured they'd all sleep well tonight.

Penetrating my musings, it slowly occurred to me that there was something odd about the person standing under a young fir some fifty feet away, at about three o'clock in my view. A family on their way out passed near him, and their little girl had to be called back from wandering over to interact with the stranger. But it was a casual recall by the parents. No tension at all. Still, my suspicious subconscious maintained scrutiny.

Abruptly, he sauntered on, and I recognized what was peculiar. He was a small man but didn't carry himself so. In fact, his stroll was more like a strut, albeit slope-shouldered and loping, which, with long hands thrust deep into his pockets, made him seem to be bouncing along with a presumptuous jauntiness.

I suddenly realized he had left the beaten snow of the pathways, and was plowing through the two-foot-deep lawns, heading directly toward me. Anxious that he had felt need to respond to my scrutiny and dreading a confrontation, I stared down at my feet in dismay.

When the effort of his excursion sounded near enough, I stole a glance up. My peek was immediately overcome by the eyes in his face: right on me, bright, alert, intensely examining. Still, my brief look could not miss the challenging gleams of intelligence crowning the vaguely triangular face. But by then he was quite close, so I retreated to lowered eyes once more, and reached into my pocket for the peanuts I had purchased on the way here.

Then, to my utter chagrin, the fellow took a seat at the other end of my bench.

Steadfastly, I gazed for lonely freedom through the broad window of my view as if his presence were a wall that separated our spaces. Although, of course, nothing he did escaped my wary side-minding of him. And, gradually, my puzzled observation became certain that his eyes and interest were only for the bag of peanuts I held.

For further evidence, I switched the bag to my right hand, away from his side. As if his stare were magnetized to it by a powerful beam, the fellow followed forward like a leaning pole to keep the bag in view. At that, I felt a melting within, and a trickle of guilt seeped out. For I had been biased to the face of strangeness. And even now, I was being selfish to the mouth of hunger. I couldn't have felt more ashamed. And, without daring to look his way, I offered the bag over.

He wasn't coy. There was no wait. The bag was swiftly from my hand. I heard the uncrimping as its wrapper yielded, the rattling of the roasted unshelled peanuts as they were scooped out. Then the bag was placed on the bench, and the evening was serene but for the urgent crackle of shells, and the rapid mouth-muffled crunch of peanuts.

From behind a pretended yawn, I sidled a glance down the bench and confirmed that the fellow had indeed placed the bag right next to his own leg, fully an arm's length away from me.

Now that I didn't like! Be he hungry or not, such was improper response to my generosity. My sympathy quickly diffused, unmasking the rudeness of his intrusion. Still, I was civilized; I did not snatch. Instead, eyes only on the bag, I leaned over, took it up, and scooped out two or three peanuts. Then I deliberately replaced the bag on the seat, halfway between us.

Didn't have to look to know he had followed my every move. His attention was a fixed stare I could feel, leaving me warm with embarrassment at my unsubtle parry. But I couldn't have allowed my good manners to be bullied by him. So, defiantly, I cracked a shell, popped a kernel in, and chewed the time I awaited his response.

All he did was stare at me. I felt the look searching my profile all through my cracking, shelling, and chewing three peanuts. I felt it score into my skin, seeking, assessing, deciding on my intent. I felt it make incorrect judgments about me, and find me close and stingy.

Recalling his fine, intelligent eyes, I pictured them now glazed with hurt and disappointment. I could almost feel his misery at my siege of the bag. So. What else to do? Again eye to bag, I took it up, removed a couple, and replaced it—that is, leaned over and pointedly spotted it quite near his leg. After all, I couldn't let the poor guy grovel.

The lightening-up of mood was marked. Tension whisked away. Graciousness mellowed the ambience as he accepted the hint and promptly lessened the bag once again, replacing it within his comfortable reach, and not too far out of mine. Then he relaxed completely into peanut consumption. By now though, distracted with curiosity, I just had to pass eyes over him.

First, it was his hands. So narrow and nimble, and swift at shelling and peeling, then flicking the peanuts into his mouth, so casual, so competent. Then it was his posture: relaxed to the point of a slouch; uncomposed, yet somehow natural and comfortable. Maybe it was the gray indistinctness of the evening that made his clothes seem ramshackle and too voluminous, shrinking him, and peculiarly explaining the boniness of those fine hands. But then I came to his face.

The sun had set off-shoulder behind him, leaving spot-bright that part of the early darkness, so some of his face remained mysterious in silhouette. Yet within that dimness were enough indications of my companion's features. A small, bearded, pointed face. Low brow. The striking eyes. The busily munching jaws. Instantly, though bewildering and ridiculous, an overall impression formed: The little guy did look uncannily like a larger monkey.

Once again my consternation sought refuge in the uniform grayness of the evening in front of me. Thinking through the blinking in my mind, I searched the darkness to see if I was being the victim of a practical joke. But the dusk remained sedately innocent. Which braved me to attempt a serious ascertaining look at my companion. For the monkey notion had left its doubtful lurk; it was poised to seize conviction as I breathed deeply and turned to find him just hopped off my bench and loping down the path.

I caught his single brief glance back, and was stunned by a queer thrill. For nothing more than smug was his look, and nothing less than amused. Those sharp monkey's eyes might've even been laughing at me. One certainly had winked.

IT'S ALL RIGHT

Davey was close to giving up for a try at some other place. That young kid was tending store this morning, and it was a lost cause to approach him. The fool would definitely go righteous on him, and Davey couldn't take on that kind of stuff at this time of morning. A rising anxiety mingled with his irritation, since this was normally the easiest place to cop. Battling frustration, he wished the young kid would go somewheres away and leave him alone.

He leaned back on the wall just outside the door, fidgeting his eyes at the street. Then, abruptly, he decided to split. As he straightened up, though, he prayed one last hopeful peek around the open door. And everything was all right. Mr. Abbot had come in.

Davey suppressed the smile that wanted to relieve his face. For Mr. Abbot was all right; he'd sell to anyone. All money was green to him.

Davey entered the store and went directly to where Mr. Abbot stood. He stepped up on a wine crate near the counter and took a deep breath, readying to run his story. But before he could speak, Mr. Abbot demanded, "What d'ya want?"

Thrown off balance, Davey paused. Then, by an impulse of truth, he took a chance. "A pint of gin," he said, rather than the wine he had intended. And it worked. Mr. Abbot turned to the shelf to get the liquor. But then the righteous punk stuck his mouth in. "Gin!" he shouted, like a cop busting a joint.

Mr. Abbot hesitated. He turned back to Davey, an accusing question sharp on his face.

Davey answered quickly before he spoke it. Pointing out the door to an older man standing near a lamppost, he said, "It's for that alky over there." Then, putting derision in his voice, he asked the kid, "You thought it was for *me*?"

The young man muttered something fresh under his breath and moved away, shaking his head. But Mr. Abbot was satisfied. He took the liquor down and presented it for Davey's examination like it was part of a magic trick. "Let's see the money!" Mr. Abbot demanded. Davey read the price tag on the bottle: $7.25. He pulled his crumpled ten-dollar bill from a coat pocket and handed it over. Then he put his face bland and waited for change. Mr. Abbot returned from the cash register and put on the counter five quarters, three pennies, and a dime, then pushed across the bagged bottle.

Davey checked the change before him, concentrating, looking nowhere else. He studied the coins slowly, as though he could count them, his whole being alert for some hint of deception from the watching Mr. Abbot. But he could sense nothing incorrect. So, surrounding himself with uneasy dignity, he pocketed the coins and walked out of the store.

As soon as he cleared the door, he slid the flat bottle inside his shirt, sticking it in his belt next to his skin. Its cool reality there suddenly evoked an urge for action. He dodged a honking car as he ran into the street and stood ready in the middle, awaiting a break in the passing traffic. At first chance, he scampered between two vehicles and gained the other side, then ran into the park. He stopped beside a bench just within the wall, and pulled out the bottle.

He had to use all his effort to break the cap's seal, but tapped strength from his great excitement now that he held accomplishment in hand. With the yielding of the cap, an acute craving forced him to swallow dryly. And, stooping low beside the park bench, he gulped down a long, gurgling drink. His eyes smarted from the searing in his throat as he recapped the bottle and deep-breathed, waiting for the more pleasant warmth to fill his belly. To help it along, he uncapped and took another small one.

As the satisfying warmth slowly bloomed in his gut, he squatted down in the nook between the bench and the wall. Only the rough dirt beneath his backside made his seat uncomfortable. Remembering, he reached farther under the bench and pulled out his schoolbag. From it he took out the fattest book and opened it at the middle. And placing it just so on his sitting spot, he reseated himself. It was much better.

He felt the familiar wooziness approaching, and a smile began fixing on his face. Although it wasn't clear what was funny. A fly was flirting with his nose, and he waved at it weakly, almost unconsciously. The fly's persistence didn't really annoy him, though, for everything was all right.

Davey leaned his head back against the cool concrete wall and closed his eyes. Automatically, his right hand hitched to his face, the thumb slipping in, snug and comforting, to fit the gentle suction of his ready mouth. As he relaxed to the gritty saltiness of fingernail grime, his left hand made a small, reflex tightening around the gin bottle's neck, and his mind receded to yesterday's birthday party.

He immediately remembered its moment of overwhelming embarrassment when, in his private concern about the little flames singeing his face, he had missed blowing out two of the candles. Even now, he cringed at how wimpy it must've looked.

Davey quickly shifted his mind away from that threatening recollection. Instead, he thought of the awesome skateboard they'd given him. Squinting in speculation, he wondered how much wine its sale would get him. Now, as they entered the view of his mind's eye, he knew a rare twinge of tolerance for them, for the hype presents they always gave him.

In their way, Mommy and Daddy, too, were all right.

CONNEXIONS

Confounded though she was, fully confused by the happenstance, her hands fiercely searched through this morning's spoils; like foraging independents, the busy grubbers expertly worked the barrels at this familiar dumping spot, now suddenly too generous for wasting.

The grosser chaff, the rough paper, Styrofoam, and stuff was set aside by her left. Then, through the jagged cans and plastic junk and grease, the right one drove for the necessary chancing. It shoved unhesitating into each newfound crater of risk. Would it be soft, edible surprise? Or the piercing electric jolt? Any moment, again and again, five soft, blind eyes would tell. Would know buttered bread, or quick red tears. For that's how they rove, do Alice Tee's assessing hands. That's how they work to keep her moving, the pincer parts that feed the old crabmouth. The energy to drive that fierce confused crabhead.

Though Alice Tee would never fault these here pizza people's barrels. They were steady delivery every other morning, as regular as train tracks, a constant source she could hardly spurn. Except this morning, as Alice Tee arrived to find they'd doubled up their output. Six barrels she confronted! And off whisked her wits in every which direction, frittering her tightly stretched schedule. For she had no space, or time, to accommodate this new abundance.

Although just leaving it was as confounding. Unthinkable. Such waste she could not allow. Especially at this stop—this heartbeat to her rounds. Ohh! Here again was Excess, the quandary as always, spoiling her system, and crimping her smooth routine.

Her hands mechanical—and Alice Tee—they tried their best. Speedily, they salvaged to new limits of her bulging cart. Though even then, she had worked only four barrels. And still, the too-much extra lay scattered there, in part swift savaged, and tormenting. All while Alice Tee could feel herself remaining overlong with all this stuff. All while it poised and tensed up her time; tigering it, preparing it to spring at her. As even now she stretched herself so very close to lateness.

And how well she could imagine the little gluttons waiting! Preening themselves; full, round with curves that glittered in rainbows, and so contained of their sleek voracity. The multitude of them, with their gleaming eyes—perfect rings of focused black and gold—blank beams blinking only when their poised heads whipped around to search another compass point for Alice Tee.

Or else they might be cocking faces one side, angling their insolent looks, scanning the pavement for their warder. Her ears conjured their surly coos, their scraping claws askittering on street concrete, on cartops. How very well she saw them readying to gobble—gathering their greediness into grim silhouettes lurking overhead on power lines; dark appetites unbalancing storefront awnings and fouling the struggling branches of avenue trees.

Ah yes! Alice Tee could almost feel their vexed reproach about her tardiness. Mm-hmm! Reproach from these city locusts, these feathered roaches. But she was now only four long blocks away, and this time, Alice Tee was ready.

The traffic lights and engined wheels never slowed down Alice Tee. The better blockers were the usual eyeballing traffic, the droves that go. They were everywhere, these well-run ones; well driven in and out of their selves, their offices, their cars, their shops, the very living street. Swift tours they made. In, out quick. On time, in time, like ticks and tocks on stone-steady duty. These staring clods. These gawkers. A silliness of bigots. It was these that weighed most mightily on Alice Tee's cart wheels, that dragged so heavily and did impede.

She never stopped though, never took them on. Was slowed somewhat, but kept on moving on regardless. She just muttered rage and mowed through 'em, scattering the blockers. Crunched through their antlines. Shattered their ugly-viewing stares. Spat at them, and on them, too. And when they hurled their splintered jibes at her back, she snarled and used that extra irritation to make her way more fiercely. She kept herself to Alice Tee's demanding rounds.

And yes, her charges, they were there. Alice Tee knew, could feel them long before she trundled her squiggly cart wheels round the corner. Their hungry anticipation fluttered on the air, making great excitement quicken all through her. That formed a harsh grin snatching at her mouth; that wrenched her mind to think of how, this time, she'd let them have their waiting's worth.

Of how she'd shed the extra bulges of her shopping cart into them, into their endless craws. Of how she'd let them stuff it down, choke after peck after straining gulp. Yes! She'd even fling them seconds, and let them cram to bursting on moldy pizza scraps. Just so, she'd deal with all their ugly greed.

Thus grimly thrilled, she pushed around the corner to her stop. And there encountered Excess again, at it in glee. Excess the interloper, invading Alice Tee's sole office, casting corn at her rightful charges, feeding them. And, of course, the feathered guts were guzzling every bit down. The plain disgust welled up in Alice Tee and full-stopped her shopping cart, all while she sought in fury for just what she should do.

Usurpers was a species Alice Tee had met before. Always a horror show, the worst was when they followed her—and others —below the city limits. Underground, into the caverns where urban bat types sleep daytimes: in sepulchers for departed subway trains. A space for dropped-out ones. A place where vagrants rest, their homes—on colder nights—well warmed from raunchy rotting batshit.

Quite down here the ravaging misfits had prowled, searching after her—and others. They trailed high-stepping through live vermin and the clammy filth, smelling this putrid mess into their memories. They came in packs. And through the garbage, charged with dazzling lights and cans spraying a stifling graffiti paint. They tagged, and roared their malice at the wakened sleepers, swung wicked bats and stinging whips. They struck down the startled frail and left. So sudden in, and swiftly gone. Only their terror being left to roost with bruised and blue-black Alice Tee—and others.

Usurpers! Huh! She'd known them.

This one on her corner, though, was no better-off eyeballer. She was not merely making fun. Her shopping bag was small—a bigger pocketbook. It held the food she fed out. And as she gathered the grain from within it, she smiled. Smiling teeth much bigger than the corn, she tossed away handfuls. The smile too wide for her gaunt, skinny face, although she kept it on: big, bone white, and irritating.

Alice Tee screamed at its excessiveness, "Get outa here, you! Go on, clear off!"

The smile didn't budge, although it must've heard her rage.

Intemperate, uncaring, it hooked back in the handbag to catch and toss more crawfuls.

Alice Tee shouted again, "I say go away from here, you! I, me, just me alone, I take care of these!"

Yet still, the smile remained the same. Alice Tee rushed forward and spat at it. The smile wouldn't yield. Instead, it wanted talk. It spoke: "I'm City College class of sixty-four, the cream . . ."

But at this, it became doubtful, then was lost in a toss of her frazzle-haired head. Now minus all the teeth, she was as thin as spines. Then, bold as a lance, she went straight for Alice Tee's cart, and tore open the topmost bulging bag.

It was too much for Alice Tee. Retaliate she did, and rammed her laden cart into the busybody. A second, harder jam stumbled the intruder to the edge of the sidewalk, through the clattering, flying bellies, scattering their rush for the fallen scrapsbag.

One more time, and then another, Alice Tee rammed the busybody firmly, staggering her into the busy street, right in the path of a busy car. Which, hard as a crunch, struck her down. Then one gurgly scream, and the interloper went quiet.

But Alice Tee could tarry there no longer; she had set rounds to keep. She shoved her cart fast through the hullabaloo of grouping eyeballers, their press yielding readily as she forged through. She had to go right now. For other expectant gluttons would be thronging at her next stop—insistent as timetables—depending themselves on Alice Tee. She'd bet this life on it.

TRANSACTION

Sitting in position being invisible had become so comfortable, Omari was nodding off. Drowsiness seeped into his will like a fog, gently misting away the vibrant insistence of his purpose. His hovering dreamtime seesawed the plans for the scam, straddling them across the borders of reality: What he had to do was also what he might've done, or what might've been done, or even what he was going to do. Time frame shifted drunkenly, as insensitive to circumstance as his backside was numb to the damp coolness of the new-mown grass.

A smooth transition—and the giddy had resolved into reassurance. And all was well. He was doing it. He was being the lookout man. First one in. Last out. His job to divine trouble at the outset, and frustrate it after that. Until the play was done. Most of all, he was the man with the Might, the .38 arm of firepower. As usual, Jangles had assigned him alone that violence option.

He had entered the small East Side park half an hour ago, so ready and alert he almost twitched through the gate, concentration like a daze around him. His eyes, jackhammer rapid, darted about, wanting to check everywhere at once. The strain was controlling it all down to common sense. So that he could be the look-see man, and not conspicuous.

What his sweating anticipation had met was an innocent summer's day, ten o'clock peaceful with a morning-airing crowd. Nannies minding lazy babies lolling off in strollers. Some senior ladies brooding close-headed with their histories and who-knows in duos and trios. A bent-over old man carefully testing the pathway as if his third leg of a walking stick had a seeing eye. A few other walkers and sitters. All were too well kept or well off or well aged to be the Undercover Man.

Omari had muttered, "Beautiful." And became aware that his palms were wet, his jaw adroop. He got himself together, then set off to double-check the fortune of their good preparations.

His saunter through the park's morning calm only reassured him it was as harmless to their plans as it was pleasant. So Omari headed for his assigned post to signal and await the rest of the crew.

The second bench on the path from the entrance gate was the spot, snuggled right next to a dense, small-leafed bush sculpted into a man-high teacup. The giant cup handle touched one of the bench's arms, and the dark green bowl gave shade and color to the intimacy of the seat. Even though it was there in the open, next to the public path, it had the privacy of a nest, except for some watching body being bold and rude.

Jangles had named this as its best advantage, that plain-sight openness with politeness shades. Folks couldn't stare at coziness, he'd said, so this love seat was the perfect lookout for his lieutenant and advance man. It had been great strategy in the meeting. There was one problem now, though. During Omari's brief double-checking circuit, a woman had come in and sat there.

She was dressed straight out of a rich store window, shirt to shoes in shades of wealthy brown. The pocketbook, too, was a mahogany suede with a fat gold clasp. The outfit advertised spending bank.

This piece of dead time was clearly expensive to her. Each tick ground her down, taking valuable toll on her patience. Wasting many nerves, making her glance at her watch and, every other minute, at the entrance gate. Whenever someone strayed into her sights, he'd get a blast from her rat-a-tat vigil for her no-show target. And with every disappointment, she was building up more heat. Fine-adjusting her temper by recrossing model legs to models' poses. Unclasping the gold hold to finger tissues from the suede and press the tension out of her makeup.

With all her action, though, it was plain that something more powerful had her in control. Otherwise she would break, flail her arms and scream to the sky with rage red to blue. If she weren't dressed chic and proper, she would.

While appraising her—and not wanting to risk winding her up further—Omari had chosen an alternative spot some twenty feet over-shoulder to her. From there, feet out long, reclining on rump and elbows, he had eyes both on his job and on the benched busy-Mizzy.

Thus it was that twenty minutes later, with nothing much changed, relaxation began its creep-up assault, and the lazybones feeling started undermining his alertness. At the first, he took to easing his eyes only a little. Then he had discovered that even with the vision resting, he was still able to maintain his sense of the importance of the watch. The nods had fully conquered when he found himself time-sliding back to the meeting the night before.

Jangles had laid out this solid plan of a scam, guaranteeing some easy pawnshop cash. It was five minutes' action, no cops, no pain, and no chase. As usual with Jangles, the promise had turned to a neat adventure by the time he ran down the situation. His magic was sweet planning, and how he told it.

Jangles had scoped this park for weeks, learning its patterns. It was small, with a private-privileged look from its well-kept lawns and trimmed hedges and fresh-turned beds of varicolored tulips and ornamented bushes. It fitted in with its neighborhood: an East Side pocket of rich society living off the icing on the cake. The park had but one gate open for entrance and exit (the other secured by a two-inch-thick steel chain, as if it could break away). That convenient one-door resemblance to a shopping bag was Jangles's final persuasion that the park was easy pickings for the crew. And it should be worth the while. For its mainstay crowd was an older, better sort. Mostly heirloom conservators with family trees of gold, and jewels around their necks and wrists and fingers.

Yes! There was a cop. His beat took him by about midday. But he had taken up with a pretty nanny, who came with her kid like clockwork to help him with his workload. To synchronize and so on, they always shifted to the park's farthest end, him with his hat in his hand, her glowing like a happy baby.

After this was related, Tari had thrown out the idea of riffraffing some pussy if it showed up. That set Jangles wild. Like forever didn't matter, he began raining on speeches. Sermons on Selfishness, on Reason, on Stupidity. Then barbecuing the Ta' on a Brotherhood and Discipline grill, using Bitterness and Sarcasm for sauce. What would the cops and robbered say? How would the media put it? Even an off-color suggestion would be made into a sexual assault. One impetuous fondle would change their Well-Coordinated Caper into a Raping Rampage. From Proficient Tacticians, they'd become Heinous Hoodlums, or a Perverse Gang. Jangles might've ranted on, but for Tari screaming, "Time out!" to plead out with forced jokes, play tears, and genuine regret about his mouth mess.

Jangles quit then, after a final stutter or two of muttered remainders. The rest of the meeting had proceeded smoothly, everyone attentive and serious and mainly avoiding Jangles's word whip. His eloquence was a gift—his talent instead of science, basketball, or whatever—and it made him the major man. But it could make him a torture, too. . . .

As if a disco's door had busted open, loud beat music exploded, blowing Omari's idle-minding away. His heart abruptly pounded awakeness through him, and wrenching his neck about, with a shamed glance he raked the entrance where Jangles would be waiting; then he relaxed to find his man absent to his lieutenant's laxness. That anxiety cleared, he turned full-scowl vexation toward the noisy offender.

It was Dolfo and his jamma-blasta, posted near the gate between the fence and a tulip patch. Last night he had been insisting and whining and begging with Jangles about bringing the box. The police band on the radio could be used for checking on the law, he'd argued. When he noticed Jangles's interest in this point, he'd needled on with it until Jangles had said okay.

Omari'd been against it all along. To his mind, Dolfo would mess up and, as always, have his excuse afterward. And just as he'd expected, here was the Murf now, louding soul sounds into this elite setup. Dolfo seemed absolutely into the music. Finger-popping the rhythm, rocking his shoulders, boogying his ass where it leaned against the iron spears linking as fence.

Fiercing up his stare, Omari sat up and concentrated disgust thoughts at the asshole. No difference. Dolfo remained deeply into the current top o' the charts.

As far as Omari could judge, the music hadn't affected the folks too much. They didn't show serious alarm. Here and there was a glance at Dolfo, but no one was getting restless. The noise was just a commonplace annoyance to tolerate and ignore. Like an upset stomach, it would pass soon. When Omari noticed one of the nannies putting a little hip-hop in her strolling gait, he admitted that the tune wasn't so bad. The number moved (still carrying Dolfo) into its honey-crooning chorus.

This recalled to Omari the time somebody'd told Dolfo how he had a black hole in his head; any sense from his brain went into another dimension. Dolfo had laughed harder than everyone else. Longer, too. All that evening, again and again, he'd erupted in giggle fits and guffaws. As if it wasn't him the joke was on. As if the joke was that sweet. As if he had tasted it at all. But that was Dolfo, a guy Mr. Spock would've found "fascinating."

Now, as Omari set to heave himself up for a reminding (but casual) saunter over by the balloon-brained, Dolfo suddenly caught himself and reduced the radio's volume. So soft, Omari couldn't hear it, and his mind faltered on the ending part of the tune to which it had been humming a backup.

Dolfo was now casting sly glances around. Probably feeling that he hadn't been noticed, and looking furtive as a mouse in the cheese cupboard. Omari shifted his eyes away from the bother. All at once, his irritation changed to an odd cheerfulness. It was kinda funny, but even the Zero-head had come through in his weird way. It seemed that matters could only get better now.

Right then the woman halfway stood up to briefly arrange skirt creases at her bottom. Then, readied for whatever, she sat again, looking straight ahead. His instant check of the gate told Omari why. A man had entered and was approaching in a rush. And once more Omari was seized by tension, while his heartbeat started its own jam session in his chest.

But the man had eyes only for the woman in brown. He hurried straight to her like a late schoolboy with his upset mama whip-waiting. Omari thought, Punk! and his muscles and mind went mellow again, his heart quieting to relief.

The Punk might've been a model, too. Or maybe they dressed from the same store windows. He looked to be a diet-watcher who probably worked out yet still remained a slight-weight. One to whom even karate couldn't pass on aggression. A vulgar belch would blow him right away.

As he neared his date, he commenced an elaborate arm-stretching, wrist-bending, and elbow-jerking action, which ended in a studied glance at his watch. Although practiced and smooth, still it was a punkish move, not hiding the wimp behind it. He had to have known he was late. And worse, he had done his glance act, and it missed his audience. For the woman never gave him eye. She had remained looking frustrated at her morning, as if the piece of day were behaving unmanageably.

Standing his distance like a Boy Scout, the Punk hailed her, and maybe got the permission to sit. Or perhaps it was manners understanding. She still wasn't looking at him.

Now Omari saw that time-checking wasn't his only gimmick. The Punk was elaborate at sitting down, too. He had to pinch-hold the front pleats of his pants' legs just so, and throw a glance behind to guide his ass to sit. Then he did a softness test before committing the sensitive backside. He ended by crossing the gentleman's legs.

All this, and not yet a play from the woman.

With all their motions and gestures, Omari couldn't but notice the Punk's hands. He would've never recognized him by them. They looked real, foreign to the magazine-ad man they serviced. The right one showed a fresh-healed scar. They had fat veins, and long, strong, knobby fingers. Big enough to palm a basketball, they looked man's hands.

Omari realized that the woman had been fussing at the Punk while still gazing away. He heard some as the off-and-on breezes allowed her voice to reach him. A bit about him demeaning reality. Something else about winter and discontent. It was speechy complaining, sounding prepared, poor-felt, and distant. Omari relaxed out of their hassle. They couldn't be trouble, not with that quarreling like no-longer lovers. They weren't the undercover police trap he was wary about, only coupled rabbits setting up as prey.

He was thinking in terms of another Jangles idea: his Natural Survival Theory. When he'd dropped out of college, Jangles had kept up his self-education, reading majorly in biology. This he used as basis for interpreting the Life's systems.

By his Survival Theory, Out Here was a great human-species natural park. It had available for every want by everybody. No one ever had to go hungry. The catch was that each one was the food for another. Whether dog eat dog, or wolf eat rabbit, or worm eat wolf, one guy had to depend on that one other for food.

Jangles saw that as a problem, this depending on one special food. As he said it, "If your burger joint closed down, y're starving!" According to him, the rats had found a solution: eat anything, live anywhere, adjust with instinct, and stay hungry. Using that plan, they owned everywhere man lived. And they never made a weapon.

Hear Jangles expound about rats, and they became most admirable. Their strength, intelligence, family ties, patience, and success against human oppression all gave them underdog glamour and heroic stature. From vermin they were changed to sophisticated social survivors. And this is how he wanted the crew to see themselves: as a gang of rats with hands, the ultimate candidates for the One Life Handicap Derby.

Something had made the Punk exert his voice. Maybe it was a squeezed ball, for he calmed down again after a fidget. But he was still talking back to her. With the breezes on hold, Omari could hear quite plainly, the Punk speaking each word FM perfect, from its beginning through to its end, extra-working his lips and tongue as if the language had bubble gum in it.

"I'm aware of my responsibilities in this. I am. Really I am.

But there are other considerations." He managed two notes into
"are." "The market is very dull. We aren't selling a thing. The
work isn't moving. The agency promised to get rid of the
'Moonlight' piece, but I regard it as . . . It's a favorite, if not
the best . . . I'm reluctant . . ."

She cut in, "Still the sentimental you, huh, always and forever?
You'd sell this, but you like it too much. That one's too good for
the money. Your pieces're like your children. You make them
from stone, or mud, and sweat. And you love them so." Here she
stopped and turned to give him the full-faced eye. "May I remind you that you have a flesh-and-blood creation that, this year,
needs eight thousand for tuition, three thousand for clothes, and
more for food and doctors. . . ."

She paused for breath, and the Punk made to slip in some
speech, but she hammered him down with, "And I cannot ask
my agent to get rid of her. You understand that? Whether she's
my favorite piece or not!"

The Punk eased his tie's knot with the active fingers and swallowed some explanations. He tried another tack, changing his
tone from explain to complain. "Well, what am I to do? You
know my extent, my resources. Father refuses to come across.
What am I supposed to do? You don't expect me to steal, do
you?"

Eye-to-eye with him, the woman surveyed his seated stature.
Up, then down, her formed eyebrows assessed him. Then,
weighted with scorn, her voice fell from proper to common
louding as she wiped him out.

"You don't have the balls!"

Omari didn't get to see the Punk's response. The distraction
was Jangles strolling into his field of vision. His major man was
smiling and relaxed, signaling all was well, and the action would
be getting on.

Putting his concentration together, Omari examined the pair on his bench and decided what items he'd be having. The pocketbook, of course. He'd clean it out. And the Punk should have a wallet. Counting the visibles, there were also two watches, bracelet(s?), earrings, and at least one neck chain. Not too bad. He could evaluate maybe four, five hundred in dollars. Plus, luck might have the Punk carrying a stash despite his crying poor pockets.

Omari looked around at the other guys. They had all cut out their posing and seemed ready for business. Emark and Tari had grounded their Frisbee. Dolfo was in his position near the fence. Jangles was heading back to the gate after his quick overlook of the situation. When he got to where he could monitor the street, it would begin.

Briefly, Omari wondered how the fine folks in the park couldn't see it coming. It seemed as obvious as rain clouds in a clear blue sky.

Jangles reached the gate and pulled its iron wings shut with a bang. Ten guys who watched it happen moved into action as one. Omari quicked over to his bench and stood close over the couple. The woman, still working the Punk, didn't notice him.

Omari wasn't loud, but his voice was hard: "Shut up!"

She looked up at his command with bigging eyes, mouth agape. The hanging jaws sagged her cheeks, giving her a fish mouth.

"Gimme what y'got!" Omari told her.

In response she slumped down on the bench, propping her head up against the backrest.

The Punk took it much better. It was the startled look, then immediate understanding. He folded his arms and didn't try a word.

"Okay, okay. It's a takeoff," Omari continued quickly. "You

don't panic, and y'don't bleed. So nothing fancy, okay? Mi' man there at the fence could blow y'fuckin' heads off anytime. Y'got it? So relax, okay?"

The woman's eyes wanted to look behind him at the fence, but they couldn't break the magnet of Omari's face. She had closed her mouth. Now a tic of a smile kept tugging it on one side only. Omari hoped she'd stay in shock and checked the Punk. He had closed his eyes and was shaking his head as if he didn't believe it was really happening to him.

She made a fart when Omari reached down and grabbed her mahogany suede pocketbook. Chuckling, he demanded her watch and earrings. Meantime he searched the pocketbook with half his eyes and five fingers. It had a checkbook, a small fold of bills, a change purse, some credit cards, and other pure feminine stuff. A second pass of his fingers found nothing but a pen. He kept the bills and chucked the suede back on the bench.

She was taking her time with the watch, slowly peeling it off as if it were wrist skin, wasting time and hoping.

"Give it here! Bitch!" Omari growled, and snatched at it.

That was enough grease, and the watch slid off immediately. Without urging, the earrings followed, offered from shaking, long-nailed fingers. Her neck chain, Omari saw, was a thin, delicate rope with a tiny pendant. As his pawnshop man bought gold by weight, he passed on it. So with the woman finished, he turned to the Punk.

"Awright, let's have it. And don't fuck up now."

The Punk took off his watch quickly. Next came a heavy gold ID band Omari hadn't even seen. Then the Punk hesitated.

"Your pockets, sucker!" Omari urged. He added a meaningful look at the Punk's jacket pockets. But turned insides out, they didn't yield the wallet Omari sought. He was growing impatient.

"I want your wallet, fuckhead!" he said.

The Punk stammered, "I . . . I, er, don't carry a, er, wallet, sir!"

Omari almost grinned. The Punk had called him "sir" as if he meant it. Mentally cursing the Luck of No Wallet, Omari was about to demand the Punk's finger ring when the woman's voice cut in.

"For God's sake, give him the damned wallet and stop trying to be a hero."

Omari shot a look at her. Her hand was reaching for her throat but wasn't quite there. It crouched nearer to her shoulder like a little animal caught undecided whether to stand or run. Her eyes slid away from his like a traitor's, and he felt a strong disgust at her. She shouldn't have blown the Punk's try. It wasn't her place to. A man had to try. But he reined in his vexation at her and turned his rage on the Punk.

"So, what's it goin' to be, huh, asshole? You want to see y'blood? Gimme it! Now!"

Omari pounced smelling-close to the Punk, staring right into the clean-shaven face, ready to break it with his fist as the anger roused by the woman's betrayal recharged from the man's attempted resistance. The combined underhandedness offended him so. He tensed himself to punch—just as the Punk gave in.

Lifting his foot to his lap, he reached inside his sock and pulled out a wallet. Loaded up to strike, breathing hard, Omari barely held in the energy. He kept the blow poised and said, "Just gimme the cash, man."

With deliberate speed, the Punk emptied his wallet and handed over the cash.

As Omari took the money, from the corner of his eye he glimpsed the woman's crouching hand still fluttering near her throat. It suddenly occurred to him that the gesture held a suspicious stealthiness. He studied her face, her eyes scurrying about wildly, like cockroaches trapped in a light cage.

"What y'got there?" he asked softly, gesturing toward her hand.

Her answer was to make a fist over what she concealed.

The stupid defiance of the little fist slacked the bonds of his control. The silly, back-squeezing bitch. His time was almost up, and here she was playing her greedy ways with him. Furious, he stooped and hissed in her face, "Gimme. Here, here. Give it up!"

She was so out-of-line. And he, near out-of-bounds of Jangles's rule, he wanted to punch the shit out of her. His fist was up, the blood charging through him.

The woman broke and sobbed, "Oh my God . . ." and she removed her hand.

It was a brooch. A golden, pinky-sized butterfly with spread wings and eyes of bulging ruby red; it was a big, beautiful, classy treasure on her chest. Now Omari realized why she had betrayed the Punk's wallet. It was to buy some opportunity to hide her fancy brooch.

As he discovered her fault, Omari beheld a crumpling of her made-up face. Cracks between where was paint and where was pallor had made a gap into her, like it was an earthquake. And he could see her greedy core. Not greedy from need, but from just wanting more. Automatic greedy, like a worm eating shit. Which was why he felt he could squash her face.

"You greedy bitch!" he snarled, and snatched at the jewel. But it was well pinned to the beige cashmere collar, so the grab only yanked her shoulder sideways, making her scream out fright and cower down.

"Don't," the Punk chimed in, "please don't. It's not her fault. . . ."

Surprised, Omari looked at him. He had raised his big, veiny hands, palms up and open, certainly not to attack. More forcing of a pause, like a guy wanting fairness, not fights. He continued talking into Omari's hesitation.

"It's my family's. An heirloom. I gave it to her as a wedding present. It's really for my daughter . . . a tradition. It's our way, sir."

He was explaining it strong-voiced, as if this was a western and he was the hero. He was being reasonable, until he got to the "sir." Only then it became appeal. The whole speech so surprised Omari that he met the fellow's eyes. And in that odd consternation—exchanging shocked, reseeing stares—they formed a wordless bargain.

Omari straightened up. "Okay, mi' man. Y'got it."

Right then he heard the scam being called. "Time! Time's out!" He stepped back onto the pavement.

"Don't move till the gate bangs, okay?" he warned them. "You're still lined up. So don't spoil it now."

Just before turning away, he jumped close and faked a violent cuff at the woman. She made a retching, asthma-attack sound and threw her arms up over her hairdo. The guy didn't even flinch at the empty gesture, just sat there testing an ambiguous half smile.

As Omari split with the gang, his parting image was of the man comforting the woman, holding her head on his chest, stroking it slowly. Omari imagined him years hence telling the daughter how he'd saved the family heirloom. He hoped the guy would tell it like a hero.

HOME IS THE HEART

Entering his homeland was like with every other country. It made Nalden Vonn feel vaguely criminal, like some felon, a person of doubtful privilege, being allowed back to anxious society. He balanced at that too-familiar point of his every voyage: intimidation time by those boundary authorities filtering which and what entered the sanctity of their country. He always had the uneasy sense of being the one who'd be dregged out.

He waited at the head of the line, while the immigration officer was taking forever at assessing a family. Spying on them from his impatience, Nalden condemned their empty-headed last-minute searching through pockets and purses for passport particulars. Just in case, he moved up his own and his son's from trousers' to shirt's pocket. He nudged their oversized carrying bag about six inches forward, and reached back to herd the boy the little bit forward to stand at his backside. "Y'see," he said to him, "soon we'll be out of here."

A short pause after, the boy replied, "It's okay, Dad. I'm not tired or anything."

Nalden studied his summertime son. The kid wasn't being brave. He seemed relaxed as usual, cool as his off-pace speaking manner. He showed none of the eager display Nalden would have preferred. If he himself were being taken to his roots-home in the Caribbean, he would have been flipping all the way down the plane's aisle this morning. On the other hand, this might be standard behaviour for a part-time son. With this kid, he was always finding out. Two summers ago, the mother had told him their kid had tested precocious in some fancy kindergarten program. Since her illustrator's job was connected with it, she had enrolled him. So, after all, the kid might be having an exuberantly great time in his quiet, smart way. What would his regular-headed father know?

"Handsome boy," said the woman behind them, following Nalden's gaze. Her face showed that pleasant sympathy automatic in modern-minded women when they encounter a father/son couple. "He looks just like you." She looked up, her eyes appraising too brightly for the end of a five-hour early-morning flight.

He reevaluated her: smooth-faced pretty, nice teeth, accent lived-abroad Trinidadian, her blue dress fresh, expensive. A sophisticated national, home for a vacation, he guessed. And was she trying to pick him up?

Her gleaming smile remained poised and open-ended. Nalden searched quickly for a smart line to impress her—her and the boy standing at the backside of his ego, the cool son whose attention he could feel on him. So lured by her readiness to listen, Nalden caught the gabbles.

"Well, we on a sort of vacation and roots search. He's been in the States since diaper days, so this is his first chance to really see the environment that made his daddy and mammy. And his grandmother, she getting old, so I figured is time he met her, y'know what I mean. It's our trip this summer."

Her smile of gentle interest slid into an approving moue. "That's wonderful. Your wife must be grateful. . . ."

"No wife, y'know . . . I only have him for the summers. They live West Coast."

The woman nodded slowly, understanding him on, jerking a string of intimate detail out of him like a hooked fish in reverse.

The boy shifted slightly, and Nalden suddenly sensed his disapproving focus on the conversation. He tried to end up. "Yes, he'll be meeting the gramma for the first time. . . ."

The woman regarded the boy. "Well, she should be really proud. She's got a fine and handsome grandson."

She reached over and fixed the kid's shirt collar, then stole a little maternal pat to his shoulder. By it, Nalden sensed the woman's initial interest in him had changed. Now she saw him less as an available man, and more as a man with a mission.

He thought to make one bold deciding play and ask her address. But as though Mr. Circumstance, jealous, had anticipated the move, the woman pointed behind him before he could speak. "The officer's calling you," she said. Her smile had a twitch of escape as Nalden turned around.

Indeed, the immigration officer was staring at him, his impatience hanging heavy as a beam between them. Again he called, "Next!"

Nalden shepherded his son forward and handed over the passports.

Automatic-voiced, the IO asked, "Length of visit?"

"Three weeks at least, but up to six."

The IO paused from stamping Nalden's passport and looked up, his face tiring of tolerance. "Listen nah, man. I ent have time to waste, y'know. Is three weeks? Is six weeks? Or is what?" The "what" sounded like a threat of expulsion.

Nalden said quickly, "Six!"

The man stamped his passport, then picked up the boy's and

examined it. "This is a U.S. passport," he said. "You can't read this is a 'Citizens Only' line?"

Nalden interjected, his voice amiable, "Is mi' son's, he living there now." He jerked his head down toward the boy, who stood about a foot shorter than the chest-high counter. The officer stood up and bent forward to glance at him. "Y'have a return ticket for him?" he asked.

"Sure, yes."

Nalden saw by this quibbling that the man really didn't have the heart to be hard. It was just that his dignity was still piqued at having to call twice. Nalden assumed his most righteous air while the man flipped through some pages of the kid's brand-new passport.

Finally, the man stamped it and shoved it over with the other one. "Nex' time let 'im use the noncitizens' line, okay?"

Pocketing the passports, Nalden reassured him, "Sure, man, yes . . . and thanks, mi' brother."

Customs was the final trial of country entry. As bidden, Nalden exposed his all; explained his special self-assembled first-aid kit for all tropic eventualities; paid duty on his portable; and consumed the orange from his kid's backpack.

Finally, they started down the exit corridor, braving the gauntlet of greeters who, as always, thronged five/six deep on either side, scrutinizing away whatever privacies the Customs hadn't invaded. Nalden didn't dare meet any of these curious eyes, for fear he would recognize someone. What civil thing could he say to such a gawker? How would he ever again call such a *maccoe* "friend"? He concentrated on carrying his bags in a practical yet macho manner, while guiding his trailing boy through the glazing gazes.

Then they were beyond them, free in the bright open halfway between the airport building and the taxi stand. He put down the bags to stretch and catch his breath, relaxing in the fact of arrival. It was nine o'clock of a sunny tropic morning. "Y'see how bright the sun is?" he observed to the boy.

"Yeah, Pops. It's hot. Can't we go in somewhere?" The kid's face was all squint against the glare, and to Nalden's great satisfaction, animated at last.

"Y'see how blue it is? Look up, yes, right over y'head. Is that blue? Or is that violet? Eh! Isn't that violet up there fading to that clear blue in the distance? That's some blue, eh? That's some tropical sky! Right?"

The kid, sweating quietly, answered, "Yeah, Pops. But it's hot, really hot. . . ."

"It's crispy hot," Nalden expanded. "Clear and stinging, but no mugginess, just pure heat . . ."

But he was talking to himself. The kid had started off to the shade of the taxi stand.

Nalden backhanded the perspiration from his forehead as he watched him go. Then, smiling at the boy's directness, he swung up the two bags and headed for transport—the ride home.

The taxi was a brilliantly polished, chrome-enhanced burgundy Japanese midsize. Compared to the others on line, it was a diamond in a junkyard. It looked priced for princes' pockets. Nalden stopped in front of the man sitting casually on the immaculate front fender—a seat only an owner or bodyguard would dare. He put the bags down. The taximan left off his bantering with the other drivers lounging around. Looking at the boy, he addressed them. "So where is the gentleman and his son off to on their vacation in this tropical paradise? Ha-ha-ha . . ."

He laughed heartily, as if he'd made a big joke. The man's smile, framed by his small-brimmed all-weather hat and highlighted by a left-side gold-capped canine, was all fun and friendly challenge. His spirits fitted well with Nalden's mood. Standing up, the hearty driver was as tall as Nalden's six feet. He had, though, some twenty pounds more weight in smooth, muscular flesh seen at his open-shirted chest and gold-chained neck. It added all the force to his hidden joke.

Nalden smiled broadly. "Ah goin' up Aripo," he answered, emphasizing his Trinidadian accent. And then, to display familiarity with the distances and geography, he tried some flattery. "All nice smooth road for this fine machine."

Strong Fun swallowed it as bears do honey. He opened the car's back door. "He-he-he. Sit down, folks, get comfy," he invited. "Out here sun too hot to talk. Leh we make a breeze in Missis Ridesmooth. Eh? Ha-ha-ha."

He clapped the kid on the shoulder, helping him into the car. "Good idea, eh. Y'thinking dat way, too, sonnyboy? Ha-ha-ha . . ."

Driver checked that they and their bags were secure. He was particular to close their doors for them: a gentle squeezed click that expressed threats of dire consequence for a careless slammer. Then he took his own seat.

Just before he pulled his door shut, he casually mentioned his fare, as if it were a mere formality. "That'd be fifty cents. Okay?"

He had used the local slang for dollars—and had overcharged by twenty of them.

The overcharge jarred awkwardly against the sense of camaraderie force-ripening between them. Nalden couldn't let the man take him twenty dollars excess just so. He felt the kid's eyes on him, waiting, and cringed at seeming cheap, and risking getting out of the fine, cool car. Still, he wouldn't let himself be fooled by Driver's expensive-laughter gimmick.

Just then Driver added, "Everything gone up, brother-man. Y'think it easy these days?"

The comment struck Nalden as a back-out hole; a defense, a plea, a confession. His courage returned. "Let's do it for thirty-five, nah," he bargained.

Rejection began to form on Driver's face, uncrinkling his twinkle and twisting the smile down off his mobile lips.

Nalden quickly upped his offer. "Okay, forty flat. All right?"

The big smile returned, signalling Driver's agreement. "All you Trinidadians don't change at all, eh! Shortchanging yuh way through heaven. Ha-ha . . ."

Caught up again in the balloon of ready amiability, Nalden tried out some of his own local repartee. "Man must man!" he explained.

He caught his son's eye appraising him. Self-satisfied with his performance, he winked at the kid. And awkwardly, as if trying out something new, his eyes agleam with conspiracy, the boy winked back.

The jets' runway, with its takeoff action, captured the boy's full attention as they paralleled the airport heading for home. Missis Ridesmooth purred like a contented pussycat and showed off her cheetah paces on the smooth roadway, well paved international style. Nalden looked around outside—at the sugarcaned or newly burnt fields; at the occasional houses, grand or crude, close-crowding the roadside with all those open acres as their backyards; at the fruit trees—mango, coconut, banana—whizzing by more regular than fence posts. Everything he saw was fill-ins of the perfect memories he sought. Faced with the need to show off his roots in truth, for the first time Nalden tried to picture them himself.

Less than twenty miles away, the hazy blue-green Northern Range seemed as distant as his youth, barely two decades gone. He remembered how, when the sun dipped below its peaks on schoolday evenings, that boy he'd been would be late. And in his household, being late was hazard time.

He'd be in that happy place between school's over and "I'm home, Mammy!" heedless of the fooling sun as it began to slip behind those blue-green mountains, still shining playful-bright, shedding lies about six o'clock. Until suddenly, it was gone! Then fear'd mount and ride him home to Mother. The farther away, the faster, the more frightened he'd be. Running to beat the timespoilt Mammy's moods, spurred by the dread of screaming and fussing and stinging licks with a freshly skinned whip.

Time had changed the importance of the Northern Range, though; had even changed its dimensions in Nalden's recall. As a kid, he had learned that the highest peak, El Techuche, was full 3,100 feet high. A few years later, as a scholar at the University of the West Indies, he had topped El Techuche in a mountain climb with the ecology class: eight guys, three girls, and the professor, a returned-from-the-Cold Trinee. At the top, while the girls had scolded them for being indecent, most of the guys had stripped bareback to cool down in the refreshing chill up that high.

This memory reminded Nalden of the end of last summer: him and the boy on the observation deck atop the Twin Towers in New York, and the kid's shivering fingers feeding coins to the telescope.

Somehow these shifting thoughts now connected unexpectedly in an impulse to reassure the kid. He caught himself, though, wondering why he'd expect the child, here in the machine-cooled tropic heat, to be concerned about a whipping for shivering.

The boy, on his side, was lost in the window's view, taking in his wish. It was last summer he had asked Nalden to see his "other" grandmother. He had spent great times with Granny— his mommy's moms—before she died, and he had promised her to meet this other one.

After the telephone discussions, they had agreed not to tell the boy anything—nothing about how the circumstances of his birth had alienated his young parents from each other—or of Nalden's mother's much-stated dislike for the woman she unfailingly referred to as Nalden's "fallen manhood"; or of the consequent destruction-by-strain of their odd-angled relationship. Any of it would be too much for any child.

So they had decided that with care and civility, he and the child could handle the situation.

After all, Nalden was her only son—a shining prince. It was only his kid's mother who had smudged his glow in her eyes. And, as everybody knew, blood always shone through mud.

Nalden saw her as Missis Ridesmooth rounded the last slight curve—slowly, since he had been pinpoint-piloting them to the house. His mother was standing on the roadside opposite it. In his excitement, he shouted, "Stop! Stop here, man! There she is!" pointing to her instead of at the house, confusing everybody.

Driver slammed on the brakes, freezing Missis Ridesmooth, and sending all inside flying and bumping. Shrieking tires behind them sounded how their rude disruption was taken by traffic's flow.

Then, as Nalden's insisting finger sought to explain all by showing them Mother, he saw her flag down a taxi heading back the way they'd just come. It stopped, she entered, and it was off again.

As the taxi receded, he tried to command his son's attention, sighting down his pointing finger: "She's there, in that car. It's your grandmother . . . She must be going downtown, or something. . . ." He ended vaguely, embarrassed to choking.

The kid pulled his arm down. "I saw her, Pops . . . sort of. . . ." he lied.

The child's protection of his disappointment touched his quick to a stinging rage at her. That she'd flout him so, after he had called and told her the very hour they were arriving home! And here he had caught her dodging them like a bad-pay.

Nalden paid Driver the fifty as always intended, apologizing, "Sorry 'bout the li'l commotion, man."

With the tip and all, Driver was Happiness Huge once more. "Thanks for the problems, homeboy, ha-ha-ha-ha. Don't feel bad, man."

Then, just before he pressed his sweet ride shut and secure, he called out, "Hey, sonnyboy. Welcome home. Ha-ha-ha-ha."

Nalden's suspicion that Mother's absence was rude evasion was reinforced when he couldn't find the key to his room. It was not in the usual place, in among the bricks above the door. Neither was it anywhere it might've fallen (unlikely!) or reasonably been misplaced (who?).

She was the only one who would've removed it, and he could think of no good reason she should have. It had to be brand-new grounds that had waited all his life past in that room to form up —either that, or plain sulking-off-in-a-taxi spite.

Nalden concealed his ire from the boy by searching around the yard and checking other likely hiding spots. The kid watched for a minute, then began searching out his own possible key places, sharing the frustration in spirit.

"Maybe she moved it in cleaning up," Nalden muttered unconvincingly.

Finally, he decided to brick in a windowpane. Just then the kid remembered something: "Pops, can't you pick locks? Moms says you can do all sorts a' things."

Under the pressure of this unfounded fame, Nalden got an idea. "Wait a minute," he said, and went to search the bags for his multibladed pocketknife.

The screwdriver blade was good for dismantling the flat lock from the door. Five minutes later, he swung open the door to the musty, cobwebbed room.

"Wow, Pops! That was neato!" the boy exclaimed.

"That was just beginnings, kid," Nalden declared grandly. "For my next trick, I'm going t'make this spiders' palace into a humble home."

With that, he set to breaking the vinelike cobwebs tying the windows shut. Attacking the general mess, as the waves of dust permitted, he sang while he worked:

> "And let the sun shine in . . .
> Do it with a grin;
> Open up the windows,
> Let the sunshine in . . ."

Two verses later, the kid had joined the work gang, chorus and all.

Leaving the boy napping, Nalden went shopping for some staples and household items. As he returned along the street, carrying the shopping bag, he glanced up from ingrained habit to her room's window. It was open. That always had been the sign. When she was in, that window remained ajar just so; sun, rain, day, night, more or less.

Nalden put down the supplies in his room. The boy was still asleep, so he went alone to meet with Mother.

The large bedroom was the Throne from which Mother had always reigned as Queen. All the young people of the neighbour-hood acknowledged her dominion. That was a village given. For him, the Queen's Jack, their feelings had varied: some admira-tion and some envy, salted with some pity.

She was feeling sick, lying in bed with a bad mood—but other

than that, the same. Directly in her rasping twang, she wanted
him to know:

> *She didn't want to see any grandchild. It wasn't the
> time. Especially not with how her ear was aching hell in
> her head. The same old trouble. The new doctor she had
> just come from was a fool—just another thief not know-
> ing his ass from his elbow. . . .*

As was her way, Mother paused only when out of breath.
Then she glared in general while recharging, and like a wheezing
bellows gave forth again. Already, Nalden found himself slipping
into his old habit of listening to her selectively, sifting in only
what he found relevant. Now he was glad the kid didn't meet
her so. She could hardly be blamed, though.

When she paused again, he broke in, voicing the notion that
nagged him. "Mammy, didn't you see us earlier, when we came
in that burgundy taxi?"

> *Oh yes. That was something she had wanted to find out
> about. What was he trying to do—stopping the car right
> on the bend so, in the centre of the road? Making acci-
> dent? Did he expect her to stand up there waving to him
> like a flag?*

Her sarcasm grated dully, without nip, like the bite of a toothless lion. It only briefly sharpened his quieted resentment. All
was basically okay, though, Nalden rationalized. She had been
sick and going to the doctor. What could he expect? After all,
she was grandmother-old.

By the by, he also learned that she had put the key in the safe
spot where the main-house key was left. She had assumed there
was the first place any fool'd look when it wasn't in the usual
spot.

She went on about her sickness:

> *It was thunder and lightning and devilry going on inside
> the ear. It was so much disgusting muck and pus draining*

> *out her nose and down her throat when she could bear the*
> *taste of hawking it up. She was certain all that could*
> *never come from a plain bad ear. It wasn't natural. It had*
> *to be Obeah. Certain People was working hard to destroy*
> *her. . . .*

The "Certain People" hung in the air like a grey storm cloud too high to bear accusations.

"What medicines you using, Mammy?" he asked, ignoring her floating charge.

> *She was diluting a little of the disinfectant she had there.*
> *A few times a day she put a few drops down the earhole.*
> *The sting alone was sure to kill any natural germs in*
> *there. It worked in the toilet every day. It had to be better*
> *than the pills from the jackass doctors. They weren't*
> *making any difference at all. . . .*

Nalden spent the rest of the daylight convincing her that he had a cure better than hers. Without identifying it, he intended to give her some wide-range antibiotics he had brought along. He was a tenth-grade science teacher and no doctor, but he reasoned that at least his pills would kill her ear germs more gently than disinfectant.

Before he went to start dinner-making, he got her promise to see the boy as soon as she felt better. She capitulated with ill grace, touching her sick ear tentatively and muttering as he left:

"In two, three days maybe, if God spares Life . . ."

While Mother's ear got better, Nalden showed off his Pride and Joy to the village he grew up in. He introduced the boy to everyone, touring him around and teaching him whereabouts of the local wonders: the myriad lizards in mating frenzy; the enormous butterflies that the kid knew official names for—fritillary, swallowtail, monarch—and reciting them, face aglow, with his avid, ever-learning air. In defense, Nalden responded with some of the prettier local names, like Sweet Oil Yellows, and Jumbie Dreams for one shade-lover sporting soft grey wings camouflaged with big, hypnotic brown eyes.

In a class by themselves were the sweet fruits; for the boy, most of them never-see new. The governor's plums, angels' nuts, *pommes cytéres, chenettes,* mangoes in endless variety, coconuts, guavas, berries by many, cherries by same, *gru-gru boeuf, topii-tambu,* and so on. Almost everything oval and coloured was also eating-sweet.

The folks good-naturedly cautioned about catching gut worms, while feeding them ripe fruit like fattening hogs. In the bush, Nalden's compromise with caution was to tell the kid, "Make sure y'see somebody else eat it before you, okay?"

He had never realized the joy in this simple place, where, as a bitty, his lot had been "Not to cry" and "Go outside and play," and generally seek life's fun. Now he was understanding.

Once, as he was walking through the village, a fine young woman ran up and embraced him warmly. "Nalden!" She grinned up at him. "You looking so good. You ent change at all."

As she stood back appraising him, he racked his memory to place her.

"So y'don't even remember me, uh? I was too small for your eye, eh?" she said.

But by then, he had. " 'Course I remember you, Mandy. Is just that you grown up so fine, and all." As in truth, she had.

The encounter reminded of something else also. Around here childhoods were brief, with parenthood hardly waiting for maturity. For some kids here, the simple playing time was a sly mocker, never mimicking the frustration of their futures' dull disillusions.

Mother had brandished that message while banning him from village girlfriends:

> *Those girls were common-breed stock and a no-out fence for men with anything more than plain bullballs. . . .*

She had shared him his portion of blows to enforce her opinion, too. It probably helped to lead him up and out to the scholarship and the university—a totally different kind of village, as he found out. A one chock-full with independent thinkers; a one where he met his kid's mother—a most glittering flame in that limelight community.

In his moving around, Nalden met up, too, with childhood friends who had flared and faltered. "P.L." was such a burnt-out ember. P.L., the Prince of Love, whose teenage charm never matured to carry true. Nalden met him on the way for a bath in a still-favoured mountain river basin. He recognized P.L. immediately but, shy about the fellow's ragged state, would've passed him straight. P.L. didn't allow it, though.

He strode up and greeted doubtfully, "Queen Jack? Is you?" and as Nalden smiled acknowledgement, went on, "Well, well, well. Look at my main man shining down the place with Yankee prosperity. So how y'doing, boy? Tell me everything."

They chatted about this and that, as P.L. walked back to the river basin with him. He also offered some good fruits and lively "get high." Nalden understood the now-for-now magnanimity: Him being temporarily back home, it was a generous exchange for great reminiscences of when they were both alike—full of youth and promise.

He had been alone that day because, by then, the boy had established himself. The kid, by himself, was most welcome in any home in the village, at almost any time. And he used the privilege, too. To some extent, this popularity was a hand-me-down from Nalden, who had always been a favourite through sports' and exploits' fame. Still, the boy's charm was his own. Here, among his father's people, he showed himself to be a seriously cheery guy. Laconic talker but with a quick laugh, he seemed ever apause, watching a funny side in everything. The children accepted him easily in games and competitions from fistfights to fancy kite flying. In this Trinidadian village of merry, goal-free childhood, his son had fitted in like cascadura to muddy waters.

During that week of recovering, Nalden established the routines of his multiple role as parent/guide/companion for the boy. Caring for Mother was, at her insistence, minimal. Other than dispensing his better-than-black-magic capsules, he did just the normal things: restocking her larder, washing up after her, sweeping the house and yard, and generally keeping the place presentable. The same as he always used to.

Mother cooked her own meals. His second morning home, he had made a try at this. Scarcely had he begun when, with a hobble to accent her earache, Mother entered the kitchen muttering resentfully. From experience, Nalden stopped, stood aside, and listened to her scattershot tirade:

> She didn't want anybody getting ideas. She wasn't no cripple. She was depending on nooobody's good graces. She was able to fend, as always. . . .

Her slippers, all the while, slip-slapped an uneven sound trail as she bustled about, very in charge of her business if-you-please.

Nalden ascribed her fractiousness to painful Revenge of the Ear for its recent disinfection. That, and combative Old Age throwing blind punches. After that, whenever she was turning so in the kitchen, he turned elsewhere, biding until she was done and gone.

On fair late afternoons, with the lessened heat, they took to the sights of the fields and wild bush around the village. As if he were the mayor's rival, Nalden showed off the natural spring that slaked folks long before the present much-interrupted water-works pipe-borne supply. Once they saw an agouti racing for cover after a chancy drink; another time they came upon some monkeys stealing ripe *chenette*. One sundown they disturbed a flock of bright green nesting parakeets and tried to catch a fledgling one. They did the climbing, and could've taken the deafening racket of protests. But they had to flee the rain of silver-white droppings. Parakeets were never again green to the kid.

Another time it was a beautiful iridescent snake they bothered. Ominous in retreat, it sliced through the grass in yellow-and-black waves and disappeared, except for its psychic shadow: jewel-eyed and diamond-headed, as deadly vipers are.

Of all the new animals he found, it was the domestic ones—fowls in the yard—that most fascinated the kid. There were about a dozen or so—a pair of roosters, a cockerel, laying hens, pullets, one clucker with new-hatched chicks, and the occasional marauding setting hen when hunger forced her to desert the clutch.

The kid couldn't get enough of them. He took to studying their ways. Being elaborately casual, he'd follow their loose group everywhere. Probably trying to fool them into letting him join the gang as a chick, so he'd get to know them better. They never let him nearer than two feet.

Then he tried catching them—stringed prop-stick-and-box traps, with boiled-rice bait—until Mother mattered. Even then he continued, covertly, to reach for the cuddly yellow peepers until the hen flapped into peck attacks, and he had to flee.

Eventually, he gave out names to his favourites: Fascination, Speckled Grey, Greedy Beaker, Baldhead—this to a clean-necked layer he thought was going bald, clean-necked hens being another "newie."

Nalden couldn't get over the kid's making so much of common yardfowl, even considering their absence where he lived in the States. To his most subtly framed enquiries, the kid was straightforward admiring: "They're just like real people, Pops. They do everything. Eat on their own. Mind themselves. They even sleep outside in the trees by themselves—in the night!" With yardfowl, everything was wondrous to the boy. They rated better than "neat." They were "excellent."

Thus were their regular days filled. After cooking and eating, and the cleanup and washup, then tucking in the chatty kid, they never saw a nine o'clock.

The only frown to mar this indulgence of Nature's facades was the thought that they were home nearly a week, and still Mother hadn't permitted the boy to meet her. She had seen others, though, Nalden himself being the crier-cum-usher to more than enough of these oldster neighbours. True, they were long-standing members of her retinue of whisperers. Yet all week she hadn't even asked after the kid. Not even a peep, although every morning Nalden took her the pill for her hobbled ear.

It only convinced him she still hoisted the grudge against his child, just because the boy was the child his mother bore, an accident of birth. And knowing her, he was death-and-sickness certain she'd soon attempt to ram him down.

She had never liked the girl. Judging only from he-say-she-say, Mother had deemed her "forward," too self-assured, ambitious, and modern-minded for the older country folks she was born to. "An old folks' spoiled darling!" Mother called her. She was "too loud," and "too bright for her own good."

That judgement didn't stand up at the university. As a student, she pulled First Class honours. Walking to classes, she was the living lure to every campus man with blood and eyes. Two years running, she was campus queen—a competition only the most-lusted-at could win. When Mother saw the campus rag's picture of the regal celebrant at an intervarsity soccer match, her scant ratings fell further—past zero; descending from mere "forward" and "brassy" to a "butch squatting between bulldogs."

The first time Nalden brought his sweetheart home, before he could even introduce her, Mother had flounced out of the living room to seal herself in the Throne. A sudden headache got the blame. But that slight was the final stoking that boiled over his cauldron of defiance.

At that time, he was living at home and saving his scholarship's boarding allowance. Second-year finals were at hand. The rest of his class seemed months ahead in assignments and reading. Thus, his every unessential minute was being pressed to catching up. Breakfast time—preparation, consumption, and washup—he had finessed down to seven minutes, even. His clock slot for bolting through the kitchen was just before eight.

Mother, to advance her current offensive against his sweetheart, began using this very time period to happen into the kitchen, and commence thinking out loud with Biblical name-slinging about how:

> hot and sweet-fleshed Jezebel was food for dogs; and how Delilah used her legs as scissors and cut down a strong, strong man; and if anybody ever took the time to wonder what really was Sheba's sweet-smelling spice, or Magdalene's shame at Big Stone Well; and about watchman Ezekiel's vision regarding Oholah and Oholibah; and that Eve never stopped teaching Serpent's ways to Womankind . . .

On and on she went. Nalden hadn't realized there was such a bad-woman record in the Good Book until Mother began to bare them from Genesis to Revelations at one a minute. With voice too bold for her pensive posing, she'd muse in loud summary:

> *Woman was a common bunch with a common trait: having to scratch their backs the crab's way for every itch of their crotch for a blood-strong fool. . . .*

What cross did Womanhood make her bear so heavily? Nalden would ask himself. But he never returned a word to Mother. He gave her wary eye and escaped to his sweetheart's room on campus, pouring out his puzzlement to her.

Why did he take the abuse, she wanted to know. "She's my mother," he'd say. "What can I do?"

Then came their own accident predicting birth, and he swallowed his misgivings and took his pregnant lady to meet Mother. And she snubbed him cold before he could even say, "Hi." So he moved out of his room, and in with his premature family. He kept the key, though, using it occasionally to air out the place, or pick up books or notes—or some of his stashed emergency money.

Those days, peace with Mother seemed a minor thing, for he was then living through the wonderful condition of a first-time expectant daddy. He lived with reckless gaiety. Love for his woman was an enormous blanket he wrapped about them. When he came out for air, it was only to study hard. This endeavour he saw as the prime determinant of his, their future. Exams passed well meant premier jobs and best salaries, equalling quality provisioning, guaranteeing happiness forever and ever. This was about all he needed. This was what he'd get. For he was smart.

With the growing evidence of their hot love, Nalden (it had to be said) offered to do the proper thing. She—Independent Woman in a Bind—refused. She claimed to be offended by the matter-of-factness of his "gentlemanly" proposal, and decided for single parenthood. This became a circumstance no one could forget. Not in little skeleton-closet Trinidad. Not with a flashy modern meeting such a glaring comeuppance—Feminism struck in the belly. No one could hide their smirks. Not her shamed and bitter folks. Not his (of course) gloating mother. Not the scandalmongers on campus. Not even Nalden, ever doubting the whole debacle was really happening to a perfect pair like them.

Right after their son's birth, they had fled it all to America. She went to the West Coast with the baby—she had cousins there. He escaped to New York and hid himself in its blessed anonymity. The pretext was doing his final year, which cover he stretched to three years while he completed a master's degree in chemistry.

The fact is, he did reassess himself during this time. And among the bleaker facts, he found he had surrendered his independent woman and his boy child, and that he was a lonely fellow.

The best he could manage to salvage up to now was this summer-father relationship. It had been working only on his trying so hard—until this time. The back-home trip had clicked for them; he had that sense of gaining his son's trust every day. So, there was no way he'd let his effort be undermined now. Even if a hidden cost was a distant Mother ignoring his kid. If that was the case, well, he'd sponsor that sad trip, too, and smile it away for his son's gaining trust.

On Monday morning of the second week, Nalden woke to the sound of Mother's slippers brisking about the kitchen. She was humming old-time calypso. He listened closely: There was no brokenness in the slippers' slaps. He grinned relief all over himself. Mother was seeming sunbeaming this morning. It was quite in her fashion: new week, new way.

He barely waited for the boy to wake up before telling him the news. He crouched down beside the boy's fat futon, all whispers and advice. "Be very polite. Remember, y'not in America. Down here they strict with children. Is speak when y're spoken to, answer when y're called . . ."

The kid, too, had awoken sunshiny. "I'll be chilly, Pops," he said. "I'll walk in backwards, bowing and wowing." Then, with patient seriousness, he mimicked his mom's voice: "Be most polite to his mother, you hear me! It is em-per-or-tive."

Nalden was taken aback some that the boy was so sensitized about the manners-to-Mother bit. He wondered briefly what the kid must think of the Old Lady. Last thing as they left the room for the slip-slaps turning in the kitchen, Nalden told him, "Call her Grandma."

It went as smoothly as the sunrise. She sat on her rocker in the living room. The boy went up and kissed her cheek. Then, sounding like a child rehearsed and nervous, he began, "I'm glad your ears are better, Grandmother." Then he stopped sharp and, with unfeigned anxiety, raised his voice. "Can you hear me?"

She couldn't have dammed her smiles if she tried. So she hid them with her hug, saying, "Of course I can hear, child." Then they chatted some. She:

> He was so big already. What class was he in? Was he smart like his daddy? His daddy used to always be the smartest one in his school. Did he like Trinidad? Was he having a good time? . . .

The kid handled it perfectly, murmuring his "Yes, ma'am," "Good, Grandmother," "Fine, Grandmother, the animals were neat."

At the proper pause, he added detail. "We saw giant lizards this big, Grandmother"—they sounded enormous—and he was off gesturing dimensions like a showman. To Nalden's happiest surprise, his boy charmed Mother into her rarest of poses—absorbed listening.

Eventually, Nalden eased away to the breakfast kitchen with a sense of regret, as if departing a great performance. Although, all the way, he did smile.

The next few days were idyllic. Nalden sponsored a beach excursion, and most of the village kids went, along with a few available teenagers to help with their minding. While he got sorely burned lying in the shade of coconut palms, his son played all day in the blinding heat, and only developed a craving for ice cream. It was another of the day-after-day good times. The fridge stayed stocked with a variety of fresh fruit juices, courtesy of Mother, reinforcing in the boy's mind the crazy notion that thirst was not a bad state to anticipate pleasure from.

Then came an incident: Saturday midmorning. Blue-bright hot as usual, with some high white clouds playing at umbrellas every now and then. In the backyard, outside the kitchen, Mother was grating dry coconut meat to flavor lunch. Nalden was shelling green corns for boiling up a snack. The kid was building castles and moats in some fine sand near the back fence—probably daydreaming over his recent outing to the seaside.

Suddenly, Mother was screaming at the child, "Stop that blasted nonsense! You confounded demon!"

Her shout was shrill and coarse, filled with violence, as if she had been attacked and was striking back. Nalden started so violently, he dropped the corn he was holding, scattering bowl and contents onto the ground. The child, terrified, looking big-eyed foolish with fear, rushed for Nalden with a bleating cry.

He, confused, dropped to his knees and caught the boy into his arms. Then, as he gentled the sobs and terror away, he looked to find Mother's cause. What had the kid done to frighten her so? There was no reason he could see.

Rage flared like wildfire inside him, searing his filled eyes, stifling his breath, making him clench the kid too tightly. Soft in his throat began a tender crooning, an eerie sound through grinding teeth clamped taut to check his speaking.

For that was his main danger—saying something. Saying, "Why?" Saying, "Don't!" Any start at all from which his raging temper could launch a rampage. Not one thing to say. Not one thing to do. He didn't even dare look at her. He really couldn't.

She continued venting screams. Through his daze, he heard:

> *Why in hell the damned harlot's seed making grave in her yard? Whose Obeah was he bringing down on her? Why didn't he go make grave under his hot-bottomed mother? . . .*

Obeah!—that was the key. For Mother, like any older Trinidadian, Obeah was a potent and malignant force. It worked referentially by endless means—fetishes, prayers, dolls, charms, foods, new grave dirt under someone's doormat, blood sacrifice, and almost anything else at all.

The boy's castles and moats had suggested grave threats to her. Naturally, she saw him as his feminist mother's spiritual assassin. It all made nonsense, but there was superstitious logic in it, too.

With his rage put well aside, Nalden tried to explain. "Is not like that, Mother."

He had to almost scream to make himself heard over her continued blast of fussing. But she only listened to his louder volume:

> *That he was shouting at her. Disrespecting her. In her own yard. Her own son, showing off his manhood in front his only beloved one. Setting him example how to treat her . . .*

She had fumed to near-hysteria now, straddling her chair, sweating rolling beads, slavering with every screech. Her eyes were squeezed small and intense, looking wet, sharp, and dangerous. She rose and began turning about the area between the kitchen door and her chair, a step into the doorway, a step back out, picking up things and putting them down another place, a pot, a knife, a paper bag, the grater she'd been using. Then, in the mad foraying, she wandered directly towards them.

The child screamed, "Run, Papa! She's going to kill us!"

Mother was holding a table fork. She stopped short, a flash of shame blinking from her eyes. Then she calmed down to her more or less normal ranting:

> She hadn't wanted them there. She wished they'd go back whence they came. Wished they'd leave right then, and let her in peace. Take their blasted togetherness with them—out her yard. She didn't want them there. She never did. . . .

Her tone lacked conviction, though. She must've realized that the boy was only playing. That she had misreacted out-of-hand and embarrassed her dignity. That she had been wrong.

Abruptly, Nalden felt sorry at her distress. He had to be patient, he told himself. It was her age. She had been earsick. So he'd make peace, restore calm and friendship.

Yet even as he thought this, he felt the boy's fear still pulsing heavily through his small frame as a throbbing shudder, insistent and straining to pull away from the ugly scene. Suddenly, Nalden caught the child's urgency, and ignoring his fine resolve just made, he released the kid to his flight. Then, with his eyes carefully avoiding her, Nalden slunk away from Mother.

Next day, when the kid said, "Good morning, Grandmother," she walked off without replying. Right away he came and reported this to Nalden, who was still lying down, dreading to open his morning's eyes.

The kid came kissing-close—Nalden could smell his curdled-milk breath—searching of eye. He said, "Papa, she doesn't like me at all. Huh, Pops? She wants me to go away. Huh, Papa! Right?"

Nalden sat up, barring out the new day with both hands. Sighing heavy as eye bags, he answered, "No, boy. Y'don't understand. Is not you. Is . . ."

He stopped, unwilling to defend her, or even to suggest a less harsh interpretation. From behind his mask of fingers, he tried preachy neutrality. "When folks're angry, sometimes they behave stupid"—he thought he should've said silly—"and rude. . . ." Once begun, talking it away was easier. Even more so as he hugged the kid close, and out of sight. "She'll come around after a few. Don't you worry about her. That's just her way—shouting, 'Go 'way, go 'way' like that. But she'll be okay. . . ."

The kid remained stubbornly stiff in his arms, forcing Nalden to wonder whom he was trying to convince.

A few minutes later, when he encountered Mother and bade her "Good morning," she stared right through his eye, then silently stalked off to the Throne.

That cleared away his concerns about pretenses. After they had breakfast—a silent one—Nalden led the kid into the privacy of the open yard. There he spoke like a captain to his team. He was plain. He was firm. "Hey, stay out your grandmother's way, y'understand? If you meet up with her, though, make sure y're polite. But you'd better stay out the yard a lot. Got it?"

Later yet, when he sent the boy off to adventure about the village, with his usual caution of "Don't touch nothing without a stick!" he reminded again, "Stay out of trouble, okay?"

Clearly understanding the latest meaning of "trouble," the kid reassured him, "Sure bet, Pops."

Nalden put the house shipshape, and was out of there by

ten. He met his son popping hot with data: "Pops, there's a fair!"

"A fair?"

"Come'n, Pops. A fair, y'know. A fair . . . with clowns, ice cream. The usual. What y'say we go, huh?"

"Definitely hits my spot!"

Organized by the village council, the fair sported no clowns, but it offered much more than ice cream to the astonished boy: like steel-band instruments in action, and hundreds of jellies and jams selling for pittance, plus events like pig wrestling and climbing the greasy pole, and an old-timers' race.

And Nalden won the old-timers' race. The prize: a case of cold beer. His own prize, the moment after he'd broken tape: his kid's voice, pipe-high with excitement, piercing through all the other commotion—"That's my pops. He's my papa!"

So he donated the beer to his cheerers, and bought some orange juice. Then he and the kid toasted the champion already drunk on triumph's glory of a son's admiration.

On the sunset-gold, gravelled backway home, they came upon a family quarrel. A new-whelped bitch dog was protecting her young from their master, the house owner. All snarling, spitting threat, she was. Sometimes even nipping yelps out of the wailing puppies she defended.

His eyes met the kid's. The scene reminded of examples of maternal instincts Nalden had pointed out on earlier strolls: nest building, suckling heifers butting teats, and so on. Now he nudged the boy, who was already grinning at the dog scene. Spontaneously, they chorused their previously made-up summary, the kid's own joke: "Just like a mother!"

Except that, as Nalden said this line, he clearly caught the boy's sotto voce variation. Instead of "a," he'd said "your"! Nalden's mind blinked, but he never wavered his grin, or his eyes from the bitch dog. He only thought how, as a kid, he'd never have taken that chance.

Sunday Sabbath Nalden awoke to morning light shining reluctant grey into their room. The gloomy clouds hung so low, their gathered darkness had fooled them. It was nearly ten o'clock, and they had been midnight sleeping. It was his bladder that called the truth to him.

He tiptoed past the sleeping boy's futon, eased open the door, and urgented to the toilet.

The light was on in there: i.e., it was occupied by Mother.

This was like a bee sting to his bladder. Anticipating sweet relief too well, now it had put him in a panic situation. He was being premature in his shorts.

The first door in, the first container was a pot in the sink. Grabbing it, Nalden let splash into it the remainders of his day's first. Halfway through the release, he thought of the window's plain view in, and quickly squatted down like a female.

Back in the room, legs chilly-damp from his necessary extra cleaning up, he eyed the pile of dirty clothes in the corner. It had grown up there slyly during the weeks. The stink of the clothes and the high of the pile proclaimed today necessarily Big Wash Day, never mind it was Sunday, the famous Rest Day.

He had just filled the washtub in the yard for the first rinse when the rain came tumbling down. Resigned, he continued in the downpour. Somehow, it reminded of washing in the shower in New York. After a while, once he got accustomed, even the chill was a thrill.

One inch later, as he was rinsing yet another batch, the faucet gurgled impotently and stopped gushing. Nalden knew why. It was a typical Trinidadian paradox. Every time there were heavy showers, the waterworks turned off its pipe-borne supply. He also knew why this situation persisted: because everybody was resigned to it. So, rights-minded him being only on vacation, all he could do was suffer while protesting, and make do.

He used all the kitchen's large pots and a few basins to catch the torrents spouting from the roof's guttering. And with this he continued the Big Wash. Only now he had to do third and fourth rinses with the hard rainwater.

About three inches of storm later, during an onset of shivers that brought out the gooseflesh on Nalden's arms, as he wrung the rain out of a small mountain of clothes, the kid awoke and came to show his well-rested face and state that he was hungry.

Nalden told him to be tough, to go eat crackers. "Don't you notice I'm doing something?" he added, spreading the chiding sarcasm extra heavy.

The kid disappeared promptly.

The rain stayed with him to the end. So he had to hang the wet clothes in the shed, all the while envisioning some stinky, musty times to come.

It was nearly three o'clock when he got back to the room for a rest, and found the kid there—sobbing on the bed.

How long had he been there in that state? His small child's face was thinned by tear-swollen eyes. He looked cried-out, and wouldn't answer questions.

"You feeling sick? Somewhere hurting? What's wrong, son? You hungry?"

The boy just shook his head to everything.

He held the kid's face in his hands. Dreading to, he asked quietly, "Tell me, son. Did she do you something?"

The boy wailed reply then. "No, Papa. No, it's you! You're angry at me!"

As he heard, his anxiety knew a fine nuance of relief. This he could handle easy. It was honest kid's stuff: mere hurt feelings from a rough rebuff on a bad wet day. It was a comfort to take that on, and he relaxed back to his mellow feeling of plain tiredness once more.

Later on, he cooked them up some everything soup. It had ground provisions (eddoes), and coconut milk, flour dumplings, and all the leftover meat in the fridge, and lentils, raisins, noodles, garden herbs, butter, salt, and good intentions. Because of the maddening aroma it emitted, he could control himself only until it had boiled down thick and bubbly like lava. Then he still scalded his tongue gobbling a sample scooped with homemade bread.

He soon took the steaming pot to their room, where they dogged the hodgepodge like the hungriest. By then, it was vespers, so they crawled back into bed.

The best of all that miserable day was that they never did see Mother.

It was bright and early Tuesday morning before Nalden confirmed his suspicions about the house's unusual ease and quiet. Mother was gone. She had probably spirited out the rained-out morning. That was why the light had been on—needing the early light to depart, she had forgotten it.

He found out for sure when the grown son of her *ma-commère* from Tamana came by to pick up Mother's reading glasses. He had the key and the specs' exact location. Still, it wasn't easy as that.

The fellow followed strict instructions to the letter: Only Nalden was to actually enter the room and pick up the glasses— the young man being just a jackass bearing gold. Before departing, the privileged fellow did allow some news: Mother'd be back in a few days.

That night, on an impulse, Nalden sprang the question. The boy was between stretch and yawn and rubbing sleepy eyes.

"Y'having a good time, son?"

The boy didn't hesitate. "I wish I could stay all year, Pops. This is the life . . . excellent."

For Nalden then, everything was fine.

The country air must've done her good. Mother returned with the vigour of running sweat, seeming set on hand-weeding the whole half-acre she called front garden. Nalden heard her, up in the early cool of day-clean, wielding her large yard knife against the stubborn roots.

Not taking chances, he reminded the kid, "Now remember, Son, don't bother your grandmother."

"Sure bet, Pops," the kid answered.

It was around midafternoon. Nalden was home to liberate the juice mug some. He had finished with the quenching when he sighted Mother marching up from the backyard. She carried something small and yellowish-white in one hand, and the big yard knife in the other. Her general bearing proclaimed, "Trouble."

Nalden looked around, his first thought to get out of there before she saw him, but he abandoned that hope when their eyes made four through the kitchen window. So he went outside to face the music.

It was a broken egg in her hand. A gouged-out part showed a wet, ready-to-hatch chick, the sparse yellow down slick against its slack body.

She held it out to him like it was a martyr's corpse.

"So! This is how he plan to torment me, eh? Well, not so! Not so at all! And he will soon find out how much not so!"

She was furious, he knew; yet she wasn't being wild. She sounded deliberate, satisfied—ominous.

All at once, Nalden became very concerned about her intentions. Playing ignorant to get a clue, he asked, "What happened to it?"

"Y'can't see what happen to it? Y'can't see?"

"Well, how it happen then?"

"Oh-ho, so you don't know, eh?"

He sucked his teeth, deliberately rude. "Come on, Mother. Stop it, okay. Say what y'want to say."

"So . . . y'tired, eh? You tired of me an' mih bothering. Well, Mr. Father, I tired, too. I'm tired of your son digging graves and killing my business in my yard."

Nalden protested immediately. "How you could say he killed the chicken. Did you see him? Did you—"

"Did I?" she stopped him. "Since when I have to have witness? Since when I have to prove and sway your judgement? You ent see him always trailing the fowls like hungry mongoose? You ent see him poking in everything he see with a stick? You ent—"

Nalden wanted no more. He tried to put it in perspective. "Look, Mother, is just a chicken. It might've died anyhow. From pox. From the rats. The hen itself might've crushed it. Look, is just one of a dozen. I'll pay you for it." He thought not to offer that as he said it, but it was too late.

"Pay me! So y'want to pay me off, eh. You that well off. You think you could just pay me off and shut up my mouth."

"I don't mean . . ." He let the words trail off. He could see he had only hardened her set intentions. "So what you going to do?" he challenged her.

Mother looked into his memory then.

It was in that long-gone way he thought he had forgotten. In her hard old eyes, he saw again that magisterial resolution—a flat determination to punish. As if a child were a criminal, or a brute.

Then she made it perfectly plain.

"When he brings his backside here, I'm going to teach his fast li'l ass how to poke."

And she stalked toward the bushy hibiscus fence.

Nalden stepped in her way. "No, Mother. You're not."

Impatiently, she tried to elbow him away. He stood firm. In a spasm of fury, she suddenly smashed the dead chicken against his chest, shoving him with the open hand. The assault—its surprise, its violence, its stink—shifted him away, allowing her to reach the fence. With the big knife, she cut from it a thick frond and began trimming it to a whip.

Nalden strode up to her, snatched the whip, and tossed it hard away. "You're not going to hit my child, Mother."

She stood before him, arms akimbo, glaring puzzledly as if not understanding.

Nalden felt her passion's equal now. For as angry as she was, he was, too; and as determined, resolute.

"You used to beat me like a snake. I didn't mind. I didn't know different. You didn't know better. So I grow up afraid of licks, taking it 'cause it was the only love you knew. It was how you cared. But my child ent growing so, afraid of who he should run to. Don't you see he ain't afraid of nothing? Not you, your licks-love, or your bad-witch behaviour. So you not touching him. You not shouting at him. You not being hard on him at all. You don't know his kind. And I don't want him to know yours!"

She swung the blade at him. Swung to cut off his talking. Shaking with rage, awkward by age, she made a slow swipe at his head. He ducked away easily, and continued spilling out what he had held for so many years.

"You shame, Mother. Yes, you hurt. So you crying. But you

earn your pain. That's all you could feel now. 'Cause you been stifling all your soft feelings—never gave them air . . ."

She came at him again, poised to strike. But now he didn't care if he was chopped. It was only important that he face her down and tell his mind. So he stood and flinched his chest, and watched her bring the big knife down.

It faltered at the last—gouging a bruise, not cutting in truth. Then she dropped the knife as if it were she who was wounded. Half-blinded with tears, she stumbled into the kitchen as if drunk. From there, in rasping voice, bitter and final as a curse, she gave her parting words.

"Well, since you despise me so. And I'm so much a wicked witch. I don't want to spoil your fine life no more. So don't come back in this house again. Not you nor yours. Don't fill my yard again. I say don't come back here. Not if I'm sick. Not if I'm dead. From this day on, I only had a son!"

Nalden stood and listened to it all. Then he watched her go hide in the Throne.

He called the airport almost immediately. If there hadn't been a flight, he would've left the house anyhow and holed out in a hotel room or somewhere.

As it was, he was lucky. This way it was easier to make a convincing lie to the kid. He decided on an urgent call from his school in New York. The kid knew he was head of the science department. There had been a problem, he could say. The future of the science program had been placed in his hands. He hated it, but there was no other way, he'd persuade. That they were having such a good time only made it worse, he'd regret. But it was really three weeks already—nearly a month. Yes, the story sounded right.

He waited until the kid was fed and washed, and close to tired sleep before busting the news on him. Instant tears sprang from the boy's widened, suddenly awake, and saddening eyes. But Nalden could feel his son's solid trust.

"Really, Pops, we have to go tonight?"

It was just a reflex try at reasonable delay. And Nalden lied on reasonably. Sudden farewells'd be too painful for him, personally, and maybe for everyone else. He would write instead. He could also get an enormous discount if he travelled by night—it would save so much money. Then, with the notion new even as he spoke it, he suggested, ". . . and we could always come again, to our own place."

The kid's incredulous "We could, Pops? Wow! That'd be the chilliest!" sealed it all. From then, it was okay. Settled.

Their bags were all packed, and they ready to sneak from the yard to a taxi. The kid took out his Mickey Mouse camera. "Pops, I want a shot of you sitting on the bed."

Nalden sat and let him shoot, well knowing the light wasn't right.

Then the kid wanted to know, "Hey, Pops. Should I leave a note and say, well, 'Thanks,' or something? Moms said to be polite."

Immediately, smoothly, Nalden told him, "I took care of that already."

They went out then. Nalden closed the door and locked it. He left the key in the lock.

About the Author

KELVIN CHRISTOPHER JAMES was born in Trinidad. He holds a B.Sc. from the University of West Indies and a doctorate in Science Education from Columbia University. His short stories have appeared in *Between C&D*, *BOMB* magazine, *American Letters and Commentary*, *Quarto*, *The Portable Lower East Side*, *The Literary Review*, and *Les Jungles d'Amerique*, in France. In 1989 he was awarded a New York Foundation for the Arts Fellowship in fiction. *Jumping Ship and Other Stories* was first published in 1992. *Secrets*, his first novel, was published in 1993. Kelvin Christopher James lives in Harlem, New York.